POWE ☞ W9-CZA-597

"Look, Steve, you've got to face it. The Republic is dying. Life is too complicated for a system that gives total power to a bunch of uninformed congressmen interested only in being returned to power. They will instinctively pander to the mob, as they are doing now, until we've driven the country into the ground. Drastic measures are called for, and no democratic parliament is going to have the courage to take them."

Doyle looked up, meeting Carlyle's brown eyes. "The president has the courage. God knows, his program is drastic enough."

"Drastic, yes. Courageous, no. He's taking the easy way out. Cutting defense costs was always a politician's easiest course in this country. He can run against the military-industrial complex, act self-righteous, and wind up leaving us helpless." He shook his head. "It won't wash, Steve. He's going to destroy us if somebody doesn't do something about it."

Also by Edward McGhee:

The Chinese Ultimatum (with Robin Moore)

THE LAST CAESAR

Edward McGhee

PINNACLE BOOKS   LOS ANGELES

This is a work of fiction. All the characters and events portrayed in this book are fictional, and any resemblance to real people or incidents is purely coincidental.

THE LAST CAESAR

An original Pinnacle Books edition, published for the first time anywhere.

First printing, April 1980

ISBN: 0-523-40663-0

Printed in the United States of America

PINNACLE BOOKS, INC.
2029 Century Park East
Los Angeles, California 90067

For Lisl, Alec, and Steven

The Last Caesar

CHAPTER ONE

The four helicopters came out of the sun in a precise line, their rotors slanting at a shallow angle as they circled the big ship and moved in echelon toward the white circles on the immense deck. The first machine touched lightly, lifted for a split second, then slumped down on its shock absorbers. As the rotors slowed, half a dozen officers in braid-encrusted blue winter uniforms moved toward the door marked with the presidential seal and came to attention in an expectant cluster. Up the deck, as the second helicopter touched down, eight men piled out and approached at a run, suit coats flopping back to reveal revolvers and snub-nosed machine guns. They spread in a half circle around the first helicopter, feet slightly apart, facing outward.

One approached the welcoming group, eyes flicking across the insignia of rank. "Captain Hammond?"

"Yes." The naval officer almost saluted the tone of command, although the young man addressing him was not much more than half his age.

"Your orders were that none of your men were to

1

wear loaded side arms. Has that order been carried out?"

"It has."

The man nodded and turned to the helicopter to raise a closed fist and open it. Immediately the blue door lowered, converting into a stairway, and a tall, slender, thin-faced man came down in an athletic bound, knees flexed as he landed on the deck. "Hello, Bill," he said, ignoring the salute and taking the hand of the four-star admiral leading the little welcoming group, nodding curtly to the others. "You know Steve Doyle, Harrison Caldwell, and Maria Vicente." He motioned toward two men and a woman who had followed him down the stairway.

The admiral nodded. "Welcome aboard, Mr. President."

"Always glad to be here, Bill," the tall man said, his pale blue eyes sweeping the deck of the world's largest aircraft carrier. "Things don't seem to have changed all that much in the last twenty-five years. Everything is just as dirty as it always was."

The naval officers around him stiffened, but the president laughed and slapped the admiral lightly on the back. "No offense, Bill. I know you can't keep the damned things clean." The smile faded and he glanced at his watch. "Well, shall we get started? No point in freezing our asses off out here."

The admiral moved to the president's left and the group strode rapidly across the deck and took positions marked lightly in chalk as navy cameramen filmed the scene. At a signal, the deck began to descend soundlessly into the hangar area of the aircraft just as a forty-millimeter cannon fired the first salvo of the twenty-one gun salute. The president started involuntarily as the first blast reverberated off the enclosed metal and his

2

bodyguards closed around him, knees flexed, weapons flashing in the cold morning sun. A touch of a smile slipped across the president's lips. "Very nice touch, Bill. Firing that salute while we're on the elevator. Multiplies the effect of that popgun until it sounds like a sixteen incher."

The admiral's face reddened, but his eyes never left the scene opening up below them. Some five hundred of the ship's six-thousand man complement were drawn up at rigid attention to the left. Its marine detail, three hundred strong, presented arms on the right as the president descended into view and the ship's band began a funereal version of "Hail to the Chief."

The elevator stopped and the president stepped off onto the metal deck where he was met by the commander of the marine detachment. "Detail ready for inspection, sir," the crew-cut young officer shouted out, sword at his shoulder.

"Very well, let's go, son," the president said. As he strode down the lines of marines, each came to attention and opened the breech of his rifle, closing it with a snap after he passed. In the background the band played "Anchors Aweigh" followed by the "Marine Hymn." At the end of the walk-through the president nodded to the admiral and the group moved across the deck to the cluster of officers.

"Very handsome ceremony, Bill. Worthy of the finest traditions of the navy. What's next on the agenda?"

"A demonstration of the ship's capabilities, Mr. President. If you'll follow me." Admiral Christman led the party across the hangar deck to the strains of "She Wore a Yellow Ribbon" and began the climb through ten decks to the ship's bridge. As they emerged into a bright early-winter sun, the president paused to catch his breath. "Christ, Bill, you're in good shape for a worn-out old fullback with a bad knee who smokes too much."

The admiral's smile was wintry. "I run three miles on this deck every morning when I'm on board, Mr. President."

The president grinned. "With the entire officer complement at your heels, no doubt. What is the operations plan?" he asked, moving off the open deck of the bridge overlooking the launch area into the glassed-in enclosure from which the ship was steered and commanded. He slipped uninvited into the captain's chair, high off the deck overlooking flight operations, and gazed down at the scene below. A thousand men in varicolored jackets and helmets were preparing to launch eighty aircraft from two forward catapults: the sharklike F-18, quick and nervous-looking even on the deck, and the all-purpose A-14, the troublesome new bomber which was not living up to expectations.

"The launch begins in one minute, Mr. President. We'll put up eighty planes, every operational aircraft on the ship, conduct a fire exercise three miles off the port side, and recover the aircraft."

"Ready to begin launch, Admiral."

"Whenever you wish, Captain," Christman said. He had begun flying off carriers forty-four years before on the old *Midway*, the year he graduated from Annapolis. He was already a year beyond mandatory retirement age, but they had kept him on as chairman of the Joint Chiefs of Staff because of his ability to command the respect of Congress. Now he leaned on the chartboard to the president's right and watched the planes emplaced on the catapults, swarms of bright-jacketed men hooking the cables, carefully avoiding the lethal stream from the jet planes' exhaust. As the launch readied, a heavy oblong metal plate rose out of the deck, blocking the jet stream, and the men gathered behind it for pro-

4

tection. Then the two catapults fired simultaneously as the planes shot off the deck with a roar, one tipping slightly to the left, the other to the right as they veered away from possible collision. As the planes left the deck, they were converted from clumsy symbols of heavy menace to graceful birds of prey, in their element now, their sharklike noses cruelly beautiful. Forty times the maneuver sent them across the whitecaps of Chesapeake Bay.

"What's their armament, Bill?" the president asked, turning toward the admiral.

"Five-inch rockets for air-to-ground work. A new version of the Falcon for killing aircraft. Laser-guided with a special electronic backup and heat-seeking when it comes within close range. Two-hundred-and-fifty pound bombs today. The A-14 also has a sixty-mm Gatling gun which carries about as much firepower as a Second World War destroyer over the short term."

"And the nukes, of course."

The admiral nodded. "And the nukes."

"Can the ship defend itself against submarines, Bill?"

The admiral shrugged. "Not by itself, no. But we would know before one got within fifty miles of us. The Soviet missiles are too crude to penetrate our electronic baffle screen. If one did we've got anti-missiles which can intercept just about anything they can throw at us with about seventy-five percent chance of success. That's about as secure as you can get in a war, Mr. President."

"What about their missile ships?"

"We'll kill any surface ship with planes or the new aircushion Corvettes before it can get within range."

"It's a little different from my days on an A-6 over Vietnam," the president said, staring down at the deck. "We had the little black box, and they told us to put the plane in its hands when the telephone poles started coming up at you. I lost a lot of friends that way."

"You would have lost more without the black box, Mr. President. Anyway, that wasn't a war. It was suicide. The man this ship was named after sent you in day after day along the same route with the same target. You weren't allowed to hit the missile complexes which were deliberately sited in the middle of dense population centers."

"He had his reasons, Bill. He had his reasons."

The admiral turned away, watching the planes gathering, tiny specks in the sky. Now they began to peel off in wings of three each, bombers first. They came in low and flat, radar scopes lining them up on the metal targets emplaced by the darting Corvettes capable of eighty knots on their cushion of air. The rockets were soundless white threads suddenly streaking out of the wings, landing on the sea with the threatening *whump, whump* of death. The bombs followed, conventional explosions, almost comforting in their familiarity. Then the Gatling guns, lifting spray in needlelike clumps, sounding like a heavy zipper ripping open. First the sight, then, delayed, the sound. It went on for an hour as the president began to pace restlessly up and down the bridge, talking to the helmsman, the officer of the deck, the orderly.

"Where are you from, son?" he asked the duty quartermaster.

"Iowa, sir."

"What brought you to the navy?"

"Couldn't get a job anywhere else, sir."

"Like it?"

"No, sir," the seaman said, lowering his voice.

The president laughed and slapped him on the shoulder. "Well, it's only four years. Maybe we'll have this country turned around before you have to re-up."

A klaxon split the quiet of the deck and a voice boomed out. "Prepare to recover aircraft. Prepare to recover aircraft." The deck crews, who had been perched like birds on the port side watching the show, leaped to their feet and dispersed across the deck in compact, ordered masses. Almost immediately the first plane appeared circling aft of the ship. A complex panel of lights told him where he was as he approached. As he crossed the trailing edge of the flight deck, his nose lifted slightly and the hook trailing behind the plane skipped over two of the raised cables before catching the third and hauling him to a stop.

"Jesus," the president said. "At full power that A-14 must tear a few cables loose."

"Everything's been strengthened," the admiral said. "But it's still the one problem nobody's been able to solve. They've got to come in at full power or they'd never be able to get off again if something went wrong. We're still experimenting with a supplementary rocket booster or something like it to give an extra thrust if it's needed, but they don't work. The pilot just hasn't got time to fool with anything sophisticated. It's got to be kept simple. Landing one of those birds is tough enough as it is."

"So I remember," the president said dryly, glancing at his watch. "I think I've seen enough, Bill. It's been fascinating, but I don't have all that much time. In any case, there must have been some other reason for getting me out here."

"Yes, Mr. President. As a matter of fact there was. If you'll follow me to the wardroom." He motioned toward a hatchway and led the president through it and down three decks into a pine-paneled conference room.

7

"Attention!" The command cracked through the room as the party entered and three general officers came out of their chairs. The president stopped and turned to the admiral. "What the hell is this, Christman? Nobody told me I was being invited to a meeting of the Joint Chiefs of Staff." He turned to the lean-faced man on his right in a bemedaled major general's uniform. "Were you in on this, Steve?"

The officer shook his head. "No, Mr. President."

"All right, Admiral." The president's voice was thin with controlled rage, his light blue eyes chilly and flat as glass. "Maybe you'd like to explain this."

The admiral, almost as tall as the president, but with the muscular body of an ex-All American football player, met his stare. "I can, Mr. President. If you'll be seated," he gestured toward the head of the wardroom table. The others scattered haphazardly around the oval as the admiral moved to the other end.

"We asked you to join us today, Mr. President, because we've been hearing some very disturbing information since the congressional elections. We arranged it here, because it's most unusual for you to meet with us as a group, and we wanted as little press coverage as possible. That is also the reason we took the liberty of not telling your staff."

"You're suggesting that my staff can't keep anything from the press?"

"Yes, Mr. President. That is exactly what I'm suggesting."

"Very well, Admiral. I'm not here to debate you. Presumably by risking your careers in this ridiculous cloak-and-dagger exercise you have something important to tell me. Can we get on with it? I've already wasted the better part of a day watching you play with your toys."

8

The admiral cleared his throat and placed a pair of half-moon glasses on his nose. "As chief of the Joint Chiefs I've been asked to speak for the entire military establishment. It should be understood that we are all in complete agreement on what I'm about to say." He glanced up at the other three officers who met his look with unspoken agreement. "Mr. President, we have received copies of a report drawn up by your Board of Economic Counselors' staff, the recommendations of which, if implemented, would cripple the defense capabilities of the nation. It recommends nothing less than the dismantling of our armed forces. I refer to Staff Study Fifteen, a copy of which is before you."

The president stared down at a thick blue folder in front of him. "That report, Admiral, was for the eyes of the president only. May I ask just how you received a copy of it?"

A wintry smile creased the lean, tanned features of the naval officer. "I came in my office one morning and found it on my desk, Mr. President."

"I see. Well, admiral, you've read the report and you don't agree with it. I presume that is why you brought me two hundred miles out into Chesapeake Bay. Is that all you have to say?"

"No, Mr. President. It isn't. My colleagues and I wish to know what, if any, possibility exists that the report will be implemented."

"When the 100th Congress meets on January 21, 1987, that report will be the basis for the defense budget I plan to submit. As you are well aware, with the massive new liberal majorities my party enjoys in both houses of Congress and given the tragic economic situation of the country, I don't think, Admiral, you will find much opposition to any program I submit designed to pull this country out of the economic morass into which it has fallen."

"Mr. President, are you aware of the implications of what you propose? The reduction of effective naval and air force units by half. Disbanding two-thirds of the army's effective manpower. Elimination of the Marine Corps as a separate entity, its contraction to one division and its incorporation into the army. The base closures alone entailed in reductions of this size will cause immense economic dislocation as well as crippling our defense capacity."

The president drummed his long, thin fingers on the highly polished table and studied the faces of the men around it. The hard edge left his voice and he leaned forward. "Gentlemen, believe me. What I am doing is not a punitive act against you and the officer corps. As a former navy flyer, I sympathize with you. And as president I respect your competence and the patriotism to which those chestfuls of medals attest. But I cannot allow my judgment to be clouded by outdated sentimentality at a time when the nation's very survival depends on drastic measures."

He paused and poured a glass of water from the silver pitcher at his side. "Are you aware of the economic statistics? Twelve million unemployed. Our productive capacity reduced by a third, inflation rampant, our balance of payments in a disastrous state." He waved a slender hand impatiently. "This is a crisis unparalleled in our history, gentlemen, worse than 1933. Drastic measures are needed to overcome it. We can't simply apply palliatives this time. There has to be a basic reform of the system."

"That doesn't alter the fact that we exist in a hostile world armed to the teeth, much of it bent on our destruction," Christman said.

10

"Jesus, Bill, you talk like somebody out of the mid-seventies. The world's changed. Nobody wants our destruction. Far from it. We're still the largest production complex in the world. They need us too badly. Without our agricultural production, a third of the world would face famine. Our markets sustain Europe and Japan. The Soviets, the Chinese, and the Third World are in desperate need of our technology. It's a new ball game, gentlemen. We're wasting energy and resources on a defense establishment of this size and I simply will not permit it to continue." He glanced down at the blue book in front of him. "Bill, I've known you for years, and at no time have you ever shown insubordination or an unwillingness to submit to the direction of the civilian administration. This exhibition today, however, is close to mutiny. I'm not sure that it's acceptable to me."

Admiral Christman glanced inquiringly around the table and received an affirmative from each of the other officers. "Mr. President, we are all loyal officers. Every one of us has risked his life more than once to preserve this nation and its precious heritage. We cannot, in good conscience, continue to serve an administration which we sincerely feel is endangering the country's very existence. If this is really your program, Mr. President, we wish to submit our resignations as of this date."

The president met Christman's eyes only briefly before turning to his military aide. "Steve, I want you to bring me the captain of this vessel. Meantime, I want a message drafted to the Secretary of Defense informing him that the Joint Chiefs of Staff have resigned and that he is to designate their temporary successors immediately. I want these men put on immediate," he paused and spoke the word again with steady force, "immediate retirement status and barred from access to the Pentagon, classified information, or any military installation in the country."

He turned to the four officers. "I will make one of my helicopters available to put you ashore. I want no announcement to the press by any of you. Is that understood? You are still under my orders as commander in chief, even after you enter reserve status, and I will not have you disrupting my programs."

The captain of the *Lyndon B. Johnson* entered, a big, handsome ex-pilot. "Mr. President?"

"I want your communications facilities put at the disposal of my aide, General Doyle. I will be leaving your ship as soon as he has transmitted his message. If you'll be good enough to accompany me to your quarters, Captain." He nodded curtly and left, stooping slightly to avoid the bulkhead of the wardroom.

CHAPTER TWO

The Brasserie Lorraine perched atop the new Hay-Adams Hotel in incongruous splendor, brass columns separating slabs of dull, almost black glass overlooking Lafayette Park. The hotel mirrored the neo-Federalist style of the brick buildings enclosing the small park facing the White House, where the statue of Andrew Jackson stood, smeared with a hundred years of pigeon droppings. The Brasserie had opened during the second Carter administration and, because of its proximity to the White House and the excellence of its French cuisine, had rapidly become the fashionable restaurant of its time. Here the shakers and movers of the capital met each day at lunch to see and be seen. Some famous, some notorious, some anonymous, they all knew each other, knew the sources of power they represented, and were in tacit agreement that it was in their personal interest to maintain the status quo no matter what constituency they represented. They were, in a word which had fallen into disuse in the eighties, the "establishment," the people who really ruled America: senators,

13

congressmen, judges, lawyers, union leaders, businessmen, lobbyists, and representatives of minority groups whose needs cut across all lines.

The interaction of these groups, and others, trading power and influence in one field for assistance in another, was the lifeblood of the American governmental system in 1986 as it had been for more than two centuries. It was a messy system, vulnerable to error, inefficient, and often unjust. But it had the great virtue of offering some influence to virtually every organized group of citizens and of giving each of them a sense of participation. It was, in the words of a previous vice-president, a "system to defang hostility with verbiage," and gave the facade, if not the substance, of that illusive political theory, democracy.

The restaurant was run, as it had been since its founding, by Jacques Moreau and his partner Athené Sauvignon, one of the truly great émigré French chefs. Moreau was the outside man, who had been a former maître d'hôtel at several of the top French restaurants of the capital for more than twenty years. He knew everyone, never forgot a face, and had the political instincts of a Talleyrand. His uncanny sense of rising power was reflected in the increasingly desirable tables accorded ascending stars in the Washington firmament. One had arrived, in Jacques's eyes, when one of the eight window tables overlooking Lafayette Park and the White House was regularly made available. The descent was usually much more swift than the rise. A shaky cabinet minister or a White House aide about to get the ax would suddenly find every table booked, though an expanse of empty white tablecloths gave the lie to Jacques's bland assurance that he was *"complet."*

Major General Steven Doyle, chief Defense Department aide to the president, was not a shaker or a mover.

14

He had eaten twice in the restaurant, both times as the guest of powerful men, but he would not be remembered, either by the young Frenchman in the Pierre Cardin suit who guarded the restaurant's private elevator in the hotel lobby or by the great Moreau himself.

"You have a reservation, Monsieur." The tone implied doubt, disdain, and boredom in the lightest of Midi accents.

"I'm a guest of Dr. Esterhazy," Doyle said.

The young man consulted a list. "General Doyle?" He snapped his fingers at the elevator operator. "Take General Doyle to the bar." The restaurant was on two levels, but the lower one was purgatory to which were relegated tourists, ambassadors from minor Third World countries and second-echelon bureaucrats on the make. The bar was on the top floor, seperated from the main dining room by a wall of mildly erotic glass panels illustrating scenes from Baudelaire's "Fleurs de Mal." It was the anteroom to the inner sanctum. Here the mighty waited to be anointed with a table by the diminutive Moreau.

It was a mark of the status of Doyle's host that the maître d'hôtel met him at the elevator. "General Doyle? Dr. Esterhazy has not yet arrived. Would you care to wait at the bar? A drink, perhaps, courtesy of the *maison, bien sûr*." The man, who spoke impeccable English, punctuated his conversation with French words carefully selected not to exceed the knowledge of a college freshman.

"A beer," Doyle said, returning the nod of a tall man in a pin-striped suit whose name he could not remember. Half the faces in the dining room, visible through the clear portions of the glass, belonged on the cover of *Time* magazine. Vice-President Joshua Harrington, his laugh booming out across the room. Secretary of the

15

Treasury George Wiesenthal. The president's adviser for National Security Affairs, Harrison Caldwell. Senate Majority leader William Bullitt. Nationally syndicated columnist Kip Dean.

"Good afternoon, General. Delighted you were able to join me."

Doyle turned to take the hand of Dr. Istvan Esterhazy, chairman of the Board of Economic Counselors and widely believed to be the author of the New Economic Plan about to be submitted to Congress. He was a tiny old man, no more than five-feet-two, a slender, elegant, white-haired figure whose fine-boned hand was engulfed in Doyle's paw.

"A pleasure, Doctor."

Jacques hovered at their elbow, voice lifted a pitch as he lapsed into French laced with a heavy Corsican accent. "*Bonjour,* Dr. Esterhazy. Your table is ready. A fino as usual, perhaps? And may I suggest the belons? Superb. Just arrived from France. With some fresh South African asparagus in an omelette. And your special stock of Pouligny-Montrachet, of course." The man chattered with servile assurance as he led them through the closely packed room to a window table glittering with silver and crystal. Below, across the square, the White House rose through the leafless winter trees.

"That sounds fine, Jacques," Esterhazy answered in slightly accented English. "Will you join me, General? The oysters are a real treat, and even Jacques doesn't have them often."

"I'd prefer a small steak, rare, no sauce. Just grilled. And a green salad sprinkled with lemon juice."

The Frenchman looked pained. "I'm afraid the menu doesn't contain those choices, General," he said stiffly. "May I suggest a pepper steak and our salade Niçoise? I'm sure you'll like it."

Doyle glanced across the table at the old man who was smiling faintly. "If you don't have steak and salad just bring me a beer and a cheese sandwich," Doyle said quietly.

The Frenchman lowered the pad and opened his mouth to speak, revealing a row of gold crowns on his molars. Esterhazy's low voice cut over his first words. "I'm sure you can find what the general wants, Jacques," he said gently, dismissing him.

"He's really beginning to think he's a source of power in this town rather than just a mirror reflecting it," Esterhazy said. "I suppose, General, you're wondering what prompted this lunch invitation?"

Doyle nodded, trying to remember the history of the little man. He had been a leading member of the Hungarian resistance in World War II and a prominent socialist political figure in his early thirties when the war ended. Four years later, divorced from his wife and at odds with the Communist regime, he had defected while attending a monetary conference in Paris.

He had emigrated to America, landing in the United States with a doctorate in economics and, as he liked to say, "two dollars in forints." By the time he was forty he was president of an electronics company which had grown spectacularly as a result of his management. Abruptly, he had sold out to one of the giants of the industry and for the next forty years had dedicated himself to teaching and serving in a variety of government posts in both Democratic and Republican administrations. As he grew older, Esterhazy had confounded theory and, instead of becoming more conservative, had grown increasingly radical.

Five years previously he had liquidated his assets and established one-million-dollar trust funds for each of the seven children he had fathered with four wives. The rest

17

he had carefully divided between a medical research foundation and a small, exquisitely elegant museum for his collection of expressionist paintings in Louisville, Kentucky. He now lived with a valet-cook-chauffeur in the aging, slightly dilapidated Watergate apartment he had bought during the Nixon administration and seldom appeared in public. His writings in scholarly economic and political science journals preached the necessity of rigid controls over the capitalist economy of the United States and confiscatory fiscal policies to redistribute income more equitably. His money had financed a series of devastating critiques of waste and inefficiency by the leftist-oriented Susquehanna Foundation for Government Reform, and he was rumored to be largely responsible for the selection of a trio of military advisers to the president who had recommended the massive budget cuts for the armed forces.

"I have been watching you for two years, General, since you became the president's military aide. My first impression of you was at one with your brilliant military record: a brave, somewhat simple soldier, dedicated to his president and his profession." The old man smiled. "I confess, I dismissed you from my mind rather quickly as one of the supernumeraries of this administration."

"I hope I've done nothing to disappoint you, Doctor," Doyle said, his sunburned face immobile.

Esterhazy leaned back and laughed. "No, General. You are a superb actor. Had I not chanced to see a dossier on you recently, I might well have continued to hold my first impression. But you are too good an actor, and the role you play doesn't fit your history. I find it inconceivable that a man who speaks Russian, French, and Vietnamese and holds a doctorate in military administration from Stanford University could be the simple soldier you pretend to be. Also, my assistant, Maria Vicente, has confirmed the error of my first analysis. It becomes even more obvious, when one reads your dissertation on psychological warfare during the Vietnam war. What was it called? 'The Limits of Terror'? Fascinating document, General. I must confess it gripped me in a way that very little does these days."

"It was hardly original, Doctor. The basic idea can be stated in one sentence and was by one of my sergeants."

"Oh? And that sentence is?"

"Grab 'em by the balls and their hearts and minds will follow. For a while."

Esterhazy began to laugh, a dry old man's laugh, coughing into his napkin. "You'll do, General. You'll do. You remind me of one of my colleagues in the Hungarian resistance movement. Charming fellow. He was accustomed to lick his knife after sticking it into a German's back."

A white-gloved waiter served a slender glass of sherry to the old man and a beer in a crystal goblet to Doyle.

"But we are not here to reminisce, are we, General? I need your help. Or I should say *we* do. The president and I."

"I work for him. All he has to do is give me an order."

"We need more than obedience, General. We need an advocate. Somebody who can go to the Pentagon and persuade the brass to accept the new military budget, if not with enthusiasm, then with grace. We don't want the military sniping behind our backs when we go up to the Hill. Not that we won't win. We will. No matter what. But the president wants a show of unity within the administration. He thinks you can help bring the military around."

"I'm only a lowly major general, Doctor. At the bottom of the seniority list. You don't know how the military works if you think the Joint Chiefs of Staff are going to listen to me. Hell, I'd be lucky to get in to see them."

Esterhazy shook his head. "If you'll pardon me, General, that is a lot of crap. You're the president's military aide. You're closer to him than anybody in the Pentagon. My information is that the hierarchy over there is in chaos since the resignation of the Joint Chiefs. They're like virgins at an orgy, disoriented. They would talk to anybody who would give them a line on the president's thinking."

"They might listen to me. Persuading them is something else."

"Look, General. Stop fencing. I know you. I've read your file from cover to cover. At forty-eight, you're the youngest major general in the army. There is nobody even faintly like you. You came out of the Virginia hills, a poverty-stricken half-Indian orphan, and got a West Point athletic scholarship. Your combat record is the best in the army. Four tours in Vietnam. Every medal in the book. Defense attaché in Moscow. Former commander of the Special Forces Brigade and the army's only combat-ready fighting force, the Eighty-Second Airborne. Brilliant academic career. You have, in the vernacular, punched every ticket, and if you keep your nose clean and don't foul up, you're sure to be the chairman of the Joint Chiefs one day."

Doyle met the man's chilly gray eyes. "All right. What do you want me to tell them? That they have to accept defense budget cuts that will emasculate the country's defense forces? They know that already. Just what kind of mesmerism am I supposed to use to make them smile as they lose their balls? And anyway, why are you so concerned with what they think? As you say, you'll win anyway. You've got the votes."

Esterhazy leaned forward, his thin old face set in hard lines. "I don't expect you to persuade them, Doyle. But you can offer them a mixture of threats and goodies that will keep them quiet and in line until the legislation gets through Congress."

Doyle frowned. "Goodies, yes. The four top jobs are still open. And after the initial shock of the chiefs resigning there has been a lot of jockeying around. I'm not so sure about the threats."

Esterhazy sipped the pale sherry, letting the liquid rest on his tongue. "God, that's good. You really should try it."

"I prefer beer. What threats can I make?"

Esterhazy twirled the empty sherry glass in his thin, veined fingers. "When the cuts go through, about half the general officers will go with them. You'll be in a position to make sure that those loyal to the president are not affected."

"Regardless of competence?" Doyle asked. "Loyalty to the president being the only criterion?"

"Yes."

"You want me to move around the top echelon of the Defense Department, pick out a group of finks who will place careerism and loyalty to the president above principle and what they think is necessary for national defense?"

"Yes," Esterhazy said. "They're probably better officers than your square-headed, straight arrows anyway, General, and you know it. But you've stated the case with your usual admirable clarity. We're not looking for great strategists or military geniuses. We want loyalty.

21

In any case our defense advisors tell us that all the premises of our strategy are outmoded myths out of the nineteenth century. We are, in effect, geared up to fight a somewhat technologically advanced Civil War. It is all going to have to go. And to get rid of it we need a group of pliable senior officers to prepare for the next generation."

"Who are your defense advisors?"

"Professor William Sibelius of Harvard, Dr. George Dent at Chicago and Captain Samuel Vogeler of the Meineck Corporation, the West Coast think tank. You know, the successor to Rand."

"Jesus Christ," Doyle muttered. "You're kidding."

Esterhazy's face hardened. "No, General. I know what you probably think of them. Eggheads. Intellectuals. Dilettantes who've never smelled cordite. But they also happen to be the most innovative and imaginative strategic thinkers of our time. And they are going to set defense policy for this administration over the next few years. So you had better get used to it. Or get out."

Doyle stared across the table, his dark face immobile and his somewhat flat gray eyes recessed behind high cheekbones. His body was still, the muscular hands surrounding the beer glass carved in stone. Esterhazy noted the long jagged scar across the back of the left one, running through the light covering of curling black hairs on the wrist and disappearing beneath the white line of his shirt cuff.

"Now look here, Doyle," Esterhazy began as a slender, hatchet-faced man with graying sideburns down to the jawline drifted up to the table. "Good afternoon, Doctor," he said, ignoring Doyle, pulling up a chair from a neighboring table and straddling it—an action which drew a look of frantic despair from Jacques who discouraged table-hopping with chilly rage.

22

"Well, if it isn't my favorite anchor man," Esterhazy said. "Hello, Dick, what can I do for you?"

"Who's your friend?" the newsman said, hooking a finger in Doyle's direction. "One of the mutineers?"

"General Steven Doyle. I'm sure you know Richard Mariani, General, Italy's gracefully aging gift to millions of television screens."

Mariani stared at Doyle, his black eyes narrowed to slits. "Doyle. Hell, I know you, General. We served in Nam together. You remember me? I was working for the Los Angeles *Times* then. I covered the relief column that came in to get you out of that trap at Dak Lo. Christ, you must remember me, huh?"

"I remember you," Doyle said.

"This guy's famous, Doctor," Mariani said, turning to Esterhazy. "The men used to call him—" He snapped his fingers in irritation. "What was it they called you, General?"

Doyle was silent, the skin over the high cheekbones of his face seeming to have drawn more taut.

"No, I remember—Apache. You're part Indian, huh, General?" Mariani turned to Esterhazy. "The general was a captain then, commanding a company." Mariani's voice changed, and he was suddenly using the oily tones of his nightly television newscast. "He and a hundred and fifty men dug in on a small hill just outside the village of Dak Lo in June 1968. By morning they were surrounded by Cong. Cut off. Nobody worried at first. The copters would come in and get them out. But within twenty-four hours there were an estimated two thousand gooks in the jungle around them, and the division was under heavy attack twenty miles away. They toughed it out for five days. Six copters went down bringing out wounded and supplying them. The Cong were about ready to wipe them out. That right, General?" Mariani asked, turning toward Doyle who did not answer.

"Yeah, well, it was bad, but the worst was the guy on the other side with the bullhorn. Spoke almost perfect British English. He spent all day and most of the night taunting them, spitting out communist propaganda, telling the blacks they were slaves, telling them what would happen if they didn't surrender. He was good, too. By about the sixth day, Doyle here was having trouble holding the men in line. It had been a problem company when he took it over just before the operation, and it looked as if they'd mutiny and surrender any minute. So, Doctor, you know what the general did?"

Esterhazy glanced at Doyle who was staring into a small space between the upper lip and nostrils of the newsman.

"Well, old Apache here blacks his face and disappears into the night just as the Cong announcer starts his harangue. He's got about thirty feet of light helicopter-lifting cable coiled over his shoulder and a knife. Well, about a half-hour later, the announcer stops. Right in the middle of a sentence. The guys up on the hill had about had it. They think the crazy goddamn Indian captain is gone and they can surrender. Then the noise stops. It's been going on for days, and the quiet is almost worse than the son-of-a-bitch telling them what's going to happen. About an hour and a half later, Doyle shows up without the wire, and everybody's a little disappointed."

Esterhazy, bored, glanced at his watch and shot Doyle, who continued to stare at the newsman, a glance. "Look, it's all very fascinating, Dick, but we're in rather a hurry," the old man said.

Mariani nodded, his thin, northern Italian face

24

creased in an evil smirk. "I'm coming to the end. When the sun came up the men didn't notice anything at first. Then they saw it. Hanging from a cottonwood tree about fifty feet in front of their lines and maybe a hundred yards from the edge of the jungle where the Cong were."

Esterhazy glanced up sharply. "What are you talking about?"

"You see, Doyle had slipped into the Cong lines, cut a couple of throats and snatched the guy who was talking over the bullhorn. The Americans just didn't do things like that normally. They hid in their trenches. So the Cong were out in front of their lines and careless. The Cong didn't weigh much, you know, and this was just a little guy. Doyle took him back to that tree, alive, and tied him up in a 'chicken' position, arms behind his back, legs laced to them. Then he attached him to that helo cable and strung him up the tree. When the sun came up, he was swinging there between the lines, a little guy in black pyjamas. Alive. And get this. Hanging from his neck was the portable bullhorn."

"Is that true?" Esterhazy turned to Doyle.

"Oh, it's true all right," Mariani said. "Christ, I saw the remnant of the guy when I came in with the relief column two days later. But you haven't heard it all. Turns out the guy was the Cong battalion commander, a big hero, and his troops kind of lost their heads when they saw him hanging there. Something which Doyle here probably had figured would happen. So they rushed the tree. In broad daylight. Only by then every MG in the company was enfilading the area. They lost about a hundred men in that first attack and a couple of hundred more during the course of the day. But they couldn't reach him. They tried for two days to get him down, before he finally ordered them to kill him. How many men did that Cong battalion lose, General? Five hundred? A thousand? You got a field promotion for that action, if I remember correctly. Well, nice seeing you again, General, Doctor. Forgot what it was I wanted to talk to you about." He stood and extended his hand to Doyle, who met his eyes briefly and turned away, ignoring it.

Mariani's teeth drew back over his lips. "Okay, General," he said. "That story never got used at the time. My paper thought I made it up. But maybe I can find a place for it in one of my broadcasts. On the evils of the military caste." He turned and moved off, weaving expertly between the closely packed tables like a waiter on vacation.

"Is that story true?"

Doyle shrugged, prying lose his fingers from the beer glass.

"You showed admirable self-control, General. I would have expected you to react violently to such rudeness."

"That's what the Cong second-in-command did when he saw his commander hanging from the tree."

Esterhazy smiled. "Did you get that particular wisdom from your Indian ancestors?"

"No. From von Clausewitz."

CHAPTER THREE

The president glanced up and down the long oval table with seats for thirty. Only ten were taken. Directly across from him a portrait of Washington in jowly middle age looked down across the left shoulder of the Secretary of the Treasury.

"Where is Coleridge?" the president asked. All the members of the president's Board of Economic Counselors were present except the Secretary of Labor, Rufus S. Coleridge.

"Plane trouble over Pittsburgh, Mr. President," the board's secretary said. "Undersecretary O'Donlan is representing Labor."

The President nodded, his chilly blue eyes focusing on the top button of Vice-President Joshua Harrington's vest across the table.

"Very well. Let's begin. First, as must be obvious, this is no normal meeting of the board. I've asked the chiefs of the defense and foreign policy liaison staffs to sit in so they can brief the Pentagon and State once we've finished. You needn't take notes, gentlemen, since you'll be provided a resumé of what Dr. Vicente is going to tell us. I might add at this point that we're not here to conduct a debate. The time for that is past. I've spoken to each of you individually and collectively for more than two years about what I want to do as president. The time for talk is past. Circumstances have now made it possible to put into practice some of the plans we have discussed at such length. They are embodied in the document you have in front of you." The president lifted a nine-hundred page blue book lying on the polished surface of the table and let it drop.

"The New Economic Plan—NEP—is the result of two years of intensive effort by the best economic brains in the nation. Dr. Istvan Esterhazy has synthesized their efforts and added yours. What you have before you is the first attempt ever made in the United States to develop a rational, integrated approach to the economic and social problems of the country. It attempts to define the goals of our society and to align its resources toward the efficient realization of those goals. It excises campaign rhetoric and, even more important, it ignores the desires of special interest groups. It is, gentlemen, a blueprint for a socio-economic revolution which will take the economic decision-making of this country out of the hands of a self-interested oligarchy and put it into those of the people. The end product will be, if we're wise and lucky, a redistribution of the economic benefits in a more equitable fashion and at the same time it will shift the emphasis of our lives from a continuing mindless consumerism into a more balanced and sensible lifestyle."

The president stopped, his icy blue eyes moving around the table, a slight smile on his thin lips. "I see a certain amount of consternation even among those of you who agree with me. I know what you're thinking.

28

Are we moving too fast? Is the country ready for it? Well, gentlemen, I think the time for dissimulation and half measures is past. We have a unique opportunity which may not come again for decades to do what must be done. The nation is ready for brutal measures. We've been deep in the worst recession since the nineteen-thirties for more than three years. The people are both angry and frightened. The business and banking communities are in complete disarray. With the overwhelming majorities we've won in both houses of Congress, we're in a position to make 1987 a watershed in American history." He paused with the practiced drama of a trained politician, his slender, handsome face deliberately hardening. "The people are behind me, gentlemen. Make no mistake about it. For two years they have seen my programs to help them frustrated by special interests. They have noted the obstructionism by men of small intelligence and little talent. They have given us a message, and I intend to heed it. This plan is a revolution, make no mistake. But it will be a revolution made by lawyers and economists using computers, not by bearded terrorists wielding grease guns. The means will be as dull and unobtrusive as we can make them: tax law, administrative reform, investment incentives, controls on wages and profits. There will be nothing dramatic, and the plan envisages a period of some fifteen to twenty years before the process is completed. But once it is begun, and we have six years to rivet it onto the economy, it will take a brave man indeed to sabotage or dismantle it."

The president paused, his long, sensitive fingers drumming lightly on the table. "History, gentlemen, may well record this gray revolution as being more exciting than 1776 or 1917. It may be written that we have wrought something far more important than the men who made those revolutions. For we will have transformed a modern capitalist state at the service of a mindless materialism in the interests of a small minority into a modern, humanistic nation dedicated to the spiritual, intellectual and cultural betterment of man. We will, in short, have put this great dynamo of witless activity, the most powerful economic unit in history, at the service of man rather than allowing it to make him its slave."

The silence was broken by a single burst of applause from across the table as the vice-president, grinning broadly, pounded his meaty palms together. After a startled moment, the others joined in.

As the applause died, the president glanced down at his notes and continued, suppressing a grimace of irritation. "I should like to add one more thing. Much of the plan has already leaked to the press. With their usual penchant for complicating the simple and finding plots where none exist, it is being made to seem that it is the work of what columnist Kip Dean calls my economic Rasputin, Dr. Esterhazy. As must be obvious to everyone here, this is utter nonsense.

"Dr. Esterhazy was my professor at Princeton. He is a distinguished economic thinker. I trust his judgment implicitly. But this plan is mine, not his, just as is the philosophy behind it. Dr. Esterhazy is chairman of the Board of Economic Counselors and my good friend. He is not the *eminence grise* of this administration but its loyal servant. As most of you know all too well, Dr. Esterhazy regards meetings such as this one as a distasteful waste of time and declines to attend." The president smiled.

"I can see that some of you agree. However, I have asked his staff chief, Dr. Maria Vicente, whom I think all of you know, to explain the broad outlines of what we are planning. Dr. Vicente."

"Thank you, Mr. President." A tall, slender woman in her mid-thirties rose from a seat behind the president and moved to one end of the cabinet room. The severe cut of her suit could not conceal her startlingly sensuous body. Her voice was crisp and uninflected. "I hope you gentlemen don't mind, but I'm going to use the screen. My presentation will be short, covering only the major points of the president's policy. The details are in the written report," she said, indicating the folders in front of each man. "Most of you already know the broad outlines of what we're planning. What may not be so clear is the methods we intend to use." As she pressed a small device in her left hand, an electronic screen descended to her right and a chart came into focus.

"This is a model of the 1986 economic year which now coincides with the calendar year. Today is December 22nd, so we're projecting the last ten days, but it's accurate to about one-tenth of one percent. As you can see, unemployment has levelled off at thirteen percent. The real gross national product is down almost twenty percent from two trillion eight hundred and eighty billion in 1983 to two trillion three hundred billion today. Real personal income has declined proportionately. Inflation continues at close to fifteen percent. The Dow Jones average today slipped below 450, a loss of almost 1600 points since the end of the last bull market in 1983. Our balance of payments shows only a fifty billion dollar deficit for the year solely because agricultural exports have been spectacular. The budget shows a deficit of 120 billion dollars on expenditures of 750 billion. Strikes and wildcat work stoppages cost the economy 200 million man days in 1986, by far the largest in our history. Only 1945 approaches this disastrous

31

loss of production and that year we lost only 125 million man days.

"In brutally down-to-earth terms all this means that average per capita income in 1983 was $12,000. Today that figure is $9,000 in constant dollars, a reduction of 25 percent.

"If we continue the policies now in effect, 1987 could well see an additional three to five percent deterioration in the economic profile. The major immediate problem is unemployment. Our plan will attack this head on. The negative income tax is today providing every wage earner in the country with a minimum of $10,000 per year based on a family of four. This will be terminated. It will be replaced by a program under which every individual seeking employment will be offered three opportunities for a government job. He may reject the first two, but if he does not accept the third, then all subsistence payments will be terminated.

"The government will institute over the next two years massive public works projects, both urban and rural, within which every able-bodied individual in the United States will be offered employment. No one will be turned away. Within this time span, there will be a job for everyone who wants it and is able to perform it. Those disabled for whatever reason will be paid a subsistence income above the poverty line. In order to make this program viable, large numbers of people will be required to relocate. Huge urban conglomerations with heavy unemployment will be gradually depopulated. An attempt will be made at the same time to strike a racial balance in the relocation areas in rough equivalency with the national profile."

The vice-president cleared his throat. "I'm not quite sure I follow that, Ms. Vicente. Could you clarify?"

The young woman smiled. "I am afraid I lapsed into

the jargon of the trade. It simply means that we'll attempt to resettle large numbers of unemployed blacks and other difficult-to-assimilate minorities in medium-sized and small communities with low minority concentrations but only in numbers equal to their percentage of the population at large. A city with a hundred thousand people with excess jobs and no minorities could expect to welcome ten thousand blacks and ten thousand from other minorities from a large metropolitan area with a population mix of fifty-fifty. This would gradually spread the problem and, hopefully, ameliorate it."

"Good God." The vice-president let his breath out explosively. "You can't be serious. You'll start a revolution."

"We'll have one if we don't do something," the president said, his dry voice sharp with irritation. "I'd appreciate it, gentlemen, if you'd let Maria finish before interrupting. We'll then take any questions you may have. I repeat, however, that the program is in final form. It will not be debated here."

"I should have made it clear that we don't propose to coerce anyone to move." Maria looked around the table at the vice-president, her slim, serious face creased by an engaging smile. "It's just that people who need and want work will have to go where it is."

"And if they don't they'll starve," the vice-president said, flushing at the warning look from the president.

"Nobody has starved in the last two years and nobody will starve under this program, Mr. Vice-President," the young woman said. "But to participate fully, individuals will have to conform to certain rules. Otherwise it's just more of the chaos we're experiencing now. Obviously, none of this will be done overnight. Please don't have visions of boxcars packed with hollow-cheeked refugees. Each move will be voluntary, dictated by the social and economic interests of the people involved. Teams of aides will move through the big city ghettos advising people of the opportunities and pointing out the disadvantages of staying. Community advisors will prepare the areas to which they will be moving to receive them.

"Obviously a program of this type will necessitate large rehousing schemes. This is deliberate. Housing is one of the most depressed areas of the economic profile. Government subsidies for housing will put large numbers of people to work and generate more employment in the private sector among the suppliers.

"The work programs will involve both economically and socially useful projects. Schools, dams, highways, and public transport systems will be heavily subsidized. However, a great deal more money will be put into programs designed to regenerate the nation socially. Parks will be built and refurbished, and combined adult education, cultural and sports centers will be constructed in every population center of more than 50,000, which means in every neighborhood containing that many people in a large city. Very large numbers of unemployed intellectuals will be employed in self-education and adult education programs revolving around these centers which we envision as becoming the intellectual and social hub of every large neighborhood.

"In the countryside, abandoned or uncultivated land will be bought at condemned rates by government corporations and reforested, converted into pasturage, or used as parkland. Vast numbers of the unemployed will be organized to eradicate both rural and urban slums, saving what is salvageable and destroying what isn't." Maria Vicente looked up from her notes and smiled. "We'll turn the country into one big garden."

The vice-president interrupted in an outraged yelp. "My God, it's all totally unconstitutional. You can't do any of these things. The law won't let you."

"Josh," the president spoke softly. "I must insist that you not interrupt. The plan envisages constitutional changes where there is a conflict. However, in the initial stages virtually everything can be done by administrative decree. We'll simply drag it out through the courts until the proper amendments can be rammed through. I don't intend to have any problems with the Supreme Court. And if we do, I'll simply add six more justices of my own choosing."

"You think you can get away with something Roosevelt couldn't manage?" Harrington asked, incredulous.

"Yes, Josh, I do. We have the votes in Congress. He didn't. But I won't have to do anything. The Court will go along, because it knows I have the power. The idea that the Supreme Court can buck a president with a congressional majority solidly behind him is, and always has been, absurd. Roosevelt didn't have that majority. I have. But a majority is nothing without the will to use it. Which I also have." He turned to the woman who had leaned against the woodpaneled wall waiting quietly. "Please go on, Maria."

"Obviously, to put this plan into effect means a major realignment of resources. The biggest single slice of money, aside from social insurance and health services, which we don't plan to reduce, is the defense budget. At two hundred and fifty billion dollars a year it represents more than ten percent of the gross national product. Our staff studies indicate that a suitable defense posture can be provided for half that amount of money." Maria Vicente looked up, her green eyes circling the room. "Our defense establishment has based its budget on certain outmoded concepts of bipolar power relationships which are no longer valid in a world of pluralist power centers." She smiled down at the vice-president. "Which in plain language means that there are no longer two power centers, Russia and the United States, but four including the China-Japan axis and a reunited nuclear-armed Germany."

The image on the electronic screen changed. "You'll note the respective force levels in these four super-power complexes. Since the Sino-Soviet conflict in 1983 and the reunification of East and West Germany following the breakup of the Soviet-Eastern European hegemony, there has been a radical realignment of force. It is no longer essential, or even desirable, for the United States to invest such a massive amount of its resources in what is an intrinsically sterile activity. Defense expenditures are economically useless in a controlled economy, and we plan to reduce them by maintaining a minimum credible nuclear deterrent which will enable us to reply with devastating force to any first strike."

"What about conventional forces?" the vice-president asked.

"They will be reduced to a marine attack force of one division integrated into the army and a five-division army of three hundred thousand men. The navy and air force will be halved."

"You'll leave us defenseless," the vice-president said, incredulous.

"No, Mr. Vice-President. We won't. It would take a foolish statesman indeed to attack us if he knew we could reply with such devastating nuclear force. The nuclear deterrent will remain unaffected."

"What about confrontations short of major war? Something in the Caribbean, Africa, the Middle East, or South America? Are we just going to concede the world outside our borders to our enemies?"

Maria Vicente's voice hardened. "Mr. Vice-President, we have not had spectacular success over the past two decades in attempting to police the world or to impose our doctrines on it. This program presupposes a foreign policy of non-intervention in the affairs of other nations."

"Josh," the president interrupted, "we are not living in a world of monolithic communist conspiracy anymore. We simply don't need to assume that hostility will result from countries which install socialist regimes. Especially if we alter our own system as drastically as this plan proposes and cease to meddle in their affairs. Now, I would appreciate it if we could allow Maria to finish her presentation without further interruptions."

"Thank you, Mr. President. Obviously, simply cutting the defense budget isn't going to free all the money we need. The process is going to entail a radical redistribution of income and capital." A new image appeared on the electronic screen outlining a complicated tax model.

"We envision an immediate increase in taxes on unearned income rising to ninety-five percent with no exemptions after the first hundred thousand dollars. Capital gains taxes will be taxed as unearned income." She smiled faintly at a gasp down the table. "Regular income taxes will rise from the present maximum of fifty percent to eighty-five percent on all earned income in excess of two hundred thousand dollars. And finally, inheritance taxes will be increased to fifty percent of everything over one hundred thousand dollars, ninety percent of everything in excess of one million dollars, and ninety-nine percent of everything in excess of five million dollars. The first hundred thousand will be free of inheritance tax. We intend to close all the loopholes allowing the transmission of money within families to avoid death duties. Tax rates on middle-class incomes from twenty to one hundred thousand dollars, which is where most of the money is, will rise gradually to levels assuring a more socially desirable distribution of income."

Secretary of the Treasury George Wiesenthal expelled a breath. "My God, you can't mean this, Mr. President. There will be a massive flight of capital. It amounts to the confiscation of all wealth."

"Yes, George. It does. But painlessly. Over two generations. Nobody will be hurt all that much immediately. As for the flight of capital, we'll stop it with heavy criminal sanctions."

"It'll never get through Congress," Vice-President Harrington said. "It's just too radical."

"Please continue, Maria. There are some compensations for the capitalist sector, particularly for the bureaucratic managers who run it as contrasted with the unproductive owners."

"To encourage capital investment, which has been one of our system's conspicuous weaknesses over the past two decades, the corporate income tax will be drastically reduced from forty-eight to twenty-five percent, and accelerated depreciating schedules will be introduced making it possible for a corporation to avoid any taxes at all provided it reinvests its profits in socially useful ways."

"What the hell does that mean? Are you going to approve all corporate investments?" The Secretary of the Treasury sounded incredulous.

"Yes, Mr. Secretary. That's precisely what we plan to do. That is, if the corporation expects tax credits. Otherwise they can do as they like." She smiled.

"But, good God, Ms. Vicente. You'll need a staff in the hundreds of thousands to police all this," Wiesenthal exploded.

"There are large numbers of unemployed, Mr. Secretary. We have a skilled labor pool more than sufficient to handle it. In any case, since wages and prices will also be rigidly controlled, we can incorporate all this in the same bureaucratic organization."

"Wages and prices will be controlled?" The question came from down the table.

"Yes. Not temporarily, but permanently. The market mechanism is simply too cumbersome. We can't allow it to dominate a major economy such as ours. It's messy, and, to put it bluntly, screws up the economic models too badly. It's got to go, gentlemen."

"Ms. Vicente, I know we've been over all this to the point of exhaustion over the past months," the Secretary of the Treasury said. "However, I had not realized that the consensus had come up with the conclusions you've just laid out. I think it's much too radical a program, particularly the tax proposals and the permanent wage and price controls. I favor a radical redistribution of income, but this program is too revolutionary. The medicine might kill the patient. The experience of Eastern European social systems has been that only with a quasi-market economy can you keep a realistic price structure. All this, combined with the confiscatory tax measure, is going to cause traumas to the economy we can't forecast."

"Mr. Secretary, the Eastern European countries were living in an economic wasteland when they tried what we're proposing. They didn't have the computer technology or the sophisticated economic models we do. Today, it's a new ball game and the sooner it gets started the sooner we'll get this economy moving again."

39

The president glanced up and down the table. "I don't think Ms. Vicente need go any further, gentlemen. You have the full program in front of you. It will be presented to Congress just after my State of the Union message on January 25th. Meantime we intend to leak it extensively. If you have any comments, please make them to Ms. Vicente who will have them staffed out before getting them to me." He glanced at his watch. "I'm afraid I've a terribly crowded schedule. I'm sure you'll forgive me if we break this up. I assume nobody has any serious reservations about the program as outlined?"

The president's chilly blue eyes swept the table as he rose.

The Secretary of the Treasury, a film of sweat on his balding forehead, cleared his throat. "Well, Mr. President, yes, I'm afraid I still do have some problems with it. For one, it doesn't reflect what the working parties from Treasury understood would be the main lines of the proposal and second—"

The president interrupted, his voice steely. "George, the program was put together by the best economic brains this country possesses. If your people were not able to get their ideas in, then their ideas weren't good enough. The question before this meeting is: can all of you give these proposals your wholehearted support? If not . . ." The president's silence was eloquent with menace.

Secretary of the Treasury George Wiesenthal lifted his bulk out of the chair facing the president, his normally florid face pale with anger. "If my remaining in your cabinet is contingent on supporting this program, you'll have my resignation on your desk within the hour. Good day, Mr. President." He turned and strode out of the room.

"Well, gentlemen." The president's voice released the

tension. "George has been his predictable choleric self. Is there anyone else among you who feels this strongly?" His gaze once again swept the table. "No? Then I take it we can all agree and get behind this program with all our force and energy. Maria will be orchestrating the public support operation and assigning each of you gentlemen a role in selling it to the people. Not, I think, that it will take much selling." The tall slender figure turned and left the room, trailed by his foreign affairs and defense counselors.

CHAPTER FOUR

Vice-President Joshua Harrington yawned discreetly and snatched a glance at his watch as the senator from California held forth in the almost empty Senate chamber, telling his three drowsy colleagues about the rape of the redwoods with an intensity which indicated that an important citizens' lobby was in the gallery.

"These trees, more than four thousand years old, the depository of our most precious heritage, nature, must be saved. And what is this government doing? Nothing. For a sum of money so small as to be ridiculous, this fifteen-hundred-acre stretch of land which is crucial to the survival of these great trees can be bought and preserved for coming generations. The time is past when the industrial giants of our society can trample on the interests of the people with impunity. The people will and must be heard. And served."

Harrington glanced up at the gallery, searching it for the group Willard Campbell must be addressing. Over to the left a dozen people stared down at the speaker with earnest intensity. Harrington hid a grin in the pile of papers in front of him. He wondered if they knew that Campbell's brother-in-law was chief attorney for the timber company being castigated on the Senate floor. Or that the bill being introduced, while saving fifteen hundred acres of virgin redwood in a high-visibility area which the company couldn't cut anyway without a public uproar, meant selective harvesting on another thirty thousand acres of protected federal parkland under the guise of weeding out sick and diseased trees. Campbell was a slick bastard, concealing his duplicity behind an unending fount of liberal clichés delivered in that earnest, straightforward style which oozed sincerity. He was the darling of the environmentalist and anti-pollution forces in California.

Campbell finished with an understated rhetorical flourish, and Harrington hastily adjourned the session, moving down across the well of the Senate to congratulate the speaker. "Great speech, Will. Really put it to 'em that time. Made them greedy capitalist bastards quake in their boots, huh?"

Campbell met the vice-president's grin with chilly suspicion. Behind the cornpone accent and backslapping, used-car-salesman facade, Harrington was noted for the painless insertion of a lethal verbal icepick. "Yes, well, sombody has to do it, Josh. Otherwise the bastards will pave over everything they don't turn into a coal mine."

"Right, Will. Absolutely right. Say, I can't figure out that bill. Too dumb, I guess. What's Anheuser going to get per acre when we buy it? That timber must be worth a bundle. You got it figured on some sort of special timber-foot calculation which don't mean much to me."

"Well," Campbell cleared his throat and looked around him, "it will work out at about fifteen million,

Josh. We couldn't just take it away from him, much as I would have liked to."

Harrington nodded, staring down at the other man, blue eyes smiling. "Well, that's just great, Will. Another victory for the forces of progress at the expense of the bloated capitalists," he said, moving off across the floor, his big athlete's body still showing the power and grace of one of the best fullbacks ever fielded at State University. The nickname "Big Cat," bestowed by a bored sports writer one lazy Saturday afternoon during a dull game, had stuck and he was still known to his intimates at the weekly Capitol poker games as "Cat."

The Chief Senate Usher intercepted him as he left the floor with a neatly folded note on heavy embossed Senate stationery. "I would greatly appreciate meeting with you immediately, if this suits your convenience," it read. The almost illegible signature perplexed Harrington for a moment.

"Where is he?"

"In your private office, Mr. Vice-President." Harrington had spent twenty years in the Senate before his election as vice-president, and during that period, along with seniority and committee assignments, he had collected a small geographic empire of hidden offices and mini-staffs which constituted his private fief. He retained many such hideaways as V.P. His "private" office was a small two-room suite hidden in a dead-end corridor which housed the clerical staff of the World War I Veterans Affairs Committee, one of the most somnolent on the Hill. It was his retreat of last resort, known only to a few intimates who respected his need for privacy and moments of solitude in a relentlessly public business. his salary, equal to that of a high-ranking civil servant,

The usher had been in the Senate for forty years, and

was earned many times over. His legendary discretion and judgment were combined with a loyalty to the institution and its members which were without price in a social order which was the closest thing in human experience to a jungle. For here the rule of the strong and the subservience of the weak was rigidly established. The old bulls wielded the power while always walking in fear of the ambush, electoral or legislative, which would bring them down. As with all such power elites, they surrounded themselves with courtiers and the perquisites of power in order to persuade themselves that it was all worth it.

"Hello, Sue," Harrington said, as he entered the outer office of the small suite. Somehow, despite everything, it always embarrassed him the first time he saw her every day. Vestiges of puritan guilt, he guessed. Hell, at sixty-two he could be not only her father, but with a little sexual precosity, her grandfather.

"Good afternoon, Mr. Vice-President," she said, her pale face haloed by the mass of dark hair gathered in a bun at the back of her neck. The white blouse was cut discreetly, offering almost no view of the small breasts pushing against it. A tiny gold cross hung from a black band drawn tight around her neck. Harrington felt his groin muscles tighten at the sight of it. The last time he'd seen her, it was all she wore.

"I understand the admiral is waiting."

"Yes. He's in your inner office." She glanced at her watch. It was six o'clock. "Do you want me to wait?"

Harrington cleared his throat, staring down into luminous brown eyes meeting his steadily. Even after a year, she was still a little unreal. She'd applied for a job as a researcher fresh from a Ph.D. in history at Stanford, a pale, slender girl with the face of a fourteen-year-old virgin, and the mores of a Singapore hooker. She made him nervous. "Would you mind?"

"No. I wouldn't mind." She turned back to a mass of papers on the desk as he entered the inner office, a panelled sanctuary of deep brown natural wood and leather chairs scuffed with age. Admiral William Christman rose to meet him, looking awkward in a blue tweed suit a size too big and a shade too bright.

"Hello, Josh," Christman said.

The vice-president took his hand, huge with a mat of curling reddish hair covering the back. They were both big men, still lean, with the craggy faces of aging athletes who had spent many hours squinting into the sun.

"Good to see you, Bill. Christ, you look silly as hell in that suit."

Christman grinned. "That's what my wife says."

Harrington motioned him to a chair. "Drink?"

"No thanks."

"Well, I'll have one," Harrington said, moving to a bar concealed in a wooden sideboard, splashing a liberal dose of a famous Tennessee sour mash into a heavy crystal glass and adding ice cubes. As he sank into one of the leather chairs he met Christman's eyes and said casually, letting his southern drawl deepen, "Well you sure fucked it up this time, Bill. Front, sideways, and ass backwards."

"You think so, Josh?"

"Yes, I think so. You turned the Defense Department over to those horses' asses behind the president. They'll dig down deep now and pull out some gutless opportunists for the Joint Chiefs who'll act like those little dolls dipping their snouts into water, bowing and scraping into eternity. That, my friend, is what you impulsive jerks have done."

"Maybe I will have that drink," Christman said, pulling his big body out of the chair and making a scotch and soda. "You realize there isn't much we could have done if we'd stayed? He didn't even ask our opinion. Christ, Josh, I'm not sure those young hotshots of his even read our budget. What came out of the economic council looks as if it had been drawn up by a butcher, not an economist."

Harrington shook his head. "No, goddamn it, Bill. You're wrong and you're kidding yourself. My staff has gone over that proposed defense budget line by line, and I'll tell you something. It's brilliant. In many ways I agree with it. Only problem is, it goes about seventy-five percent too far. But the principles behind that budgeting process are sound. The Pentagon has been pissing away the taxpayer's money ever since the Second World War. This is just about the first time since McNamara anybody has tried to get it under control."

Christman shrugged wearily, taking a long pull on the scotch. "Look, Josh. There are three million people involved. It's the biggest business in the country. There's bound to be some fat. You think General Motors is a model of efficiency? Hell, I've read studies that say they've got three managers for every job. Even we're not that bad. And we're not a fifth as well paid."

Harrington grinned. "I'm on your side, Bill. That is, if you've still got a side. But resigning was just plain brilliant. All you've done is given up any worthwhile platform to fight from, opted out, and killed any influence you might have up here on the Hill, which is where you might have stopped him."

"You think this Congress would buck him? You really think so, Josh?"

Harrington shook his head. "No. I've got to say, I don't. He's got the House in his pocket, at least for the first six months, and these new senators are going to go down the line with him in the beginning. He's in command, no question about it. Everybody is scared shitless, and he's the only one with a plan."

Christman stared down into the half-melted ice cubes at the bottom of his glass. "That's the way I figured it, Josh. He can't be stopped. Not by any conventional methods, anyway."

Harrington's big head shot up. "Just what the hell does that mean?"

Christman met his look. "It means, Josh, that I'm not ready to settle for the end of the United States as a world power. I'm not willing to tuck my tail and scuttle away because that skinny-assed, arrogant intellectual tells me he's God. If this plan goes through, the United States is finished as an influence in the world. It may not even survive, given the level of defense he's proposing. The temptation for our enemies to hit us will become intense over the next few years as they watch us deliberately courting suicide. Nobody's going to believe we'll continue to cut off our own balls forever. And they'll decide to take us out while we're weak." Christman shook his head. "Hell, there are times when I think he must be doing it deliberately. That he really wants us to lose."

Harrington stared at the big man slumped in his chair across the room tilting his glass back and forth. "Just what are you planning, Bill?" His voice was soft and gentle.

Christman stood up, shrugging the ill-fitting tweed jacket into place. "I'm not sure. There's probably nothing I can do. But I'm not alone, Josh. Just about every general officer in the army and air force as well as the command staff of the navy has panicked over this thing. It's not going to be as easy as he thinks."

"You're still under his orders, Bill," Harrington

warned. "You'll get yourself in real trouble if you're not careful. He's a ruthless bastard behind that prissy exterior. He won't hesitate to cut you down if you cross him."

"I know that. What I wanted to hear from you was that there was no other way. That it couldn't be done in the normal democratic fashion." Christman picked up an old-fashioned gray fedora from the leather seat and extended his hand. "Thanks for seeing me, Josh."

Harrington took the hand and gripped the naval officer's upper arm with his left. "Relax, Bill. Don't take it so hard. We usually wind up with a livable compromise in this country. It's one of our marks of political genius. You're too close to this thing to take an objective view. What about going to the Sugar Bowl game with us over New Year's? You and Martha. It's Navy's year. First bowl in years. I've got tickets in the presidential box. He won't be going. Hates football. We can take Air Force One to New Orleans."

Christman started to laugh. "You're something else, Josh. What would that bastard say if he knew you'd invited me to sit in his box?"

Harrington's jovial face suddenly hardened into flat, muscular planes and his blue eyes lost all expression. "Bill, I'm vice-president, not his personal servant. If you can make the game, let me know. And don't do anything stupid."

He watched the other man leave, wide shoulders turning slightly to go through the door, remembering how he'd looked moving into the line ahead of him to block. They'd both been on the unbeaten Great Lakes Naval Air Station team of 1945. It had been one of the most awesome football teams ever assembled, filled with former college stars waiting to be discharged and young hotshots eager to make a name. He and Christman, a former Annapolis fullback, had come back from the Pacific and played together for three months, beginning a friendship which had lasted for more than forty years.

"You wanted me to stay?"

Harrington turned, annoyed at himself. Nostalgia was getting to be a disease. It was a fatal sign of age, if not senility.

She leaned back against the door, smiling, as she turned the lock behind her. Then, very slowly, she unbuttoned the blouse and flipped it carelessly across the back of a chair. Her small, upturned breasts, quickly freed of the brassiere, stood out against the remnants of a summer tan. She slipped out of the skirt and spread her legs, fists on her hips, grinning at him now, a black garter belt holding up dark stockings, the tops ending several inches below the strip of white which her bikini had covered. She wore no pants.

"Jesus, baby you are something else," Harrington said, feeling the words force themselves out of his constricted throat.

She moved over, grinning widely now, letting the mass of thick black hair loose around her shoulders until it fell to her hips, and dropped to her knees between his legs, deftly freed him and leaned forward.

He lifted her gently onto his lap and kissed her. "If it's all the same to you, honey, I'd rather fuck."

CHAPTER FIVE

Doyle leaned back in his chair, positioned his feet on the desk and took a pull from the heavy coffee mug marked with the presidential seal. It was the best time of the day. At seven-thirty in the morning the White House offices were still empty except for an occasional weary duty officer waiting out his shift and the inevitable guards. Even the poker game in the press room had usually wound down as the members of the "death watch" prepared to call it a night. Outside it was still dark, and the traffic on Pennsylvania Avenue was beginning to pick up as the mass of civil servants flowed in from the bedroom communities around the capital.

He stretched, enjoying the weariness in his muscles. The three-mile morning run was getting tougher every year. It had stopped being fun three or four years ago and become a chore. Now, some mornings, it was torture. He wondered why he bothered. He'd realized years ago that through some luck of metabolism, his body would probably never run to fat. And the chances of his leading a division in combat were now remote, eliminating his only professional reason to continue the physical fitness nonsense. But over the years it had become an essential discipline, an intellectual as well as a physical need.

The messenger opened his office door without knocking, nodding familiarly. "Morning, General."

"Hello, Sam."

"Lousy weather, huh, General? Looks like it might snow." He handed Doyle the green plastic folder containing the International Intelligence Estimates put out daily by the Intelligence Advisory Group—IAG—successor to the Central Intelligence Agency and perennial congressional whipping boy.

"Anything new?"

The messenger grinned. "You know I can't read, General. See you tomorrow."

Doyle flipped through the book, a running summary of political conditions in the world on December 23, 1986. It landed on the desk of fifty senior officials in the government every morning, and its receipt was a greater indication of status than a chauffeured limousine, a corner office, or a place on the presidential plane. The spooks guarded distribution with jealous regard for real power. In Congress, only two men were on the list, the chairman of the Senate Foreign Relations Committee and the chairman of the House International Affairs Committee. Five members of the cabinet, despite angry howls, were excluded and in the economic community only the chairman of the Federal Reserve Board was privileged to read its arcane lore.

It was, Doyle knew, largely useless. Its base was a condensation of millions of words picked up by the Federal Broadcast Information Service, which monitored every national radio and television station in the world and translated its broadcasts, and millions of nuggets of information culled from publications around the world. This amorphous mass was seasoned by the much smaller input of covert agents infiltrated into the bureaucracies of foreign governments, reports from diplomatic and military attachés, and a few items traded by other intelligence organizations. At its best, it gave a quick, relatively accurate, overview of what was happening in the world at any given moment. At its worst, it was a collection of unverified gossip, character assassination, and lies planted by the opposition.

It was the first thing Doyle read every morning, and he now turned to the summary.

"Troop movements along the Siberian frontier from Khabarovsk to Lake Baikal indicate a continuing Soviet nervousness as to Chinese intentions in the area. Chinese violations of the neutral zone established following the 1983 war are now so blatant as to make the agreement a dead letter, and the Soviets have once again begun to fortify forward positions along the frontier. All indications point to a situation of continuing strain throughout the area as neither side shows any indications of wishing to resume the deadlocked Geneva negotiations to settle the frontier question.

"In South Africa Prime Minister Heinrich Goelet announced at a secret cabinet meeting that the nation's first hydrogen bomb would be ready for testing at an underground site within two weeks. Israeli scientific advisors will help with the final preparations but will leave the country before the explosion takes place. Goelet also gave a report on the status of the proposed nuclear fence to seal off South Africa from surrounding hostile regimes. He said the proposal, while technically feasible, was too expensive and would not be implemented at this time. The minister of nationalities reported that the continuing drive to force black South Africans into enclaves in the north was meeting with more and more resistance. Security forces would have to be increased by twenty percent over the next year. Efforts to establish a de facto partition of the races will continue despite international criticism.

"In Germany, friction between the officer corps of reunited East and West Germany continues. Defense Minister Egon Fritsch told American Ambassador Harold Manning that the problem was not a serious one and did not affect the fighting potential of the army of the new Germany. However, the three years since reunification had not been sufficient to integrate the armed forces completely. Comment: Fritsch is an optimist. A small but influential minority of East German officers continue to sympathize with the Soviet Union. This feeling is heightened by the class structure of the West German officer corps which is dominated by descendants of the landed aristocracy who hold the former communists in contempt. Fritsch is believed to be preparing a purge in the spring which will drive most East German dissidents out of the German armed forces.

"The escalating border war between Thailand and Cambodia, backed by Vietnam, has resulted in the fall of the Siriket government and its replacement by a military junta in which General Pham is dominant. Reports from the front indicate that the fall of Phra Don Chai is imminent and that the Thai forces are breaking before the Cambodian attack all along the line. Only Thai air superiority has contained the defeat to date. The Cambodians are poised to protest the presence of American contract mercenaries flying for the Thai air force at today's session of the United Nations.

"Despite the local frontier victories over the past week, the Cambodians are unlikely to push much deeper into Thailand. The Vietnamese have assured us that their main concern was the destruction of the hostile Siriket government, not a full-scale military campaign.

"In Canada, Prime Minister William Gannon survived the third attempt on his life by members of the Quebec Liberation Army (QLA) as he addressed a meeting of the Loyalist Society in Toronto. As Gannon began to speak, three members of the QLA eluded security guards and began to fire at the prime minister who was saved only by the bulletproof glass shield behind which he was speaking. The three terrorists were killed by members of his security team.

"In Quebec, the military governor, General Foster McPherson, warned that he would put down the proposed independence demonstrations on Sunday with force if necessary and refused to say when he would lift the eight P.M. to dawn curfew. Quebec's imprisoned governor, René Cartier, continues his hunger strike, now in its twelfth day, and his condition is reported to be degenerating. McPherson indicated he would not release Cartier without a pledge from the French Canadian leader that he would cease inciting violence.

"The FBI reports that teams of arms buyers from Quebec are continuing to smuggle weapons across the U.S.-Canadian border in preparation for an armed uprising in the spring.

"In the Pacific the inhabitants of the island republic of Nauru have completed negotiations for the sale of their desolate island home to Japan for two hundred million dollars. The seven thousand islanders will move over the next few months to portions of the Solomon Islands archipelago which they have purchased for more than one billion dollars from the Solomon Island government. The Nauru Trust, with assets totalling more than five billion dollars, has moved its headquarters from Canberra to Geneva because of Australian protests over the move which will give the Japanese a military base in the South Pacific for the first time since the Second World War. Exhaustion of the phosphate deposits on Nauru, source of the trust's wealth, left the islanders little choice but to immigrate.

"In the Middle East, the situation continues tense." Doyle glanced up from the report as his secretary entered.

"Good morning, General."

"Good morning, Louise. What's up?"

"The president wants to see you."

Doyle nodded, unwinding from his chair and shrugging into the gray herringbone suit jacket draped over the back of a chair. He, like many military men, had tended to buy his civilian clothes at Sears until he came to the White House. There, surrounded by the relaxed sartorial grace epitomized by Brooks Brothers, he had realized something was going to have to be done. The transition had been helped by a short affair with a columnist for the Washington *Herald* who had left him with an image of expensive elegance along with an incipient case of impotence before they broke it off. One of his colleagues had described the lady as a cross between Delilah and a barracuda.

Doyle's office, a small suite containing his own cubbyhole, that of two aides and his secretary, occupied a portion of the old press room in the west wing of the White House. His predecessor had intrigued for three months to obtain the coveted space when President Carter, in a rage over persistent leaks from his personal staff, had ordered the press rooms moved to the ornate old Executive Office Building shortly after his election to a second term in 1980. The decision had stuck despite howls of pain from the press corps. And the leaks had continued.

56

It was only a short walk through an inner corridor and up a flight of stairs to the anteroom of the Oval Office. Hidden closed-circuit television cameras watched him all the way, monitored in a basement cubicle twenty-four hours a day by a team of secret service men. The system had been installed in 1981 after the mentally deranged chauffeur of a North African ambassador presenting his credentials at the White House had eluded security precautions and penetrated to within ten feet of the president's outer office before being cut down in a gun battle which left two secret service men and the president's appointments secretary bleeding to death on one of the thick carpets bearing motifs of the presidential seal.

The White House curator had repaired the bullet holes in the woodwork in such a way as to leave them faintly visible. An historical record, he called it.

Doyle entered the outer office and nodded to Catherine Howland. She had been the president's secretary for more than twenty years, a slender, elegant woman with pale blue eyes who was reputed to have had an affair with him many years before, between his second and third marriages. Her office, lined with paneled walls concealing top secret file cabinets, was decorated with nineteenth-century lithographs of navy sailing ships donated to former President Carter by the Naval Reserve Officer Association and retained by his successor. Funny, Doyle thought. All of the last five presidents had been navy officers.

"Good morning, General. Please go right in. The president is waiting for you."

Doyle was never able to enter the Oval Office without an almost physical awareness that it housed the world's most powerful man. Despite diminishing relative military might and the rise of world powers such as a reunited Germany and the China-Japan alliance, the combined military-economic clout of the United States was still unequalled, and the man now slumped in a comfortable leather arm chair sucking on an empty pipe had virtually dictatorial power over it.

"Morning, Steve. Have a seat." The president waved toward a sofa on his left. "You know Harlan Worth."

Doyle nodded to the short, balding FBI director.

"Tell him what you've just told me, Harlan."

Worth cleared his throat, and glanced uneasily at the president. "You are aware, Mr. President, that my sources are risking their careers. I don't question Doyle's loyalty, but these men have come forward for patriotic reasons, and I'd hate to have them hurt by their actions."

"If they hadn't come forward they would be traitors, Harlan. I can assure you nobody is going to be hurt by what they've done as loyal officers. However, you can leave out the names of your informants."

Worth cleared his throat and fumbled for a moment with the sheaf of papers in his lap. "Well, General, we began getting some rather odd reports from our sources over at the Pentagon just after the election. As you probably know the defense establishment has been pretty unhappy for a couple of years. Ever since this administration came in, in fact. But the grumbling didn't amount to much more than a few wild-eyed colonels blowing off to each other." He glanced up and met Doyle's eyes. Worth was an ex-Los Angeles cop who had worked his way through the ranks to chief. He had been tapped to head the FBI during Carter's second administration because of his reputation for impeccable honesty, courage and administrative efficiency. During his four years as head of the agency, morale had soared and criticism virtually ceased. He had three years to go on a seven-year term and would almost certainly be re-appointed. He was utterly humorless.

"Then, following that meeting with the Joint Chiefs last month on the *Lyndon B. Johnson* and the mass resignation of the Chiefs, we began to get a different set of reports. Maybe you've heard something yourself, General?"

"A lot of people are unhappy," Doyle said. "What sort of reports are you talking about?"

"Reports that a coup is being planned," Worth said, expelling the sentence heavily.

"A coup?" Worth pronounced it coop. "You mean a military takeover of the United States?" Doyle suppressed a grin, wondering what some drunken colonel had, in his cups, suggested. That only the military really knew how to run the country, and, by God, ought to take it over before those pansies over at the White House had sold it lock, stock, and barrel to the communists?

"You've heard nothing?" the president asked.

Doyle met the chilly blue eyes and realized that the president, at least, didn't think it was a joke.

"No. I haven't heard anything," Doyle said, thinking back over his weekly conferences with the Strategic Planning Staff, the lunches with colleagues and conversations over coffee. "Are you sure this isn't some jerk shooting off his mouth? It happens at every army post. The system tends to produce some pretty conservative types who think in terms of simple solutions. But nobody I've known has ever been really serious. It's a form of relieving frustration. At the war college once a few years ago several of the officers staffed out a coup d'état as a joke."

"I know," Worth said. "I've got a copy of it. Damned scary document, too."

59

Doyle stared at the man in disbelief. "It was a joke, Harlan. They did it over coffee in the cafeteria. Took maybe half an hour," Doyle said gently.

"Maybe so. But what's going on now is no joke, General. Admiral William Christman's travel schedule over the past month has taken him to every key military installation in the country. In every instance he was accompanied by the former commander of the branch he was visiting. They consulted privately with more than thirty general and flag rank officers, each of whom occupies a strategic command. Would you like to see the list, General?"

Doyle glanced down at the single sheet of paper Worth handed him. Vice Admiral Clark, Pensacola. Lieutenant-General Salvador Curselli, Fort Benning. Marine Major General Harold Cushing, Parris Island. Lieutenant-General Bailey Sadler, Strategic Air Command. Admiral Simms Monroe, Commander, Atlantic Fleet. And it continued to name every important line commander in the United States armed forces.

"And that's not all, General. The visits are continuing. Down to division and brigade commanders and captains of major naval units."

"What are they talking about?" Doyle asked, his tanned face immobile.

"We're not absolutely sure, Steve," the president interrupted. "Nobody who was actually in one of the meetings has reported on them. But some of the junior officers around them have picked up some very disturbing information. Christman seems to be telling these men that my defense program will gut the armed forces and leave us defenseless. He is implying that I may, in fact, be disloyal to the United States. That I may wish to see it destroyed. Either that or I'm irrational. He's saying there is no other explanation for my actions.

And he is implying that it is the patriotic duty of the armed forces to save the country. From me." The president's voice snapped off the last two words with bitter force.

"Has the word *coup* come up?" Doyle asked turning to Worth.

"Yes," the FBI man said. "It has. But only from secondary sources. Not one of these men has come forward," he said tapping the list which Doyle passed back after trying to memorize most of the names.

"Isn't that a little strange, Steve? That none of these men would report to me or to his superiors if officers who have left the service are attempting to subvert them?"

Doyle shrugged. "We don't know what was said. I doubt if Admiral Christman would just walk in off the street and lay out a plan for a takeover of the government, even if that's what he'd like to do. He'd have with him a man who less than a month ago was the highest ranking member of that service. The commander they would be talking to would be five or ten years their junior. He'd be a little nervous about the visit to begin with. And in most cases he'd be sympathetic to the older officers. You must understand, Mr. President, that most senior military men are badly shaken by your program. Even those who can accept the end of their personal careers are deeply concerned about the security of the country. And they would be bound by loyalty to men they respect and under whom they served often in combat. It's a complex situation. Especially since I doubt if participation in a coup or takeover was proposed. Not the first time around, anyway."

The president nodded. "Precisely. You confirm my own feelings. It could be just a bunch of frustrated, aging men attempting to sabotage my program by gaining support among the military brass. The program has to go up to Congress, and although I'm sure it will win, a united front on the part of the military could cause endless difficulties."

Doyle said nothing, watching Worth twitch restlessly in his chair across the room. The president had chosen not to understand him accurately, to put the best face possible on the situation. It was a human reaction. In combat, men always did it. Hope for the best. Worth was not going to buy it, however.

"Mr. President, with all due respect to General Doyle here, I'm afraid I can't agree. The reports I have indicate something much more serious than this."

"You mean you think a coup d'état is definitely being prepared? An effort by the military to take over this government? My God, man, they'd have to be insane. They couldn't run it for a day. The people would rebel. The unions would strike. Every public service would come to a standstill. The police forces would rise against them. Nobody would support them. It would be total anarchy."

"Not entirely, Mr. President," Worth said, polite but stubborn. "Admiral Christman and his group have also been in contact with some of the most powerful business leaders in the country. A great many of them disagree with your proposed economic program, as you know. As for the police forces, I'm afraid most policemen are pretty conservative, Mr. President. And right now there is a crime wave induced by unemployment and a rise in poverty which is making some of them pretty desperate. The big cities are on the verge of revolt. Christman's people have been quietly contacting key police officials, particularly the paramilitary state police forces." Worth paused and looked up. "It's my feeling that he'll encounter a great deal of sympathy from some of these men."

"Why didn't you tell me this earlier?"

"I didn't have time, Mr. President. You called in General Doyle in the middle of my report."

"Are they preaching a takeover to these groups? Do you know what's being said?"

Worth again shook his head.

"Not in so many words. They're feeling these men out, trying to find out how they would react to what they describe as an 'emergency' in Washington. It's all pretty transparent, though. And I'm reasonably sure they're getting a surprising amount of support. The police in this country have been taking it on the chin for two decades, Mr. President. They feel that they're held in contempt both by the criminal element and by the people they're supposed to protect. They think the minorities which produce most of the criminals are being coddled because of their voting power. There's just one hell of a lot of frustration there, and these military men are appealing to it."

The president unfolded his long, thin body from the depths of the chair and began to pace back and forth across the presidential seal woven into the huge rug which covered the Oval Office. "It's ridiculous, of course. They'd never be able to bring it off. But I simply can't afford to have something like this explode right now. It might delay my program for a year while Congress dealt with it. You know that organization's penchant for ignoring work for spectacle." His dry voice dripped contempt for the legislative branch. "Can't we do something to stop them, Harlan? Haven't they broken some law that would allow you to arrest them or at least scare the hell out of them?"

The FBI director shook his head. "I've got nothing

actionable under the law at this time. Conspiracy charges are almost impossible to make stick. Not one person was convicted at the time of the Vietnam war, if you'll recall. And anyway, bringing it out into the open is just what you don't want. Legally, since the Warren Court reforms, it's almost impossible to bring extra legal pressure to bear the way Hoover used to. They'd throw me in jail."

The president nodded. "Any ideas, Steve?"

"Why don't I check around and find out just exactly what is going on before we decide to do anything? I'm due at the Strategic Planning Staff session at the Pentagon at ten. Let me nose around and find out what Admiral Christman has been saying."

"You think they'll tell you?" the president asked. "You're tarred with the White House brush, aren't you? Won't they be suspicious?"

Doyle met the president's eyes, his lean face impassive. "If they're planning a coup, I'd be one of the key men, Mr. President. I'm on the inside."

CHAPTER SIX

Maria Vicente caught up with him as he left the presidential office. "What about a cup of coffee, Steve? Or do affairs of state weigh too heavily on your shoulders to take a break?"

"Those are my years, not my affairs."

She grinned up at him. "Your place or mine, General?"

"Yours. Sgt. McBain's coffee tastes more like shellac every day."

She opened the door to her inner office and stood with one hand at the knob, the other doubled in a fist on her hip, her large green eyes focusing on him like weapons. She was a beautiful woman. Her oval face, honey-colored skin, and coal-black hair pulled back in a bun were set off by the severely tailored turquoise suit which tried unsuccessfully to mask the ripe curves of her body.

Her dark unplucked eyebrows arched in a frown as she looked at him. "You goddamn male chauvinist pig.

Are you suggesting that my role in your life is similar to that of your sergeant's?"

"The army would frown on McBain's doing for me what you do, Maria," he said.

She relaxed. "At least I finally seem to have your attention. Won't you come in?"

"Said the spider to the fly," he murmured moving past her, feeling her breasts brush against him as she let him pass. As the door closed, he encircled her waist and pulled her toward him.

She dug an elbow into his navel, looking over his shoulder at the closed door. "Steve, cut it out. Martha will be here any second with the coffee." They had been sleeping together for more than a year, but the touch of her body was still like a match striking in his groin.

She slipped out of his arms, and he watched her move behind her desk, hips rolling slightly. She might be a member of Mensa with a mind like a well-honed razor blade, but behind the chilly intellectual facade there was the remnant of a Sicilian woman—an amalgam of Greek, Carthagenian, Roman, Visigothic, French, and Spanish, all melded in the hot unforgiving Mediterranean sun. She was also the president's stiletto, honed, perfumed, and lethal.

Her angular secretary brought in two of the distinctive mugs embossed with the White House seal, and Maria watched him over the rim. "Well, Steve. What do you think? Are they really going to pull something or is it just a bunch of disappointed old men stirring up trouble?"

Doyle stared into the coffee, holding the mug in both hands. "Sorry, you lost me," he said, looking up to meet her cool green eyes.

"Knock it off, Steve. He showed me Harlan's preliminary report three days ago," she said softly. "Me and

Caldwell and two or three others. You weren't brought in because he wasn't totally sure of you. He had to have you checked out. After all, you're the very model of a modern major general. How could he know that you weren't part of it?"

"Did you think I was?"

She grinned. "Steve, darling, what I know about you doesn't say much about what you would do in a situation like this. Anyway, nobody asked me. Harlan had you followed, put a bug on your phone and combed your record. Aside from considerable evidence that you're not human, which could be an asset in a crisis, you're spotless. About the only thing that isn't in the image of an all-American boy is your divorce. But your ex-wife is an obvious tramp, so you're pretty much in the tradition there as well."

She hesitated. "Oh, and they found out about us, of course."

Doyle frowned. "Then why the charade in his office? Pretending Harlan was letting him in on it for the first time. To make me feel like one of the palace guard, I suppose."

"Sure. He plays games all the time. Every politician does. You want some simple-minded honest man as president? But what do you think? Is there anything to it?"

Doyle hesitated, sipping the bitter black coffee with a touch of chicory. "I don't know. It's possible. The officer corps never really recovered from the Vietnam war. They were blamed for losing it at a time when they felt they were not being allowed to win. The flyers in the air force and the navy were sent on suicide missions, practically advertised in advance, with orders not to take out the anti-aircraft missile sites because they were deliberately emplaced in the middle of population centers. On the ground," he shrugged, "you can't fight an enemy which can retire to protected sanctuaries. There was no way to win."

"Steve, you disappoint me," Maria Vicente said, putting the heavy coffee mug down on the round glass cocktail table with an audible click. "It was an immoral war fought out of pride and arrogance, utterly devoid of strategic merit, against our self-interest."

"Perhaps," Doyle said, his voice still. "But the men who fought it were asked to die by their political leaders in conditions it's very difficult for soldiers to accept. Out in the middle of that jungle it didn't matter much who was right or just. It mattered who got killed and who did the killing. The men who led the troops, those who thought about it at all, believed in the geopolitical rationale of war. I know I did. And they're coming into positions of command now. It's been eighteen years since the Tet offensive. Nineteen-sixty-eight. But in the officers' club bars it's remembered. And so are the ones who died. And the biased press coverage which pictured it as a defeat when we won hands down and left the North Vietnamese on the ropes. We could have won it then, if we'd been ruthless enough. Now it looks again as if the politicians are about to disarm us, leave the country defenseless in the face of a hostile, implacable enemy. At least that's the perception of a majority of my generation of soldiers."

"So you think it might be serious?"

"Look, Maria. I'm going over to the Pentagon for a Strategic Policy Staff meeting. I'll nose around, and I'll report back to the president. Chances are it's a lot of hot air. Harlan is a typical cop with about as much imagination as a stone idol. It's probably nothing more than the usual rightwing bombast that you get from most army colonels who've been passed over for general and are too greedy to retire and too soured to accept their fate with grace."

Maria frowned. "I had no idea you were so bitter. You've never talked about the war before."

He shrugged. "I found out a long time ago that disagreeing with a woman is the same as telling her you don't love her."

Doyle ducked as the heavy coffee mug sailed across the room at his head and smacked against the wall behind him leaving a dark stain on the cracked plaster.

"You insufferable son-of-a-bitch." She was on her feet, eyes blazing.

Doyle grinned. "That makes us even. Next time somebody has Harlan's hounds sicked on me, you might let me know."

"I wanted to, Steve," she said, contrite. "But, Jesus, I wasn't sure either. You're an inscrutable bastard, you know. And after the way you've been talking, I'm still not sure of you."

"And you, my dear, are the devious, scheming, ambitious, loyal servant of the president. And you would drop me or anybody else down a well, if it suited your purposes, without losing thirty seconds sleep over it. The administration's golden girl. Dr. Esterhazy's alter ego. One of the three or four most trusted aides to the president."

Unexpectedly she giggled. Doyle was taken aback. She looked about eighteen as she moved around the desk and put her arms around his neck. "And you, General, are the biggest fucking fraud I've ever seen. Here I thought I was getting involved with a virile redman, a simple soldier, an uncomplicated fuck, if you will. Something to take my mind off the office. And what do I wind up with? A goddamn phony with a doctorate in management, an IQ in the hundred and sixties, and to top it all off you're only a quarter Indian. Behind that impassive mask lies another three-quarters of wild Irish coal miner. You see, I've read the report, Steve," she was laughing. "Nothing is hidden from me. So will you please cut the crap?"

"What does that mean?"

"Suppose it's true. Suppose they're planning a coup? Where do you stand? With them or with us?"

He grinned, the lean planes of his face breaking up. "Reminds me of a whore I once knew in Naples. When somebody asked her how much, you know what she said?"

"No."

"Make me an offer."

The Strategic Policy Staff meeting was misnamed. No policy was made, no planning was done and the only strategy involved was in jockeying for the prestigious seats near the control area of the situation room in which it was held. The meetings had begun early in the Carter administration to bring together the top strategic thinkers of the four services. They had continued for almost ten years, although it had become immediately apparent that they were useless as a strategic exercise. Too many high-ranking officers with bloated egos and carefully guarded personal turfs were involved. And the ever-present danger of press leaks made realistic assessments difficult before a group of thirty to fifty people.

The meetings had served one purpose, however, and had survived because of it. They were almost the only forum in the Pentagon where senior members of all branches of the armed forces could size each other up and develop a sense of just how good or how bad they all were. A format patterned after the Harvard Business School Case Study had evolved. Three of the four monthly sessions were devoted to a specific military problem. The Strategic Policy Staff presented an initial assessment, with various options, and a general discussion followed. The problems ranged from a combined air-amphibious invasion of Alaska to the rescue of an American ambassador held hostage in a small African country.

Once each month, the planning staff reviewed the current military strength of the world's military powers and pinpointed possible flash points. This was on the agenda today as Doyle showed his special pass and was allowed into the two-story, circular, windowless situation room. Maps covered the walls, fronted by plastic panels threaded with invisible grids of tiny electronic circuitry which enabled programmers at consoles located along the walls to show instantaneous operations changes on the maps in a variety of formats. Two massive ten-by-ten television screens on opposite sides of the room were used for projecting aerial reconnaissance film strips and, occasionally, battlefield scenes from the Pentagon archives to illustrate a point.

Doyle surveyed the scene, some thirty general and flag rank officers milling about among the armchairs equipped with mikes and earphones, and decided for the fiftieth time that it represented one more example of a special American genius. Doyle's first law: having overeducated large numbers of people who were now unemployed, the country invented useless organizations and functions to provide them with work.

"Morning, Steve." Doyle turned to greet a former West Point classmate, Brigadier General Samuel Paddington Carlyle, scion of a rich and powerful Virginia family and one of the best polo players in the army.

"Hello, Sam. What great strategic insights are in store for us this morning?"

71

"We're going to be told, once again, just how much weaker we are than the Soviet Union, Germany and the China-Japan axis and how, if we don't stop cutting our defense budget and begin serious rearmament, we'll soon find ourselves as helpless as Finland."

Doyle met his friend's eyes. The normally indolent cynicism with which this southern aristocrat faced the world was replaced by a tense bitterness.

"What about lunch after this is over?"

Carlyle nodded. "Great idea, Steve. Since you joined the enemy across the river, I never see you any more. Meet you at the Anabasis Club about one?"

Doyle nodded and Carlyle moved across to his seat. The room was filling up now, gold-braided hats piling up on a table near the door, coffee and doughnuts being dispensed by waiters in white jackets. Gradually the groups broke up and drifted toward their seats. Each was assigned in strict hierarchical order, the inner seats surrounding the bank of sunken control consoles at the center of the room being the most choice since the occupants had to crane their necks the least.

A disembodied, crisply military voice flowed out of hidden speakers. "Please take your seats, gentlemen. The briefing begins in one minute." Doyle watched the second hand on the clock giving Washington time move in exact unison with those of the two dozen other time zones around the world. When the second hand touched twenty-four, a map on the left wall came alive as the electronic grid was activated. A southern-accented voice filled the room.

"Good morning, gentlemen. This is Colonel Papaladopolous. We'll start with Europe today. Since the last briefing the German order of battle has altered slightly. The tenth Panzer division has moved southeast of Berlin along the east bank of the Neisse and replaced the fourth Panzer which is moving to Dresden for training on the new nuclear-armed tank. Tenth Panzer was formerly at Wusterhausen. We're not sure which division will be replacing them. These reserve divisions are rotating through the Dresden training facility to learn how to handle the new nuclear-armed guided missile tank before going back into the forward areas. There has been no basic change in the German defense posture which has held in all essentials since the reunification of East and West Germany in 1983. The Polish areas they reincorporated after the Russo-German division of Poland are still regarded as essentially hostile despite vigorous efforts at settling ethnic Germans in these regions and the attempted Germanization of the native population. A one-hundred-mile-wide zone along the Soviet-German border continues to be regarded as the likely battlefield. Obstacles to quick-moving tank divisions continue to be removed, all bridges are mined, and strong points along the roads are being strengthened.

"The Germans have done an impressive job over the three-year period they have been in control. Heavy unemployment among the Polish working class has enabled them to recruit sufficient cheap labor for military purposes and within eighteen months they will have completed an interlocking defense system, based on nuclear mines, from Koenigsberg on the Baltic to Trieste on the Adriatic. A limited tactical nuclear strike against these defenses would be suicidal.

"Their defenses against a conventional non-nuclear attack are somewhat more problematical. The German general staff continues to feel that static defense is disastrous. They have, therefore, based their conventional defense to a Soviet non-nuclear attack on large concentrations of tanks and motorized infantry spotted at strategic points along the frontier." Scarlet circles appeared on the map, indicating the sites of the German armor. Geographic names were in Polish followed by the new German designation, since the United States still had not recognized the German-Soviet partition of Poland which took place in 1983.

"This refusal to accept the efficacy of the new laser- and television-guided anti-tank missiles and the various other sophisticated anti-tank weapons available to motorized infantry makes their whole concept of defense along this line somewhat dubious. However, these are superb troops, disciplined, motivated, superbly officered. A classic German army. The unification of the East and West German armies is now complete. Within the next year-to-eighteen months the purge of East German officers still believed sympathetic to the Soviet Union will have been completed and the last serious problem of integration will evaporate."

Papaladopolous's soft southern voice droned on as several older officers yawned surreptitiously and motioned for more coffee. His assessment of German naval and air power was followed by a detailed analysis of Soviet dispositions.

"In sum, then, the Soviets and Germans are both in a posture of relaxed defensiveness. Both know that a surprise attack, either with tactical nukes or conventional weapons, is impossible. Full mobilization for a major war would immediately alert the other side. There are no major outstanding political problems. Additionally the symbiotic economic relationship in which West Germany takes Soviet raw materials and supplies them with finished goods and technology seems likely to continue for the forseeable future. Thus, no war is likely."

After a brief review of the force levels and dispositions of the other European nations Papaladopolous illuminated a map of Siberia and the northern frontier of China.

He's a brilliant intelligence specialist, Doyle thought. Son of a Greek sponge fisherman who had immigrated to Tampa, Florida, in the nineteen-thirties, Papaladopolous had graduated first in his class at Annapolis in 1966. He had lost a leg with the Marines at Khe Sanh in Vietnam, ending a brilliant early career as a combat officer. He was now one of the Pentagon's leading intelligence experts. Fluent in German, Russian, Greek and with excellent Chinese, he represented the military intellectual at his best.

"Since the 1983 frontier war between the Soviet Union and China the whole seven-thousand mile border has remained closed," Papaladopolous continued. "Thirty-seven incidents of armed conflict have occurred. Soviet losses over this period are estimated at fifty thousand dead and two hundred thousand incapacitated. The frontier is an open wound, draining Soviet manpower and resources in an unending war of attrition. Chinese losses in men have undoubtedly been greater, perhaps double. But with their interior lines and inexhaustible reserves, they are able to put almost unbearable pressure on the single track Siberian rail line. Soviet morale is bad and worsening."

A three-star general with close-cropped white hair and a ruddy face pulled the mike on his chair to his mouth. "They are also blooding a new generation of officers and men, turning the whole Soviet army into hardened veterans by rotating unit after unit into the battles. They'll soon have the most seasoned modern fighting force in the world."

Papaladopolous's soft, even voice came over the concealed speakers. "True, General but, as with us in Vietnam, the people are restive and the army wants to go in

75

and finish it. There is immense frustration at being handcuffed. We're not sure a twentieth-century nation state can fight an open-ended war of attrition, not even one with a totalitarian regime. The Chinese are beaming direct transmissions of the Russian battlefield dead onto Soviet television screens from their broadcast satellites. And they warn that the war won't stop until their Siberian territorial demands are met."

Papaladopolous continued. "In the Middle East Israeli dominance in Egypt is seriously threatened. As the Egyptian population approaches fifty million, Israeli backup control forces are becoming increasingly inundated in a sea of people. The danger of a massacre of Israeli security forces during a massive demonstration is great. In any event, internal strains within the Israeli regime make more stringent repressive measures impossible. Israeli-controlled portions of Lebanon and Syria continue quiet with the exception of an occasional student demonstration in Damascus. The Israeli puppet government, dominated by the Alawite and Christian minorities, continues to keep effective control of all sectors by means of brutal repressive measures. Ten more dissidents were publicly executed in front of Damascus' Semiramis Hotel in November.

"The situation in Iran continues tense following the assassination of the Ayatollah Muhamab in September. The revolutionary council, headed by General Gharamani, is in only nominal control of the country as factions within the army, airforce and navy vie for preeminence. The execution on December 4 of former Premier Khoragan indicates that progressive forces may be gaining the upper hand. This view is supported by the massive flight of capital reportedly flowing into Zurich and by the continuing immigration of remaining members of the middle class.

"The Soviet-supported Persian Progressive Alliance (PPA), which dominates the illegal labor organizations, has threatened a general strike if its demands are not met. There are strong indications that the fighting arm of this labor group, the Front for the Liberation of Persia (FLP), has penetrated heavily among the junior officers of the army and air force. Comment: the situation is fluid and dangerous. Panic among the upper classes is compounded by uncertainty as to the tendencies among the lower echelons of the armed forces. The only organized political force in the country is the PPA. No attractive options present themselves for U.S. policy other than support of the status quo and efforts to stabilize the situation in such a manner as to deny the Soviets decisive influence over this vital oil-producing area. Not since the days of the hostage crisis has the situation in Iran been so critical.

"The Israelis are convinced that Colonel Fereydan Djam and his group, who are supported by the Chinese, are the real power and regard General Gharamani as a figurehead. However, their information comes from Israeli agents in the Persian intelligence service, SAVAK, who managed to escape the service's virtual annihilation following the Khomeini coup.

"Israeli nerves are understandable, however. Their hold on the Middle East is at its weakest since their takeover of Egypt in 1983. Only in Saudi Arabia is their puppet regime really in charge, and there it maintains itself with the kind of brutal repression, aided by Mossad, Israeli CIA and FBI combined, which probably can't continue indefinitely. The pro-Israeli regime is in a state of siege. Demonstrators are overrunning the streets on an almost daily basis demanding the withdrawal of Israeli troops who are confined to barracks. It's an explosive situation, no question about it.

77

"The rump Syrian-Jordanian state is quiet, mostly because the Mossad forces have penetrated their resistance groups so thoroughly that they are paralyzed. But the situation throughout the area is explosive. Persia may hold the match. If it begins active support of terrorist groups aimed at overthrowing the Israeli hegemony, we would have to be prepared for a confrontation between these two Middle Eastern nuclear powers. At the moment Israel, with its estimated one hundred fission bombs and a fusion weapon about to come on stream, is by far the more powerful. Its Dayan missile can reach up to two thousand miles with a light payload, and the Persians are no match for Israeli ground forces in a conventional non-nuclear conflict. In any event their internal problems make a near-term confrontation unlikely."

Doyle's attention wandered. The briefing varied little from month to month. Since the Sino-Soviet border war in Siberia in 1983, the world had settled into five troubled power centers. The United States, the Soviet Union, the China-Japan axis, a re-united Germany dominating Western Europe and, on a lesser scale, Israel astride the oil of the Middle East. Another power source was beginning to emerge in Latin America as Brazil's nuclear armaments program moved into high gear.

It was, as elder statesman Henry Kissinger continued to maintain in his scholarly writings, a pluralistic world in which the United States must seek its allies regardless of ideology and without paying too much attention to moral imperatives. Survival was the name of the game, and to survive meant, in his view, a ruthless and single-minded devotion to national self-interest.

"In South Africa the situation has eased somewhat since the last meeting," Papaladopolous's soft voice had put one admiral and two generals to sleep. They drowsed peacefully in the comfortable chairs as the shadows from the maps flickered across their aging faces. The briefing ended shortly after noon, and the discussion was mercifully short. Doyle retrieved his hat and threaded his way through the crowd, exchanging cryptic greetings. Escaping, he headed for an area on the third floor which was sometimes cynically referred to as the "Second State Department." More military officers worked in this section than there were American diplomats overseas. Here reports from a network of military attachés plus masses of publications from all over the world were combined with State Department and intelligence reports to form a military foreign policy. Originally the SSD's purpose had been the collection and analysis of political and economic information of military significance, but, since this could be stretched to cover virtually every conceivable piece of data, the mission and the section had been expanded exponentially over the years. It was headed by an assistant secretary who, before coming to the job, had been chairman of the political science department at the large western university where Doyle had taken his M.A.

Dr. Jordan Cummings was a natural. Short, fat, balding, he was utterly fearless and irreverent to the point of anarchy. He was also a talented administrator who had brought intellectual order out of the neat military chaos he had inherited and was now a powerful, if shadowy, figure in the Washington foreign affairs community.

Cummings's secretary motioned Doyle into the inner office. "He's waiting for you, General."

"Hello, Jordan."

"Good to see you, Steve," Cummings said, coming out from behind a huge desk and motioning him to a chair. "Cigar?" he asked, offering a box of almost black Uppmans.

"No thanks."

"What brings you to the fount of all knowledge?"

"We're going to be at the same table tonight at the White House dinner for the Israeli prime minister."

"With that greedy bastard Shimon, I assume?"

"You assume right. What do they want now?"

Cummings shrugged. "Reassurance. Everybody is worried, Steve. Despite all their apparent self-confidence and the immense successes of the last few years, the Israelis know as well as the Europeans that their ultimate survival depends on us. They see the president weakening our defenses, pulling back into what they perceive as a neo-isolationism. And they're scared."

"They may have reasons to be. Jordan, what do you hear from the grapevine these days? The White House has been getting some odd reports from your funny farm."

"So the president has decided to trust you?"

"Apparently only after everybody else."

Cummings grinned. "Steve, you're a general. At least on the surface you're a composite of the military establishment. The president doesn't know your secret vices—Vivaldi and gin, Schopenhauer and schnapps, Spengler and snatch. He just thinks you're another straight arrow in the bent quiver of the Pentagon."

Cummings's shirt was half out of his belt, his tie was undone and slightly soiled, and a film of perspiration covered his balding head despite the chilliness of his office. He was suffering from an incipient case of emphysema and still smoked twenty cigars a day, inhaling every puff.

"You think there is something to it, Jordan?"

The fat man shrugged. "There's a lot of talk. But I'd be the last one to hear about it, of course, and my nest of military intellectuals here are outside the chain of command. Anybody planning a coup would go for line officers. Outfits like this would fall in their lap anyway once they took over. Bureaucrats gravitate to power like pricks to pussy."

"Nobody's stupid enough to try it," Doyle said. "The country's too big, the people too undisciplined. You couldn't control it."

"Don't be too sure. You'd be amazed at just how few levers of real power there are in an advanced industrial society. You control the media, the communications systems, the water, the electricity, transportation, and the police and you control everything. Never forget Steve, all societies, no matter how free, base themselves on police power. It may be almost invisible, and in many places may be benevolent, but in the last analysis, the man who controls the cops, controls the country. The military are the cops of last resort."

"Maybe so. But controlling something and running it are two different things. The labor unions would strike, resistance groups would form, people would go up into the hills with guns, the universities would riot." Doyle shook his head. "I can't believe anybody would seriously try it."

"Steve, for a man who has spent most of his life dealing with violence, you're fantastically naïve. How did you control that bunch of savages in Special Services? The ones you used to take out that terrorist group which kidnapped the vice-president in Houston. From what I've heard you collected a group of criminals, misfits, incorrigibles and quasi-psychotics and turned them into one of the most disciplined units in the army. How'd you do it, with kindness? Bullshit you did."

81

Doyle smiled, remembering the thousand-man unit he had commanded for two years. It had developed out of the old Green Berets, an anti-insurgency, anti-terrorist commando group on twenty-four hour call to do anything from rescuing a kidnapped ambassador to taking over an airfield and holding it while American citizens were evacuated from a trouble spot. The unit was born following the Israeli Entebbe raid in Uganda which freed a planeload of passengers from a guerrilla group of the old Palestine Liberation Army.

"Well, how'd you do it?"

"Fear, mostly," he acknowledged. "A combination of heavy, brutal punishment and small rewards. You can't train men to die the way you do circus animals, with kindness and patience. They're too intelligent. They have to know that the alternative to cowardice is worse than death—humiliation, contempt and physical pain. The German army does it better than any I've ever seen, a mix of brutality and the subtle building of a group ethic which instills a Pavlovian reaction and makes death more acceptable than disgracing the group."

"Exactly. And that highly disciplined, motivated force, disembodied from the populace, is the United States Army today. They're mercenaries, recruited largely from the dregs of our society, unable to make it on the outside, seeking the comfort of discipline, resentful of the prosperity and success of the civilians, members of a persecuted but powerful group. Praetorians in search of a Caesar." He shook his head. "And they're not alone. Every police force in the country thinks of itself as an embattled army for good against a better-armed group of criminals who often get more sympathy and admiration from the populace than they, the police, do. It's a natural alliance, the police and the army. Almost never in the history of coups have they not failed to cooperate. After all, they're the forces of order."

"What about the people? Hell, Jordan, you know every goddamn second household has a gun in it. They'd take to the streets. It would be a bloodbath."

Cummings smiled. "You know that's a lot of crap. What can an undisciplined mob do against trained soldiers? Look what the Israelis have done in the Middle East. They've kept control over seventy-five million captive Arabs for almost ten years using doses of intense and brutal power backed by the populace's realization that they were absolutely ruthless and capable of anything. It's Grobakov's law."

"What the hell is that?" Doyle asked.

"Grobakov was a Czarist police officer. At the Tiflis police academy in January 1906, he came up with this formulation." Cummings imitated a heavy Russian accent. "One man with machine gun can control one hundred without. If he is willing to use it."

"Goddamn it, Jordan, you made that up."

"I made up Grobakov. But his law is the law of the land, Steve. You'd better realize that a large number of determined, ruthless men in command of a loyal army could take this country over in twenty-four hours."

Jordan glanced at his watch. "I've got a meeting with the secretary. I'll see what he knows and we can compare notes at the White House dinner for the Israeli prime minister."

CHAPTER SEVEN

Sgt. Buck McBain held the door to the black Chevrolet, one of the first of General Motors's production diesels and a perk of which the president was about to deprive him and all senior military officers.

"The Anabasis club, Buck," Doyle said, staring at the driver's red neck, its corded muscles now encased in a layer of fat. Buck McBain and a handful of officers and NCOs he had collected from the old disbanded Green Beret units had been the training staff for the new Special Projects Unit which President Carter had secretly authorized late in 1978 after a series of incidents culminating in the capture and torture of an American envoy in a Central American nation. The regular army, ever resentful of such special forces, had come up with a collection of a thousand "volunteers" to staff the new force. Almost to a man they were petty criminals, signed on to avoid court-martial, chronic alcoholics, misfits, troublemakers, or the psychically troubled. It was fortunate, Doyle had thought, as he surveyed them on the muddy parade ground of an abandoned Second World War training base in the mountains of North Carolina, that such men were historically the best suited for the kind of duty they might have to perform. As a famous British commando leader in the Second World War had said, "Give me men who are a little mad, for I am going to lead them into hell."

In the first miserable February days, McBain, a former army light heavyweight boxing champion, had gathered the two dozen toughest, most incorrigible men in the camp into a punishment detail. The base, unused for twenty years, was a mess and the men had been divided up into squads for painting, carpentry, roofing, landscaping. This group had been designated to unclog the stopped-up sewers, unusable since it had been put in operation temporarily to house a thousand Vietnamese refugees in 1974. It was the classic shit detail.

They had stood at attention in the rain on the parade ground, dominated by the hulking figure of a six-foot, six-inch, two-hundred-and-sixty-pound former tackle on the Chicago Bears who had enlisted in the army following a scandal in which he was accused of raping a teammate's wife. Charges had not been pressed, but he had been barred from football for life.

Instill fear and respect. The first order of business. Doyle had stood before the group, his voice hardly audible over the rain and wind. "Since you've been cleaning sewers all morning I thought you men would like to take a break, have a little fun. The sergeant tells me you're the toughest men on the camp. Real men."

He surveyed the faces above the shit-stained uniforms, a wild-eyed psychopath on the left chewing compulsively at his lower lip, looking for something to lash out at, the football player, a mop of blonde hair beginning about an inch above his jutting brows, a hulking black man, body tense with hostility. It was now or never.

"Well, I happen to think you're a bunch of pussies." As he spoke, groups repairing the barracks on either side of the street had stopped and were watching the little scene. "And I intend to prove it to you once and for all. Right now. When you walk away from here you're going to know one thing. And that is that I'm the head motherfucker in charge in this battalion from now until the day you leave it." He'd practiced the speech with some amusement the night before, but it seemed even more absurd now. "So, who's the meanest, toughest son of a bitch among you?"

The big former tackle had finally come awake, his blue eyes wide in disbelief as he stared at the crazy Indian officer mouthing off at them. Somebody in the second row pushed him forward, and his massive face broke up in a grin when he recognized what was taking place. "Ah, shit, Colonel. You don't want to fight me. Old man like you. Shit, I might hurt you bad. That fucking judo and all that horseshit ain't gonna do you any good with me."

"Are you ready, Sims?"

"Yeah, sure," the big man had said, holding out arms corded with muscle in an imitation of an old-fashioned boxing stance, turning to grin over his shoulder at the group behind. Doyle balanced himself on his left leg and kicked out, catching the big tackle in the balls with the steel-reinforced toe of his construction worker's boot, calculating the force needed to drive a stab of unbearable pain to the man's brain without damaging him permanently. The big man's scream tore through the winter rain like the ripping of canvas, cut off as he bent double. Doyle forced himself to wait for a count of five before casually slipping the slender leather covered sap out of his back pocket and swinging it in a small arc, careful to hit the nerve near the base of the football player's skull, not touching the delicate bone covering the brain pan. The big man collapsed in a heap face down in the mud.

Doyle stood staring at the remaining men in the group. If there was among them, or in the silent staring crowd working on the barracks, a former law student or an otherwise educated man, his career could slip away in this moment. The physical abuse of enlisted men was strictly forbidden in army regulations.

A southern voice lifted out of the group. "That wasn't a fair fight, Colonel."

Doyle smiled at the men, his lined face taking on an almost wolfish look. "No. And I don't expect any son of a bitch in this unit ever to be stupid enough to fight fair. You're here to learn to kill, not play games. And I goddamn well expect you to learn it. Now, the sergeant here has a switchblade knife. If there is among you somebody who thinks he knows how to use one, let him step forward."

His luck had gone a little bad then. The young Chicano had been superb with the knife. Doyle fingered the thin, almost invisible scar extending from his left eyebrow to the curve of his chin. He had deliberately taken the cut and broken the kid's arm, but another second and it would have been his throat. By nightfall, everybody in the camp had heard about the two encounters. It was the beginning of the "Special Group" legend that culminated with the rescue of the vice-president at the Texas Tower a year and a half later.

They had taken over the building on July 5th, 1981, at four o'clock in the afternoon, ten members of the United Front for the Liberation of the Republic of Seychelles. Only four were natives of the Seychelles. Three were members of the Rosa Luxembourg cell of the German Trotskyist Front, two belonged to the decimated remnants of the Japanese Red Guard, and one was a South Moluccan who, following the murder of a Dutch policeman, had become a freelance gunman. They had infiltrated the thirtieth floor of the Affiliated Houston Insurance Companies Building, more familiarly known as the Texas Tower, the world's tallest building, put up with Arab oil money as an unofficial monument to the oil field roughnecks who had made them all rich.

Despite tight security, the ten terrorists had entered the building, fully armed and laden with explosives, disguised as waiters for a posh cocktail party scheduled to take place on the building's fiftieth floor. They had debarked from the freight elevator into the service area of the thirtieth floor where control panels for the bank of elevators encircling the inner core of the immense skyscraper were located. In a matter of minutes they had immobilized the twelve elevators servicing floor thirty to fifty at the thirtieth floor landing. The terrorists had first rounded up the elevator passengers and imprisoned them in a large conference room before methodically moving around the outer offices of the circular building and adding the occupants of each office to a growing mob of prisoners.

In the outer office of the chairman of the Johnson Foundation three Secret Service agents were gunned down before they could react and in the inner boardroom the terrorists had taken prisoner fifteen of the leading industrialists of the United States along with the honorary chairman of the cultural foundation, Lawrence L. Hundertwasser, scion of the Hundertwasser department store clan and first Jewish vice-president of the United States.

88

Hundertwasser had taken the place of former Vice-President Mondale on the Democratic ticket in 1980, ostensibly because the crucial Jewish vote was threatening to go to President Carter's Republican opponent for the first time in history. In reality, Mondale was replaced because Carter had become enraged at his independence and popularity in the later years of his first term. Hundertwasser, a liberal New Yorker who had been elected mayor on a reform ticket, was an elegant Princetonian with an impeccable record of mediocrity and obedience to his political superiors. Since his election he had played the role of the servile vice-president to perfection. Hence his presence at the headquarters of the Johnson Foundation at a board meeting to decide where and how the three hundred and twenty-five million dollars at the group's disposal would be spent.

The board members were finishing a leisurely three-hour lunch when the bearded gunman burst in. "Everyone remain seated," he had said in slightly German-accented English. "We have taken over the building. The elevators have been brought to this floor and immobilized. The fire exits are blocked with explosive charges which will be set off at the first sign of a rescue attempt. You are my prisoners. Please do not be alarmed. If my orders are followed, you will not be injured."

The terrorists moved with practiced efficiency, neutralizing all means of communication and keeping only one telephone line open. Within minutes of the takeover, panic had broken out in the upper stories of the building. A man and woman leaped to their deaths from a fifty-second story apartment block and a psychiatric clinic on the forty-fifth story was overwhelmed with cases of hysteria. Police encircled the building below and made their way up the fire stairs to the twenty-

89

ninth floor where a spray-painted sign on the wall warned them that if they moved further an electronic device would set off an explosion.

At four thirty-five, the terrorists contacted the mayor of Houston, Tom Hochschwanz, and made their demands. Twenty-five million dollars, divided equally among the yen, the deutschemark, the dollar, the Swiss franc and the Canadian dollar. The release of fifty terrorists held around the world and their transport by Concorde to the Houston airport. This must be done within twenty-four hours. Once the Concorde arrived, half the terrorists would leave accompanied by a dozen hostages. They would board the Concorde and once it was beyond U.S. airspace, the remaining five would leave to board another plane, protected again by a dozen hostages. The hostages would be released once the planes had reached a neutral point.

At five P.M. the anti-terrorist special forces group under the command of Colonel Steven Doyle was activated. One hundred and fifty members of the thousand-man group emplaned for Houston and arrived at ten P.M. A meeting was in progress in the air-conditioned control van of the Houston chief of police. In attendance were the commander of the state National Guard, Major General James "Alamo" Jackson, the chief of police, the mayor of Houston, the FBI special agent in charge and the Houston fire chief.

"Evening, Colonel," the mayor said. "Glad you and your men could join us. We're just going over the battle plan."

Doyle shook hands all around. "What's the situation?"

The Houston police chief, a beefy man in a tight-fitting beige summer uniform, cleared his throat and

90

spat into a decorative spittoon in one corner. "It's a fucking mess, General."

"Colonel," Doyle said automatically.

"Yeah, Colonel. Well anyway, it's a fucking mess. They got a fort up there full of civilians, and they got the damn thing mined with enough explosives to blow up the whole goddamn building." He moved to a picture window in the trailer and pointed up. "See that hole." Doyle stared up at an ugly gash torn out of the side of the immense building. "That's what they did to show us what they could do. Explosive charge equivalent to about two hundred pounds of TNT. Ripped out the curtain wall of the building and a steel strut about a foot thick. They've placed similar charges around the structural supports of the building and are threatening to blow it up."

"Have you got the building plans?"

The chief nodded, unrolling one of a mass of blueprints stacked against the wall. "This shows you a cross section of the building. It's built around a circular core which carries all the stress. Revolutionary concept, I am told. Anyway, all the services, communications, elevators, etc., are carried in this core with the offices cantilevered out around it." The policeman stabbed a finger at the cross-section of the building representing the thirtieth floor. "This is where they are. They seem to have grouped all the prisoners except the veep and a few of the wheels in these two conference rooms. The vice-president and the others are in the foundation boardroom, here."

"Where are the explosive charges?"

"They are marked, according to what the asshole told us on the phone. We've got the building architect outside, and he pinpointed them for us. He thinks they had to have professional architectural help and maybe access to the plans, because they've placed the charges in such a way that the goddamn building will be cracked apart if they set off the charges. All the upper stories will topple here into the plaza. It'll kill thousands of people."

"Maybe you'd better clear those crowds out of the plaza, Chief," Doyle murmured.

The chief bristled. "Listen, General," he began.

"Colonel," Doyle said.

"Yeah, Colonel, I'll run this operation the way I see fit without any goddamned advice from you."

"No, chief. You won't," Doyle said quietly. "I'm empowered by the president to take command of all rescue operations on this site. He's declared a national emergency in order to rescue the vice-president. I would greatly appreciate all you gentlemen's cooperation. But if I don't get it, I must ask you to vacate the site. If you refuse, I'll have you removed. My men and I will be moving in to inspect the building immediately. In the meantime, I want the area cleared of everybody, including all other police forces. We'll do this our way and I would prefer not to have any confusion from other elements." Doyle turned to the chief who seemed about to suffocate with rage. "I need all your city helicopters to lift a hundred of my men to the roof. Another fifty will take over the floor below the thirtieth. Now if you don't mind, I'd like to talk to the architect."

"Get moving, Chief," the mayor said, looking relieved. "I had a call from the president just before this meeting indicating that Colonel Doyle would be taking over. We'll all be glad to assist, Colonel. You may chair the meeting if you prefer."

"Thanks, Mr. Mayor. But I'd like to end the meeting. My men are trained specifically for just such operations. What I need to know is how I can obtain access to the thirtieth floor of that building, neutralize the explosive charges, and kill the terrorists."

"Kill? You're not going to take prisoners?"

"We will if they surrender," Doyle said quietly. "Once the operation starts I expect them to wind up dead."

"Along with everybody else in the building, you hardheaded dummy," the chief said. "You think we haven't checked out how to get in? There's no way that won't give them time to set off the explosives. You're gonna kill a couple of thousand people. I say we give them the money and the fucking goons they want liberated and get them the hell out of here."

"We will not give them the money," Doyle said. "If we do, it will be an open invitation to continued attacks of this kind. The president has decided that no more bribes will be paid. Any terrorist who pulls a stunt like this has to know that he will almost certainly be killed. That way we can possibly discourage them. Now I'd like to talk to the architect."

A slender young Japanese of indeterminate age entered the trailer as the other men filed out. "I'm Harry Michekawa, Colonel."

"You designed the building?"

Michekawa smiled. "It doesn't quite work that way, Colonel. I'm a member of the firm that designed it, and I had overall management responsibility for the project. No one man designs one of these monsters. However, I know more about the structural makeup of the building than anybody else."

Doyle motioned toward the plans on the table. "Have you seen these?"

Michekawa nodded.

"Have they placed the explosives in a way to destroy the building?"

93

"Yes. There must be an architect among them who had access to the plans. There's no way they could have done it so well without expert help. They're pretty sure of themselves, telling us about the location of the charges."

"Can you get us onto the thirtieth floor?"

Michekawa stared at him. "Sorry, Colonel, I don't understand. The elevators and stairwells are blocked."

"Is there another way up to that floor? Can we get inside this core holding the service area and from there onto the thirtieth floor?"

Michekawa leaned over the plans and stared down at the concrete circle which was the center of the building. "It's packed with wires and pipes. You can get into it, for servicing, of course, but there's no way out onto the thirtieth floor. Every five floors there is a hatch into one of the elevator shafts through which repair man get in. Inside there are a series of ladders. But the thirtieth floor is not an entry way."

Doyle took a pencil and marked a small triangle between two elevators. "What's this?"

"Dead space. We couldn't make the elevators quite fit in a perfect circle. So there's a small decorative panel between these two."

"Made of what?"

"Synthetic wood. Something decorative."

"Could we get through it in a hurry?"

Michekawa looked up from the plans. "Look, Colonel. Let's get something straight. They've mined the damned building. You go busting in there, and they're going to blow it up. A couple of thousand people are going to die."

"Mr. Michekawa, I'm not here to commit suicide. I'll be the first one in, if we make the attempt. We won't go busting in. We'll cut the electric power in the building temporarily, and we'll move in without lights. A team of demolition experts will head for the explosives. We will try to locate the explosion control point before we move. And if possible we'll neutralize it. With luck we can stop enough of the charges from going off to save the building."

"And if you don't?"

Doyle ignored him, turning back to the plans. "Can you get me the exact specifications of the panel material, how it's mounted, all the details. I want a mockup here in a couple of hours if possible. We'll be doing this tonight. Right now I want to take my second in command, Captain Pruitt, and show him the access route through the inner shaft. I appreciate your help, Mr. Michekawa. Please don't mention this conversation. All we need is to have the press get hold of the plan, announce it on television, and blow it to hell and gone."

"Colonel, I think you are a little nuts. It won't work. You're going to blow up that building."

"Mr. Michekawa, you make the mistake those men want you to make. You believe them to be infallible. In fact they are right now in a cold sweat, scared shitless. Decisions are being made with increasing difficulty. They don't want to die. Nor are they trained military men who do suicidal acts as a matter of routine. They're agonizing intellectuals who will hesitate as any sane man will in the face of death. That hesitation is going to kill them."

Doyle moved to the door of the trailer and motioned Pruitt over, explaining what had to be done. "Where's the police chief?"

"Right here, Colonel. Waiting to pick up the fucking pieces after you kill two thousand of the citizens."

"You were talking to the terrorists on the telephone. How do I make contact?"

95

"There's a switchboard in there," the chief said, pointing to a panel divider. "One of my men is monitoring an open line. But they won't talk to us until they're ready. You want to talk to the psychologist?"

"Psychologist?"

"Yeah. We got an expert on terrorists. Analyzes their reactions, offers advice on how to handle them." The chief had calmed down now. The responsibility was no longer his, and the resentment was residual.

The chief turned and scanned the crowd outside the command trailer, motioning to a youngish-looking bearded man wearing a white turtleneck shirt and an elegant blue blazer. "Professor Manuel Gutierrez, Colonel Doyle. Professor Gutierrez teaches abnormal psychology at the state university."

"Glad to meet you, Colonel. Can I be of any help?"

"Have you talked to the terrorists?"

"No. But I've heard the tapes. Only one talks. Calls himself 'Red Devil'."

"What's his problem?"

The psychologist frowned. "I'm not sure what you mean, Colonel."

"There's got to be some reason why he's up there holding two thousand people hostage and threatening to kill them. What's his hangup? Power? Sublimated sex problems? Early toilet training? A mother who didn't love him?" Doyle spoke without inflection but the psychologist stiffened with irritation.

"I don't think this is the time for jokes in bad taste, Colonel. He says he is a Marxian socialist whose goal is to free the masses from fascist domination. I have no reason to doubt his sincerity or his sanity."

"You think terrorism is a normal reaction to the twentieth century environment then, Professor? A rational approach to solving our problems?"

"Obviously not, Colonel. On the other hand I don't regard the men whose decisions preceding and during the Second World War resulted in the death of thirty million people as totally rational either."

Doyle grinned. "Do you think he'll do it?"

"Blow up the building? Undoubtedly. I don't think there is any question as to their sincerity or determination. All indications are that they have a precise plan which they will carry out ruthlessly."

"Okay. Let's try to get them on the phone. I need certain information." He led the chief of police, Michekawa, and the psychologist into a small space packed with electronic gear. The young policeman at the control panel started to rise.

"Keep your seat, son. Can you tell me which room they are in?" Doyle asked, unfolding the floor plan of the thirtieth floor.

"The extension they're using is in the board chairman's office."

"Can you raise him?"

"That's an open line. Press the button at the base of the phone and he'll hear you. They've got it hooked up to one of those loudspeaker devices you use on conference calls. Everybody in the room can hear it."

Doyle picked up the phone. "Red Devil, this is police control. Can you hear me?"

"Red Devil here." The voice filled the small control room, deep and resonant. "What do you want, fascist pig?"

"We can't make your deadline on the money or the hostages, Red Devil," Doyle said. "We've got to have more time."

"Either you meet it or two thousand people in this building, including your vice-president, die. We are serious men, and we expect to be taken seriously."

Doyle's voice was low and unemotional. "It's a problem of time, Red Devil. We're having to negotiate the release of the prisoners. Some of the governments don't want to go along. It's going to take more time."

"No," the word came across the room with explosive force. "You're lying. You're playing for time, hoping for a break." The man spoke excellent English with an accent that sounded German or Central European. "You meet the deadline or else." The line went dead.

"See what I mean?" the psychologist said. "I don't think there's any question that they'll do it."

"Our experience is that virtually anybody except highly trained soldiers, paramilitary police, and the most hardened criminals will hesitate briefly before killing. It's an instinctive reaction which only long practice in the suppression of normal inhibitions will change. Can you tell me from what you heard whether this man is such a professional?"

"No," Gutierrez said, frowning. "But I don't think he is. His English is accented but virtually perfect. He sounds like a young intellectual."

Doyle nodded. "Well let's hope so. If he's a pro what we're going to try may not work. If he's not, there's a chance. Their discipline and organization seem to be excellent, but as individuals they are anarchists. They must have problems of language and cultural communications. If we can take them by surprise, move very fast, the chances are good that they will, like most nonprofessionals, hesitate that crucial moment before they push the plunger. That's our edge."

"You really plan to kill them?"

"Yes."

The architect nodded. "Okay. I'll get my people ready right away. Where's Captain Pruitt?"

Two hours later, the huge building was sealed off,

and the area at its base was empty except for half a dozen special forces men hidden behind shrubbery and statuary in the plaza. All fire trucks, command trailers and other paraphernalia had been removed. If the building fell, it would fall on nothing. Thirty men, their faces distorted by the projecting prisms of infrared goggles, had made their way from the twenty-fifth and thirty-fifth floors up and down through the inner core of the building and were waiting at the thirtieth floor level at the hole which had been carefully cut in the aluminum siding of the inner tunnel. The hole led to a plastic panel which opened onto the elevator landing. Each man on the team had rehearsed with a floor plan what he would do as he moved into the area.

Doyle waited behind the two demolition specialists who would cut the panel quickly and move out first as the lights in the big building were cut. The second hand on his watch moved toward "twenty-three," and as it touched the building was plunged into darkness. An almost soundless battery-driven high-speed saw broke through the partition and circled the paneling which fell outward onto the pile carpeting of the darkened windowless corridor. The demolition men moved quickly through, followed by Doyle, Pruitt, and the remaining members of the team. Their glasses cut through the darkness revealing an empty corridor circling the elevator well with others leading off like spokes in a wheel. The demolition squads scattered, some heading for the explosives, others moving out along the spokes of the building's wheel in an attempt to cut the detonation wires.

Pruitt moved with a team of five men toward the main prisoner holding area. Doyle and three others headed at a run for the office of the foundation chairman where the terrorist leader had his headquarters.

Doyle tried the door of the outer office and motioned to the soldier at his side. The man's .45 caliber Marietta submachine gun, equipped with a massive silencer, an antique out of production for more than a decade, burped gently and the lock disintegrated.

On schedule the lights in the building came on and Doyle flipped up his night glasses as he moved into the boardroom. The vice-president, a tall, elegant man in a dark suit, was standing with his back to the window. Half a dozen others were seated at the long boardroom table. At its head a clean-shaven blond young man was screaming into a telephone. "If we don't get lights in five seconds the building blows—"

Doyle's .223 Heckler and Koch submachine gun chattered briefly, stitching a neat pattern across his chest, shattering the phone. The heavy Marietta burped a split second later, slamming him back against the heavy glass windows of the room which shattered from the force of the bullets leaving his body. The two terrorists with him stood frozen as Doyle's men cut them down.

Doyle moved to the triggering device standing on the table and cut the wires leading from it. He turned to the group. "My men are taking care of the remaining terrorists. I think it will all be over in a couple of minutes."

"My God," the vice-president said, his face white with horror. "You shot them down like animals. Without giving them a chance to surrender."

As he spoke, Pruitt came through the door in a crouch, hazel eyes sweeping the room. "What about the others?"

"Shot trying to escape," Pruitt said, winking.

"I'm going to report this to your superior," the vice-president said, his slender, elegant figure quivering with rage. "You shot these men down without giving them a chance. I've never seen such callous brutality."

"Anabasis Club, General," Buck McBain said as they drove up the half-circular drive of one of Washington's most prestigious men's clubs. Some years before the club had taken over the immense Massachussets Avenue mansion of a nineteenth century secretary of state, leaving intact the Victorian decorations and much of the furniture. Two black marble statues of nude Numidian slaves, male and female, flanked the entry hall, each carrying on its shoulders a basket of ceramic fruit. Glittering crystal chandeliers which once graced the palace of a Hungarian count in Vienna dripped light from the two-story-high hallway. A uniformed concierge presided over a teak pulpit to one side.

"General Doyle? General Carlyle is waiting for you in the Jefferson Davis room, sir. Turn right at the end of the hall, last door on your left."

Doyle walked past nineteenth-century British boxing prints along the corridor wall as his feet sank almost to his ankles in the thick carpeting. The Anabasis was the closest thing to a traditional British club in Washington. It had resisted with glacial disdain attempts to force it to accept blacks and women, although there were four token Jewish members. Founded shortly after the Civil War by a group of Southern legislators, its membership now cut across the spectrum of Washington society, but it was still a very southern institution.

General Samuel Paddington Carlyle met him at the door of the small salon named after the president of the Confederacy. A large log was burning in the fireplace imported from a sixteenth century English manor house, and in the center of the room a small table, glistening with white linen, silver, and crystal was set for

101

two. "Thought you might like to get away from the roar of the crowd, Steve. Anyway, we're probably not going to be able to enjoy such degenerate capitalist pleasures much longer if our communist president has his way."

"Knock it off, Sam. He's no communist and you know it."

"Doesn't really matter whether he is or not. His policies are drawing the country inevitably in that direction. But let's not argue until we've had a drink. What's your pleasure?"

"Bourbon and water," Doyle said. He disliked drinking at noon, but Sam Carlyle was a near alcoholic, and he refused to drink alone. It would have been torture to refuse.

Carlyle touched a button to the left of the fireplace and the two men dropped into pleasantly worn brown leather armchairs.

"Well, Steve, what have you heard?"

Doyle smiled. Sam Carlyle, despite his politics, which were to the right of Ashurbanipal, and the mild alcoholic daze in which he lived, was one of the most intelligent men in the army. And it was an intelligence informed by sensitivity and a keen appreciation of his fellow man's foibles.

"The word is that some of our brilliant colleagues are planning a coup d'état." There was no point in fencing with Carlyle. "The White House is uptight. I've been asked to nose around and find out what's going on."

"And you think I'd know? Or, more to the point, would tell you if I did know?"

"Look, Sam," Doyle said, stopping to take a tall frosted glass from the silver tray presented by the waiter, watching him leave before continuing. "You know as well as I do it wouldn't work, and I assume you're not fool enough to allow yourself to get sucked into such romantic nonsense."

Carlyle drank a mixture of orange juice and scotch, nursing each weak drink carefully. He was thus able to maintain just the right level of alcohol in his blood to deaden whatever pain he was escaping without ceasing to function. "First, Steve, if there is a coup, I'm not in on it. Everybody knows Sam Carlyle is a hopeless drunk, so nobody would trust him with the time of day. That's understood, right?"

Doyle said nothing, staring into the glass, remembering his friend holding a dying soldier in his arms in the Khe Sanh mud and comforting the man in his soft southern drawl, his uniform jacket gradually becoming soaked from the bloody spittle of the dying man's cough.

"So I don't know what's going on, if anything is. However, I can tell you this and you can take it back to that chilly son of a bitch in the White House. There are people in this country who are not yet ready to turn it over to that coalition of Central European socialists, blacks, chicanos, Zionists, big city deadbeats, ethnic intellectuals, Ivy League assholes, crooked union leaders and the lumpen proletariat who put him in office."

"Who would you substitute? A bunch of ignorant, redneck John Birchers? The upper echelons of our own esteemed army, most of whom can't tell a nuclear missile from a horseshoe nail? Who would you turn it over to?"

"I'd turn it over to the descendants of the people who settled it, tore it from the Indians and nature and built it. The solid, if confused, majority who work hard, don't steal, don't beg, raise their children in decent homes, and are sick and tired of being treated like pariahs in their own country. The silent, unrepresented majority."

"White Anglo-Saxon Protestants haven't been a majority in the United States since the nineteen-twenties," Doyle said wearily.

"Don't patronize me, Steve. I'm not talking about ethnic groups. The people I'm talking about cut across the whole spectrum. There are among them members of every group I mentioned earlier, but they have accepted the responsibility of citizenship, and the paramount necessity of defending what you've got from the ones who want to take it from you. Christ, Steve, have you completely forgotten your history? We're the most powerful country on earth and the richest. You think anybody is going to let us alone, let us keep all these goodies if we're too weak and lacking in will to defend them? Well, you're simpleminded if you do."

Doyle realized with a shock that Carlyle bored him. He'd heard it all before. The wealthy Virginia patrician had watched his world crumble around him over the past thirty years. He now rode to the hounds with a group of Yankees with bad seats and worse accents. His golf club had finally succumbed to a deluge of *arrivistes*, his ancestral land had withered away under the impact of tract housing, and his beautiful young wife had left him for a second-rate Rumanian tennis pro.

"Look. Steve, you've got to face it. The republic is dying. Life is too complicated for a system which gives total power to a bunch of uninformed congressmen interested only in being returned to power. They will instinctively pander to the mob, as they are doing now, until we've driven the country into the ground. Drastic measures are called for and no democratic parliament is going to have the courage to take them."

Doyle looked up, meeting Carlyle's brown eyes. "The president has the courage. God knows, his program is drastic enough."

"Drastic, yes. Courageous, no. He's taking the easy

way out. Cutting defense costs was always a politician's easiest course in this country. He can run against the military-industrial complex, act self-righteous and wind up leaving us helpless." He shook his head. "It won't wash, Steve. He's going to destroy us if somebody doesn't do something about it."

"And somebody is?"

Carlyle met his look, his pale, almost-too-fine face thoughtful. "Steve, I've known you for thirty years. You are the best professional soldier in the army. There's nobody I'd rather have next to me in battle. But you have sold yourself to this man, and I know you well enough to realize that you'll never betray him. If there were an attempt to take over the government, I wouldn't tell you. Shall we have lunch?"

As he stood up, steadying himself on the mantelpiece, Carlyle's eyes focused on Doyle. "By the way, what do you hear from Nadia? I hear she's doing very well."

CHAPTER EIGHT

He had met her at the Cercle Sportif in Saigon in 1967 six months after separating from his wife. He'd just spent ten weeks with a Montagnard group in the Central Highlands behind the Cong lines, and he'd picked up some sort of bug which had dropped him from a normal one-seventy to one-fifty. The medics had prescribed a month's convalescent leave. He'd decided to spend it in Saigon, and a friend had wangled him a temporary membership at the famous tennis club in the center of the city.

It was a nineteenth-century monument to the French occupation, a green and white termite-ridden wooden relic, creaky with age and decay. A musty odor of stale perfume and tropical rot had pervaded the main salon with its low square tables, heavy armchairs and huge dark metal fans turning lazily on the ceiling. Outside, on a long terrace, a melange of Vietnamese, French, and Americans sipped drinks and waited for a free court.

He had made his way past the tennis court to a low

concrete building and beyond to the large swimming pool. Stripped, Doyle glanced at himself briefly in the full-length mirror in the dressing room. His body was emaciated and the grayish scar tissue was more evident. Then he had done the fifty laps recommended by the therapist and dropped on a towel beside the pool, ignoring the delicate beauty of the young Vietnamese girls in wispy bikinis, moving with provocative grace among the watching males.

Six months before he had flown into Bangkok unannounced on a special mission, intending to surprise his wife and two young sons who were living there with most of the other military and State Department families. It was midnight before he had located the air force general, delivered the plan and maps for a special air strike, and been told he was free until the following morning. The house had been dark except for a light in the bedroom. Doyle had felt the tightening of his groin muscles as he moved through the unfamiliar surroundings, stumbling over a flimsy chair before finally reaching the bedroom door. He would normally have heard the noise, but his mind was blurred by anticipated desire.

"Oh shit." Mary Ann had seen him over the young naval officer's shoulder, her eyes widening above a mouth pulled back with strain and desire. The nude body on top of her had continued to pump briefly as she struggled to free herself. The young navy pilot had rolled over then and leapt awkwardly to his feet.

He had stood for a brief moment beside the bed before reaching for the uniform flung in a heap on a chair. The fight had been short and vicious. His opponent was bigger, but untrained and out of shape. Instinctively, Doyle moved inside the swinging arms, chopping at the soft unprotected lower body with the strokes designed to kill, not hearing the sudden scream of agony as the man doubled with searing pain, slashing with the edges of his hands, probing for the final spot which would end it. He had come out of it with Mary Ann on his back, clawing at his face, screaming and sobbing at him.

"Don't kill him, Steve. Goddamn it, don't kill him," in a refrain, over and over. He had flung her off and watched her nude body bounce off the edge of the bed and land in a sprawl on the floor. The naval officer was a crumpled silent heap at his feet.

They had hushed it up with the skilled efficiency of the military. The navy pilot had survived four broken ribs, a ruptured spleen, and a fractured neck vertebra. He was back in action within two months and died in a Cong prison camp two years after his F-4 was shot down trying to take out a truck convoy just north of the DMZ. Mary Ann had married an investment counselor in San Francisco and had two more children by him before divorcing again a decade later.

One of his sons, whom he saw irregularly in meetings marked by mutual embarrassment and incomprehension, was in a West Coast college majoring in, as he put it, "pussy, pot, and parties." The other played guitar in a Washington nightclub.

He had gone back to Vietnam and volunteered for the assignment in the Highlands. The objective had been to organize a Montagnard group which would disrupt the Vietcong supply pipeline from Cambodia, forcing them to divert forces from an accelerating campaign against the communications of the South Vietnamese army. It had worked for a while until the Cong lost patience and moved in on one of the Montagnard villages with flame throwers and incinerated five hundred women and children. That had ended his last mission as the men in his group had melted away into the forest taking with them all their equipment. He and two NCOs had moved by night out of the area of highest Cong concentration and finally called in a chopper to pull them out.

He had been half-asleep, the mid-morning sun eating into him, when the Vietnamese girl tripped over his legs and landed on the newly healed wound in his side. He had suppressed a scream of agony, turning to face the lithe young body which sprawled across him. She had excused herself in exquisite French and moved quickly to collect suntan oil, comb, fingernail polish, lipstick, and assorted coins she had carried wrapped in a small towel. He had helped and when the little pile of artifacts was neatly arranged on the towel, invited her for a drink, pointing out, when she was about to refuse, that the gods must have intended them to meet.

She had laughed at that as they headed for one of the glass-topped tables surrounded by filigreed metal chairs protected from the sun by a striped sun umbrella. "Somehow I do not think my Russian Orthodox God acts in such subtle ways," she had said. The drink had stretched into lunch as she told him of her White Russian grandfather who had followed the detritus of the Russian revolution, first into China and then into Vietnam. He had married her Vietnamese grandmother and founded a dynasty based on rubber plantations and an import-export business now owned and run by her brothers.

His only legacy to her were the hazel eyes which turned almost yellow as the sun reflected off them. That and a certain Slavic gravity and sadness which underlay the Vietnamese animation.

"You speak Russian?"

"Yes. He taught us all before he died. He was a marvelous old man, always longing to go back to the snow and cold. He said no people could become great living in a climate like this. It does not develop the steel of character, he always said." She laughed at this, the lines in her lovely, delicate face turning upward.

"Maybe we could do with a few less steely characters. They seem to be the ones who cause all the trouble."

"That is traitorous to all you puritan Americans believe in, is it not?"

Doyle had suppressed a smile. The Saigon of 1967 showed few evidences of American puritanism. "You don't want to confuse the pretensions with the reality. Hypocrisy is the grease which makes the wheels of Anglo-Saxon society turn. Without it, nothing would work."

"That's what my French professors used to say in Paris. Only the French, with their impeccable realism and logic, operate a society rationally. Everywhere else it is chaos. Especially in the Anglo-Saxon countries."

As they talked he became aware that she affected him as no woman had since the night in his wife's bedroom six months before—the honeyed texture of her skin, the points of her small uptilted breasts outlined through the thin fabric of her wispy bikini top, accentuated by a fine film of perspiration combined with a musky perfume. A few strands of curling black hair escaped around the edges of the small triangle of cloth which barely covered her pubic mound. As were many Vietnamese women, she was a jewel of miniature perfection, muscular but with a fine layer of softness concealing the edges.

"That's why they do so well at governing themselves and others," he said.

"Oh, they don't do so badly," the girl said. "Most of my father's friends say Vietnam was better off economi-

110

cally when the French ran things, even if they did skim a lot off the top."

"But nobody wants them back."

"No." Her lovely face was serious. "Nobody wants them back. Or anybody else, really. We just want to be left alone. That's Vietnamese history for the last four thousand years. Nobody will leave us alone."

She was a student of medicine in her fourth year, twenty-three years old, unmarried and unattached. Her family was becoming increasingly worried that she would wind up a spinster.

"I don't think I can marry a Vietnamese," she had said.

"Why not? Too domineering?"

She hesitated, frowning. "No. I don't mind being dominated. My French training is, after all, only a little patina on top of my education as a Vietnamese woman. Domination I can accept. But not contempt. You know, in the Far East a woman is no better than an animal, and sometimes the animals are more important. You know what the Chinese say?"

"No."

"Feeding a woman is like feeding a cowbird." She had shrugged. "That is also the attitude of the Vietnamese, and that I find hard to accept."

Over the next days she had met him at the club each morning, and they had played tennis, swam, and ate at one of the myriad small restaurants she knew in the teeming native quarter. Then she had suggested a Russian restaurant, Chez Romanoff, a rundown antique of a place which had once been chic but which now was patronized by the aging remnants of the White Russian community and a few East European ex-legionnaires who had married Vietnamese and settled in Saigon.

"I reserved a room upstairs," she said. "Otherwise

we'll be constantly interrupted by my grandfather's old friends."

The ancient maître d'hôtel had greeted her in a flood of Russian, bending low over her hand, and she had introduced them gravely. He led them up a flight of creaky stairs to a windowless room lined in red plush and furnished in stained, decrepit fin de siècle furniture. Badly faked icons and cheap Russian religious statuary decorated the walls. A bottle of Polish vodka encased in a layer of ice was fighting a losing battle with the heat, despite an ancient air conditioner on a low table surrounded by plush cushions. Against the opposite wall an elegantly delicate table was set with an array of crystal and Chinese porcelain.

"I ordered cold borscht and a chicken-and-rice dish they're famous for. Is that all right?"

He nodded, dropping onto one of the cushions. "Christ, it looks like a Turkish opium peddler's dream of paradise."

"You don't like it?" She was frowning.

"Sure, I like it. My father was a Turk."

"Very funny," she said, pouring two tiny glasses full of the icy vodka and toasting him silently. It was mellow, the searing of raw alcohol muted, and the aftertaste somehow carried with it the memory of northern steppes.

"It's true. The Indians came across the Bering strait from North Central Asia. The Turks originated in the same area. My mother was half Indian. So I'm a Turk."

"In that case I am God," the girl said. "The Vietnamese race was founded by a union of a noble girl and a god."

"I wonder what would happen if you united a god and a Turk," he said, grinning.

The girl stared down at her vodka glass and was silent

as the antique maître d'hôtel led in a pair of white-coated waiters laden with silver dishes.

The borscht, deep red and clear, was ice cold. The chicken, a curious mixture of Russian and oriental flavors based on curry, was superb. "Why did you bring me here?" Doyle asked, admiring the delicate line of her neck where the silk ao dai ended.

"I thought you might be tired of Vietnamese food. And I like it. My grandfather would bring us here as a great treat. It was his window to Russia. The old waiters would gather around and they would speak Russian and after lunch he and Vassily would play chess."

Doyle had reached for her then, half expecting a rebuff, but she had smiled and slipped under his arm, rising gracefully, the silk dress, split on one side almost to her waist, riding high up over the lace of her pants. "There are conventions," she said, moving to the door and sliding a wooden panel into a slot. "They won't bother us now," she said, turning to him, hands hanging limply at her sides. He rose and crossed the room, taking the slim body in his arms, feeling its stiffness.

He let her go and moved back. "You're not very interested, are you? This is some kind of an act."

The girl looked startled, her hazel eyes widening. Then quickly she moved forward against him. "No. No, that's not true. It's just that I haven't had much experience. Especially with round eyes." She was grinning up at him now, her body soft against him. "You must be a little patient. Our customs are so different." She moved back then and crossed her hand in front of her, lifting the dress over her head in one graceful motion, revealing the same body he'd seen many times in a bikini. She slipped out of her pants and stood before him, long hair loosened and hanging down over her shoulders.

They had made love throughout the afternoon and

into early evening, sipping dry, cold champagne and exploring each other's bodies like perverse, precocious children. "Why me?" Doyle had asked at one point, lying on his back staring up at her oval face surrounded by a tangled halo of hair. She ran her hand down his chest, entwining her fingers in the curly black hair which began at his navel.

"It was an accident," she said, shrugging. "I didn't deliberately fall over you, although I know you think I did. I was bored. Since my grandfather died, I've seen almost no Europeans except a few of his old friends like Vassily. And the Vietnamese regard me as some sort of exotic. My skin is lighter and everybody wants to sleep with me, but their families would be horrified if they tried to marry me. And besides, women are nothing in this society. Beasts of burden or just something to pass an hour or two. It's different in the West. I've read about all the new things that are happening. So when I fell over your big feet, I thought, what the hell, why not?" Her hand now reached its goal and she began to stroke him with infinite gentleness, leaning over to kiss him, her tongue a live thing across his lips, into his mouth. Her mouth moved down across his face, following the trail of her hand earlier, across his nipples like the wings of a butterfly, teasing his skin. Gradually she moved down across his body until he felt his stomach tighten into a sudden knot of tension as she took him in her mouth.

"Are you happy with your Vietnamese, roundeye?" she asked, pushing herself up, elbows digging into his chest. "Do you still think it goes crossways?"

Doyle had begun to laugh, almost throwing her off him. "Where did you hear that?"

"I read it in some stupid book," she said. "And the

114

next day I stood with my back to the full-length mirror in my mother's room and bent over to look."

"Was it true?"

"No. It just looks like raw beefsteak," she said, giggling and pulling him over on top of her. "Come. It's time you did some of the work."

"Christ, Nadia. I think he's dead," he protested.

She moved her body across his in triumph, slipping him in in a quick movement of immense delicacy and skill. "Only a little worn down," she said, giggling as she began to move her body in a rotating motion which gradually converted his semi-limp member into a hard demanding cylinder. Her hands moved his body, touching him gently, running her fingers over his skin as her mouth held his in an insistent, prolonged vise.

"Jesus, woman, you are something else," he said as the sudden draining spasm came and she gave a little gasp which sounded almost like a reaction to pain and slid off him onto the cushions.

"We Vietnamese are supposed to be very good at it," she agreed matter of factly. "Something about Oriental decadence, my grandfather used to say."

"He discussed the subject with you?"

"He warned me about untrustworthy Westerners such as you," she said, digging her fingernails into his side in a quick, catlike gesture. "He said they would take me for their pleasure and then abandon me to my vile fate." She was on top of him again now, her slim body seeming to fill every crevice of his.

At the end of his leave, he'd been posted to Hue, and he'd taken her with him. They had shared a house with another Green Beret and his Vietnamese girl friend, coming back to it from missions into the highlands like Lond Island commuters. The house had become a meeting place for old Vietnamese hands passing through, newspapermen, State Department political officers, psychological warfare types, and Green Berets about to go into the jungle.

Nadia and Xueng Chi had moved like delicate wraiths through the throng of men, avoiding outstretched hands, bringing drinks and the spicy Vietnamese food and sitting quietly to listen to the tales of war.

It had lasted almost six months. Toward the end Doyle had begun to feel the tension building up around them throughout the ancient city, a foreboding almost like the feeling in the air in the West Virginia mountains just before a summer thunderstorm would break. They all knew something was about to happen, but intelligence was so bad or contradictory that nobody had forecast it when it came.

The traditional three-day truce to celebrate the lunar New Year, Tet, began on January 29, 1968. On the following day Doyle had returned from a week-long reconnaissance deep in the Tamlinhat mountain area where, with a group of Montagnards, he had unsuccessfully tracked a mobile Vietcong communications base.

He had found Vince Carroll, the Green Beret captain who shared the house, stoned to the eyeballs in mid-afternoon nursing a half-filled bottle of bourbon and cursing the Vietnamese in a quiet unending monologue as the two women watched.

"What's eating Vince?" Doyle had asked, taking Nadia in his arms, feeling her stiff against him.

She had shrugged. "Somebody got killed. That stupid helicopter pilot who used to come here and quote poetry. You remember him?"

Doyle nodded wearily. He remembered the carrot-headed kid who couldn't hold his liquor and was forever quoting "Abdul Abulbul Amir" in his cups. He'd put his Huey down in the middle of a firefight to bring Carroll and three of his men out from sure death once. He'd fallen in love with Nadia and, whenever he could get to Hue, would come and get drunk and stare at her. She had disliked him intensely.

He'd put Vince to bed, sodden with bourbon, and listened briefly to the evening news. The Tet truce had been broken off because of Vietcong attacks at My Tho and Vinh Long. A general offensive was expected, the Armed Forces Network reporter said. He had reached for Nadia finally, overcoming the fatigue, but she had slipped out of his arms, body taut and unyielding, and he had fallen asleep almost instantly.

He never knew why he awakened. Some atavistic instinct out of the depths of his Indian ancestors may have spoken to him of death. He opened his eyes to see her beside him holding the knife. Her eyes were closed and her lips drawn back over her small even teeth as they did when she was in the final agony of love. He had gripped her wrist, and she had come alive, fighting, clawing in silent frenzy as she tried to bury the knife in him. Only half awake, he almost let her slip from his grip as she worked the knife against his arm, drawing a spurt of blood as she severed a vein.

He'd hit her then, at the base of the jaw, and she had slumped limp in his arms. He had fumbled in a medicine chest for a bandage, cursing in the dark, and headed for Carroll's room. He'd found him lying spread-eagled on the bed, throat cut, his private parts stuffed clumsily in his mouth, the sheet around him soaked with blood.

Sounds of fighting from the city were filtering through the night. He had moved back to his own bedroom and found Nadia fumbling with the mechanism of the miniature Israeli machine gun he carried with him in the jungle. He had taken the weapon from her and she stood up to face him, hazel eyes blazing.

"Xueng killed him?"

"Yes."

"And you were supposed to kill me?"

"Yes."

"Why didn't you?"

"I would have. But I'm a sentimental half-European fool. I looked at your face, and I had to suppress my bourgeois emotions for a moment. Then you woke up. Are you a fool, too? Kill me."

"Why?"

"Why what? You mean why would I want to kill you? God, you are a fool, Steve. Don't you know who I am? Why I'm here with you? I was assigned to you. To find out what operations you were leading and warn the Viet Cong. Your goddamned unit had killed more cadres than any in Vietnam. And eventually I was to kill you when I'd learned all I could."

She stood silent in front of him, slim and beautiful in the silk ao dai.

"But why? Why the Vietcong? They'll ruin your family if they take power."

Her head snapped back. "All my brothers are members. So am I. I have been since the lycée. We'll all be leaders when we win. And we'll be free of foreign domination for the first time in our history. I've turned my back on Europe. I'm a Vietnamese. You'd better kill me, Steve. The town is full of cadres killing fools like you right now. You can't last long. Hue will fall almost immediately. And so will the rest of Vietnam. This is our last major offensive. You'll all die."

He'd lifted the little gun and slotted a cartridge, meeting her eyes. "Would you have killed me?"

"Yes, Steve. I would. Even though I love you." Her

118

face crumpled and tears began to stream down her face. "For God's sake, kill me quickly, you fool."

He'd moved across the room and taken her in his arms, kissing her gently on the eyes. "You'd better get out of here. I'm going to tell the military police what happened. You and Xueng were gone. That's all I know. Good luck, Nadia."

He'd pushed her out the door, dressed quickly, and went out into the night and war.

CHAPTER NINE

Major Mason Pruitt was in a half-crouch as the target flipped up. He wheeled to face it and the Smith and Wesson .357 spat six times, stitching a pattern in the target area the size of a man's hand. He tossed the empty gun to an enlisted man standing behind him and picked up another loaded weapon, nodding to the target controller. The second target came up to his left, in profile, and he put six neat holes in its head from jaw to hairline.

"Nice shooting, Major," the target controller said, stepping out of his bullet-proof booth and moving behind the wall to replace the pasteboard covers on the metal backings. It was a closed room, its white cement walls lighted from the floor. Around three sides a waist-high wall hid a series of twenty flip-up targets of men in various poses. Major Mason Pruitt had just finished the full series, firing six shots at each of the targets, 120 rounds.

"Shit," Pruitt said coldly. "I missed the target completely four times and on half a dozen others the son of a bitch would have lived."

"Not with that cannon you're using, Major. Hell, the wind from it would knock most people down. Why not try that new Czech .25 magnum? It'll kill 'em just as dead and you don't have to work so damned hard with it."

"I like the weight, Larry," Pruitt said, running a hand through his close-cropped, wiry red hair. "I want that kick in my hand. The .25 millimeter is a pansy gun." He turned toward the glass wall behind him and came to instant attention, saluting the figure in civilian clothes standing outside watching.

Admiral William Christman waved him out of the shooting enclosure in a half salute.

"Hello, Pruitt. How have you been?"

"Fine, Admiral. Just fine. I was sorry to hear about your resignation."

Christman nodded. "So was I. That was pretty good shooting. You haven't lost your touch."

Pruitt shrugged. "Kind of a useless exercise, standing in there blowing down paper targets with a handgun. But it keeps your eye in. What are you doing here, Admiral?"

Christman glanced around. "Is there someplace we can have a coffee and talk? Someplace private?"

"Sure, Admiral." He was not a big man, but his every movement gave the impression of repressed force and energy. He packed one hundred and ninety pounds on a five-foot nine-inch body which looked like a block of steel-reinforced concrete. He led the way to the small office of the range duty officer, a young lieutenant who shot to attention at the sight of Pruitt and Christman.

"Get lost, Wilson. The Admiral and I want to talk."

"Yes, sir," the lieutenant said, saluting, wondering

what the hell a former chairman of the Joint Chiefs of Staff was doing at this godforsaken base in the mountains of North Carolina.

"I hear you're in the doghouse again, Pruitt."

"You mean killing that hijacker?" The red-headed man shrugged, his freckled face a mask of irritation. "What the fuck did they want me to do? Let the son of a bitch walk off with two million dollars? The country's full of mushheads, Admiral."

"Four passengers died along with him," Christman said mildly, taking a cigar out of his inside coat pocket and offering one to Pruitt, who declined.

"Yeah. And maybe all two hundred of them would have bought the farm if we hadn't taken him out." He shook his bullet-shaped head in a violent motion. "You know what we ought to do with the shitheads, Admiral? One way we could stop hijacking once and for all?"

Christman smiled faintly. Major Mason Pruitt had a reputation of being a man who liked final solutions. "How would you do that?"

"I'd set up a team. Six to ten men. Recruit them from all over the world. The best hit men we could find. Bring them over here and give them some solid paramilitary training. Get the cooperation of Interpol and as many of the world's governments as we could. Every time there was a hijacking or a kidnapping, we'd pay. Get the hostages back."

Christman frowned. "How's that going to stop anything? It's an invitation to more."

Pruitt grinned, his hard, freckled face turning wolfish. "Once we had the hostages back, we'd turn loose this team. They'd hunt the hijackers down, no matter where they were, and burn them. Leave the bodies in a public place with a note pinned to them that it would happen to anybody else who tried it. No legal due pro-

122

cess or any of that horseshit. Just a little round hole in the forehead."

It was, Christman reflected, a typical Pruitt suggestion. "I understand you've been restored to command."

"Yeah. They can't find anybody else crazy enough to take it on. We're down to five hundred men now." Pruitt shook his head. "Nothing like the good old days when Steve Doyle was here. Goddamn, we were a fighting outfit then."

"I wasn't aware that Doyle was one of your favorites, Pruitt. Didn't he almost have you court-martialed after the rescue of the vice-president?"

Pruitt shrugged. "We had a disagreement over tactics. I guess I sort of disobeyed orders a little." Pruitt smiled a sardonic smile, revealing badly capped front teeth. "But I'll tell you something, Admiral. Nobody I'd rather have next to me in the front lines than that fucking Indian."

"He's the president's military advisor now."

"Yeah. If he keeps his nose clean he'll have your old job some day, Admiral. Smart son of a bitch. And cold as a whore's heart. But you didn't come up here to talk about Doyle, Admiral." Pruitt's brutal, intelligent face split in a slight smile. "You must have some dirty work you want done."

"I read your article in the last issue of *Military Quarterly*. After that, I am surprised you're still on active duty."

"You forget the new regulations on freedom of expression. There's not a fucking thing they can do to me. Except not promote me, of course, which they won't do anyway. But I've got a right to express my opinion, and by Christ I intend to keep doing it."

"They'll select you out next time around."

Pruitt shrugged. "I'm tired of the peacetime army anyway. I've got a standing offer from South Africa to command a battalion. I'm thinking about taking them up on it. There's no future for me in this man's army. All I can do is hang on until I get my twenty years in. But I'm a soldier, and it's the only game going."

"Is that article of yours bullshit or do you really believe it, Pruitt?" Christman refused to meet the younger officer's eyes as he spoke, staring at the lengthening ash on the thick Montechristo he held with great care.

"You mean about the army being the guardian of the nation's soul?" He smiled sardonically. "Yeah. I believe it. I think we've reached a point where either we shape up or somebody's going to ship us out. Life's too easy. We've been winning too long. Nobody's willing to fight for what he's got anymore. Every empire goes through the same thing. Lean and hungry at first, willing to kill, rape and pillage. A period of consolidation and maturity when the old warrior ethic still motivates the upper classes to supply intelligent, well-trained officers embued with a sense of abstract honor and all that bullshit. Then the final phase when defense is turned over to mercenaries and the ruling classes are spineless voluptuaries."

Christman still stared at his cigar. "And you think we're in that phase, do you, Pruitt?"

"You read my article, Admiral. Vietnam was the first war we ever fought where the upper classes refused to officer our armies. They hid in universities, deserted, went overseas. All under the cover of some sort of bullshit 'morality'. The rioting ended the day the draft did. Hell, we never fought a moral war in our history and neither did anybody else. Eighteen-forty-six was pure imperialism and so was the Civil War and 1898. The First and Second World Wars were fought to establish us as a world power, and in his guts everybody who took part in them knew it. So what's different about Vietnam? We were out there protecting our geopolitical interests, but we'd lost the nerve to do it. Shit, more men between 18 and 25 got killed in automobile accidents in one year than died in that whole fucking penny ante war. It was safer to have your son in Nam than behind the wheel of a car, but nobody suggested doing away with cars. We just lost our fucking guts."

"And you think we can arrest the rot of our spirit?"

"You read my article, Admiral. I want every fucking young man in the country in the army for two years of the toughest possible mandatory military training. Not this chickenshit half-assed stuff we pull today. Real, assbreaking, physical, old-style military training. Every eighteen-year-old, regardless of his condition unless he's a basket case, gets the training. It'll do two things. First, it'll stiffen their pansy spines and second it'll bring everybody down to the same level at least once in his lifetime. The rich goddamn upper-class kid will get his jaw broken by a plumber's son, and he'll never again treat him with the supercilious contempt that some of the young jerks feel today. Blacks, Chicanos, Jews, you name it, they'll all be in the same pit once in their lives."

"Admirable, Pruitt. I must say, an admirable program. You know it's impossible, of course. No Congress would vote it even if a president suggested it. They'd laugh you out of the country."

Pruitt shrugged, massaging his wrist, sore from the kick of the magnum. "Sure. I know that. I just wrote the article to get it off my chest. Like masturbation. Fun but it doesn't get you anywhere." He grinned. "But you didn't come down here to discuss my literary prowess, Admiral. You've got to have something else on your mind."

Christman stubbed out the cigar and met Pruitt's flat steely blue eyes. "You're right, Pruitt. I didn't come down here to talk about literature. I came down to look you over. And, if you measure up, make you a proposal."

CHAPTER TEN

Doyle moved through the reception line, his black dress uniform glittering with tiny medals and the green sunburst star which indicated he had once served on the Pentagon staff. Here and there a faint whiff of mothballs came his way from somebody's long-unused tailcoat. The president's blonde wife, distracted and tense, took his hand as if she'd never seen him and passed him along the line with the practiced half push, half pull handshake developed to an art by harried politicians and diplomats. The president winked at him and leaned forward to pass along a message in a low voice.

"Steve, see if you can feel out Shimon Rabin. I hear he's going to be making some impossible demands over at the Pentagon, and I want some advance warning if the prime minister brings new arms up tonight."

Doyle nodded and found himself propelled into the dazzling public rooms of the White House. Recent presidents' wives each had contributed to an increasing opulence and luxury under the careful eye of the building's curator, and now the silk-paneled walls set off a series of carefully restored Peale and Stewart historical paintings in a setting of eighteenth and nineteenth century antiques which made the place look increasingly like an English country home during the Empire's golden age. Glancing around at the colorful uniforms and elaborately coiffed women, Doyle narrowed his eyes and could almost imagine the place filled with men in powdered hair and silk knee breeches, ceremonial swords trailing behind.

"It's a little much, huh?" Maria Vicente said, coming up behind him and taking his arm.

"You read my mind."

"I know. It showed on your face."

"Oh?" Doyle said, a little startled.

"I was only kidding. That phony Indian mask of yours works even when you're making love," Maria said smiling up at him. "Speaking of which, I'm beginning to feel like a neglected wife."

Doyle suppressed a twitch of irritation, then was amused at his reaction. Hell, why shouldn't women be the aggressors? Still, he preferred making the moves.

"Do you mind going by to take in a set at the disco after this? I promised Bob. He's doing something new."

Maria laughed, throwing her head back to reveal the lovely slender column of her neck. "Don't be so stiff-necked, Steve. We ladies get the itch occasionally, too, you know. Without being invited. But I'd love to hear Bob."

Istvan Esterhazy joined them, his miniature figure immaculate in midnight blue tails. "Good evening, Maria, General. Where does one find a glass of that abominable champagne the president serves? Or is he rationing it again?"

"I'll find a waiter," Maria said, moving off quickly

128

through the crowd, her green dress moving against her body like the pelt of a finely trained racehorse.

"I've been meaning to speak to you about your intentions toward my assistant, General," Esterhazy said, his almost lineless pink face smiling up at Doyle. "Are you planning to make an honest woman out of her? My reasons for asking are more practical than moral, I hasten to assure you. Married she would get a great deal more sleep and be of considerable more use to me."

"I'm only a simple soldier, Doctor. I doubt if Maria would find in me the complexity of spirit which she probably needs in a permanent partner."

"She's a Sicilian woman, Doyle," Esterhazy said drily. "She needs above all else a rough if tender hand on the bridle. And I suspect, after those young assistant professor types to whom she was accustomed, you are providing in abundant measure just what it is that has been lacking in her life. I only hope you'll resolve your personal problems soon. We must keep our perspective these days and not waste too much time and energy on nonessentials. We're entering a really crucial period right now. Unless we're very careful and have some luck, this country may not survive it."

"I've been thinking over the suggestion you made at lunch, Doctor. I can't see being able to do much. Partly because I'm not totally convinced myself that the cuts in the military budget aren't dangerous."

The old man nodded. He moved easily but without abrupt gestures, as if he knew his ancient body to be fragile and easily broken or bruised. "You're in the grip of habitual stereotypes, General. You and your colleagues. There is probably no single task more difficult than reforming the viewpoint of an entrenched military bureaucracy. One as massive and protected by tradition as the Pentagon presents some very special problems.

129

That doesn't alter the validity of Clemenceau's aphorism that war is too serious a matter to be left to generals. Certainly today, classic military strategy is as irrelevant as the lance to modern war. All the old shibboleths about courage and will are absurd in an age when one man at a console can fire two thousand missiles and kill five hundred million people over a period of fifteen minutes."

"We've managed to avoid that scenario for the past forty years, Doctor. Just possibly because there were ways of settling disputes short of atomic weapons."

The old man waved his thin hand, a matrix of blue veins standing out against the translucent parchment of his skin. "No, Doyle. You are wrong. Nobody is going to be foolish enough to use nuclear weapons barring some maniac or an accident. But the existence of these so-called conventional toys offers unbearable temptation to the intellectual infants who run the armies on all sides. If we take the first step, and we can do it without danger of becoming enslaved, then the political leaders of the other world powers will also be able to pull back, cut their defense expenditures and devote the resources to improving their citizens' lives. In fact they will have no choice. If they don't follow our lead we'll outstrip them in every economic and social category within a short time."

"Doctor, you're a student of history. Where in human experience has a strong, aggressive, relatively poor country not taken advantage of a weak, passive, rich one when the opportunity presented itself? If we disarm to the extent you recommend, we'll leave our clients in Latin America, which is about the only place we have any left, at the mercy of our enemies. They'll quickly make their accommodations, and it won't be pleasant to see. We'll be at the mercy of our enemies for the supply of just about every vital metal and mineral resource we need."

"I doubt it, Doyle. I really doubt it. The Soviets have their hands full with China at their back and Germany looking down their throats. Germany has not yet digested its dominant role in Europe and is in no mood for overseas involvement. The China-Japan alliance is too alien to the Latins to make any penetrations, and in any case it has too many internal strains and must concentrate too much on the Soviet Union to indulge in imperialist adventures." He shook his head. "I don't agree with your fears, Doyle. Never in our history has the world balance of power been more favorable. I think we can safely cut back and devote ourselves to the economic reorganization of the country. We'll come out of that once again the strongest nation in the world economically and with an inner social peace unknown in human history. We'll be invulnerable to the tensions and strains which are besetting our allies and our enemies if we use our resources rationally. If we don't," he shrugged. "I think violent revolution is more than a possibility. It's probable."

"Istvan, you're full of shit, as usual," a big voice rasped out behind him.

Esterhazy turned, his fine features tightened into a mask of distaste. "You know Mr. Cooley, General Doyle. Ralph Cooley, president of the Federal Steel Corporation. To what do we owe the very dubious pleasure of your presence, Ralph?"

Cooley grinned. He was the antithesis of Esterhazy, six-feet-four or five, his massive belly protruding against a once elegantly tailored white vest yellowing and frazzled with age. "It wasn't voluntary, Istvan. You can bet on that. Yitshak twisted my arm. He said he needed some support in this nest of socialist vipers."

"Yitshak is like all heretics or converts. He's worse than those born to the faith. The Israeli socialists have become downright disgusting lately since their momentarily successful imperialist venture in the Middle East. Are you advising him?"

"No. Just holding his hand. Got to know him well when we put in the rolling mill a few years ago. Found out we share the same taste in cigars. Cuban Montechristos." Cooley's laugh boomed out across the room.

Esterhazy stared the big man up and down, and his face softened. "Ralph, you should lose some weight. You must be close to three hundred. You'll drop dead of a heart attack."

"Yeah, I know, Istvan. But the only things I really enjoy outside of the job are eating and drinking and screwing. I just hope I go on the upstroke." He turned to Doyle, his eyes tiny knots of steel buried in the suet of his cheeks. "I see we're sharing the same table, General. It will be an honor and a privilege to dine with one of the few genuine military heroes this country has produced since the Second World War."

Doyle searched his voice and face for irony but found none. Most businessmen he'd come in contact with showed only amused contempt for the military unless they were seeking a contract. Then it was, as one procurement officer put it, "wall-to-wall booze and broads."

Cooley moved off and Esterhazy shook his head at his back. "Brilliant man, General. One of the finest minds in American business. I had him as a student at Harvard when I first arrived in this country. Immense appetites. For everything. Studied twenty hours a day. Played tackle on the football team. Ate gargantuan amounts of food, and was noted for his exploits with the fair sex. Inside that mass of fat and muscle is the soul of an ascetic imprisoned by flesh. It's really a great shame.

132

He could have accomplished so much more. As it is all he's done is produce more and better steel cheaper than anybody else. Sometimes I see in him a symbol of the United States in our age."

Doyle was irritated and about to reply when Maria appeared with a waiter in tow. "Champagne, Doctor Esterhazy. But I'm afraid you're right. It's California."

Esterhazy sighed and picked up a slender fluted crystal glass. "He really carries things to extremes, our good president. There is nothing immoral in serving Piper Heidsieck. However," he sipped delicately, "it could be worse. With whom have they seated me, Maria?"

"The Israeli finance minister, the French ambassador and somebody with an Armenian name. I think he owns some tankers. Lots of tankers."

"Well, that should be a stimulating evening. The Frenchman and the Israeli will shout recriminations at each other and I will be left to discuss load factors with an Armenian rug peddler."

Esterhazy excused himself and headed across the room to a small group around the president.

"That man Cooley is gross. What were you talking about?"

"I'm not sure. He and your boss seem to have a father-son relationship heavily tinged with Oedipal overtones."

"They do. When Dr. Esterhazy was a professor, Cooley was his finest student. But after he took his doctorate, he decided against an academic life and went into business. I don't think Dr. Esterhazy ever quite got over how he's developed."

"Sort of a caricature of a greedy, imperialist capitalist, I gather," Doyle said trying to remember what he'd read about the industrialist in a *Time* magazine cover story several years earlier. Tough, ruthless, efficient, utterly without illusions. A patron of the Bach festival in Darien, Connecticut. Honorable mention All-America from an Ivy League college. Reads Xenophon in the original Greek for relaxation. It had all sounded like some public relations man's dream of the Renaissance capitalist.

The last guest had arrived and some fifty people were milling through the two reception rooms. Groups formed and dissolved as the crowd moved past a small table near the dining room where the ten table seating arrangements were mounted on elegantly understated leather holders. The arrangement had the advantage of bruising feelings less than the traditional long table, and it also led to an easier interchange among more people.

The White House protocol officer and the president's wife had spent a full day arranging the seating to separate obvious enemies and make sure a man's wife and mistress were not at the same table.

"Christ, I'd give a lot for a beer," Doyle said, placing his empty champagne glass on a passing tray. During the Carter administration the president's wife had instituted the custom of serving only wine, and his successor had continued the practice.

"Steve, you really are plebeian."

"Why is beer plebeian? Because it's cheap?"

"And why don't you ever eat anything but steak?"

Doyle grinned at her, thinking that they might as well be married. "I read somewhere that your so-called gourmet cooking developed only to conceal the rotten taste of the meat in an age before refrigeration. Truly fine palates prefer the fresh, unmarred taste of natural foods."

"Steve, you made that up. But you're in trouble tonight. Wait until you see the menu. We're at the same table, you know. Along with Cooley."

"Who else?" Doyle was picturing the state dining room with its portrait of a pensive Lincoln over the fireplace and its off-white paneling. A recent decorator had covered the walls in an eighteenth century French fleur-de-lis wallpaper in a muted lavender. "Shimon Rabin, the Israeli defense minister. You know him, don't you?"

"Yes."

"Dr. Jordan Cummings from Defense and Jim Stansbury."

Doyle was surprised at the last name. The head of the Intelligence Advisory Group, successor to the CIA, Defense Intelligence Agency and a host of other competing intelligence organizations, was almost a recluse. He had taken over the IAG toward the end of the first Carter administration following a reorganization of the defense communities which had left U.S. intelligence in a shambles. He was a professional. Still in his early sixties, Stansbury was an authentic anachronism. Scion of an old New England family, he had fought with distinction in the Second World War as an OSS officer behind the lines in Italy and France. In the shadowy cold war days his name figured in almost every successful covert operation from the overthrow of Mossadegh and Arbanz to the final destabilization of Chile. He had spent six years in Vietnam, and it was there that Doyle had known him and there that he had left the agency in disgrace, barely escaping a prison sentence. Carter had resurrected him in a desperate move to bring some order out of the chaos into which the intelligence community had fallen.

"Kathy Caldwell and Nicole de Matignon, the French ambassador's wife, finish it off," Maria said, taking his arm. "It really should be a jolly little evening. All stilettos and perfumed icepicks."

They entered the State Dining Room behind the president, the Israeli prime minister's elegant second wife on his arm, talking animatedly. Yitshak Grosz and the president's wife followed, she looking around the room with distracted nervousness as if half expecting to find the tables unset. Protocol broke down following the entry of the secretary of state and Doyle followed Maria to a table in one corner.

After a flurry of introductions Doyle found himself seated at the round table between Stansbury and the French ambassador's bored-looking wife. Stansbury had taken his hand with a wintry grin. "Hello, Doyle. A little different from the last meal we had together, huh?"

Doyle nodded, remembering the shared tin of cold stew under a shelter half in the Central Highlands following a disastrous Green Beret operation mounted with the help of the CIA. Five dead men had lain in front of them in green plastic body bags as they ate waiting for the helicopter to arrive.

"You know Madame de Matignon?" Stansbury asked, lapsing into impeccable French. Doyle shook the slender hand and found himself facing the examination every mature Frenchwoman makes of a new male. He had once decided it was about equally composed of an estimate of his net worth, his potential powers as a stud, and his ability to carry on a civilized conversation. The order changed depending on the woman and the circumstances but the ingredients were almost always the same.

"*Très heureux*, General," she said in French, adding with negligent insolence, "You do speak French?"

Doyle had nodded, smiling faintly. Nicole de Matignon was in her late forties, dressed in a simple, elegant black evening gown and a collar of diamonds which set off her slim, unlined neck. Lines of weariness and boredom marked her eyes and the corners of her mouth. He wondered how many similar functions she had attended over the last quarter century.

Maria Vicente winked at him from across the table as around the room people waited for the president to take his seat. As Doyle held the chair for the Frenchwoman, he heard a muttered *"merde"* slip from her.

"I beg your pardon?" he said.

She smiled at him, her rather grim face lighting up as a startling array of very white teeth suddenly appeared and all the lines in her face went up. She looked ten years younger. "I said *merde*, General. A word you presumably learned at that fantastic language school where your army teaches you French, no?" She gestured toward the menu. "I was referring to the meal of which I will be able to eat almost nothing, as usual. I do not understand why you Americans feel you must imitate all the sauceladen garbage of the French haute cuisine when you have such lovely dishes of your own. You really must grow up, you know," she said, extracting an ivory cigarette holder from a silver bag, inserting a Gauloise and holding it for Doyle to light as an embarrassed laugh fluttered around the table.

"You look very heroic, General, with your little baubles. What is that one?" she asked, pointing to a Silver Star.

"Good conduct medal," Doyle said smiling.

"My God, they give you a medal for that? In the French army they would cashier you." She turned to Cooley on her right, lapsing into heavily accented English and slipping her arm through his. As she talked her right breast lightly brushed the big man's arm.

"How are things at the center of power, Steve?" Stansbury asked as the waiter deftly slipped a bowl of oxtail soup in front of him.

"Powerful," Doyle said.

"And a touch nervous, I should judge."

Doyle met the older man's look. "You know something?"

"No. Nothing definite. But Christman has been talking to some of my people. Some of the kooks on the far right. But he's also been dealing with the Cubans and the exile groups. Nothing concrete. Just sounding them out on their feelings about the president and his program. And hints of more . . ."

"Have you told the president?"

"I've got a meeting with him tomorrow on another subject. I plan to bring it up. Difficulty is that there is nothing really specific. Bill Christman's no fool. If he's really preparing something, he wouldn't be wandering across the country preaching it. He'd first sound out the landscape to see where his possible support might be, compromising nobody. Then, at the last moment he'd bring together a tight little group of leaders, lay out the plan, and put it into immediate action. That's the way a successful coup is run. He knows it, and we know it."

"What's your gut feeling, Jim? Is it serious or are they just letting off steam?"

"Hard to tell, Steve. The frustration is real. You know that. These budget cuts are going to leave us essentially defenseless except for some sort of Armageddon. We're abdicating as one of the two most powerful nations on earth. It's extremely hard for the military to take. And not only the military." He nodded across the table, voice low. "Take Cooley for example. He's here tonight because he's hoping for a chance to talk privately with the president. Cooley hates the man, but Rabin insisted that he be invited. But make no mistake. He's the bitter enemy of this administration, not only for defense reasons but also because he regards the economic program as the beginnings of a totalitarian regime."

"How much support does he have among the business community?"

Stansbury sipped the soup and made a face. "Too much salt. A lot, Steve. And not only the munitions makers. The whole business community is well aware that the president plans to move toward a Swedish-style welfare state with total bureaucratic control of the means of production. Not nationalization in the classic sense, but a sort of state capitalism which will amount to the same thing. Obviously they are unhappy. Some may even be contemplating treason."

The Israeli defense minister leaned toward Stansbury. "Did I hear the word treason, Jim?"

"Yes, Shimon. You did. I said it's a form of treason to print the White House menu in French. Been going on for years, and it's ridiculous."

The Israeli grinned. "What do you make of the latest Soviet moves along the Amur? You think it is going to start again?"

Stansbury shook his head. "No. Not now. Neither one is ready for another bloodletting as bad as 1983. But you'd better be paying some attention to the Iranian border. The Soviets are suffering from a really critical oil shortage. The worst they've ever had, and those new Siberian fields are years away from production. With the mess in Iran, it's not inconceivable that they might move. There isn't anybody around to stop them any more," he added grimly.

Rabin was startled. "You mean right into the Gulf? But that's ridiculous, Jim. They wouldn't dare! The Japanese get half their oil from the Gulf. It would mean instant war."

"Suppose they were invited in?"

"The new Persian regime?" Rabin frowned. "I suppose it's possible. There are some wild men on the junta. But we've heard nothing as radical as this. Are you speculating, Jim, or do you have something?"

"We'll talk tomorrow, Shimon," Stansbury said glancing around the table where the conversation only partially masked what they were saying.

"Oh, but that's ridiculous, Mr. Cooley. And you know it." Maria's low, almost husky, voice had risen suddenly, slicing through the babble of voices in high-pitched anger. Across the table Jordan Cummings lifted his head out of his soup in amusement.

"What foul sexual perversion has he suggested to you, Maria?"

Maria Vicente had herself under instant control. "More political than sensual, Jordan."

"I merely suggested to Maria that among those around the president, there might be those whose motives were less than pure." Cooley's big, virile voice dominated the table.

"You said they might be traitors. Men who believed that the United States was a degenerate, materialistic society without any redeeming virtues which deserved to succumb to its socialist enemies," Maria Vicente said, face aflame with anger.

"True, I did say that." Cooley acknowledged. "Twenty years ago this nation went through one of those moments of truth that every empire faces. The ones with guts, brains and, above all, the will to dominate, regenerate themselves. The others wind up on the garbage dump of history. Or subside into fifth-rate nonpowers given to ritualistic moralizing as with Sweden and the Netherlands. Right now there are dozens of people in the upper echelons of this government who are members of something which used to be called the

140

counterculture in the sixties and seventies. They've cut their hair, got their degrees, and dropped back into society. But fundamentally they are enemies of this society, and they want it destroyed. I think that's one of the influences which is working on the president." Cooley lifted a spoonful of soup, a grim smile creasing his heavy face as the table sat in immobilized silence around him.

Kathy Caldwell, wife of the president's national security advisor, stared across at Cooley in astonishment, her china-blue eyes wide with disbelief. "Mr. Cooley, that is nonsense. My son was one of the young men you are talking about. He let his hair grow, smoked pot, and took part in the demonstrations to free the blacks. He wasn't then and isn't now a traitor. He believes that bigotry, inequality, injustice, and war are evil things and he has devoted his life to doing something about it. But he is no traitor." She spoke with serene self-assurance, never raising her voice.

"Bravo, Kathy," Nicole de Matignon said, applauding.

"Yes, bravo. I hope you, and he, are equally happy when the people he wants to turn this government over to stand him up against a wall. Because it's people such as he who get it first. The mush-headed idealists and spouters of foolish slogans. You've lived a sheltered life, Mrs. Caldwell. Rich, insulated, able to afford the luxury of idealism. Well, I haven't. And let me tell you, my dear lady, that in my experience bigotry is universal, inequality normal, and injustice a part of the human condition. As for war," his glance swept around the table, "without it we would all be slaves." Although Cooley's voice had not risen and his tone was mild, there was no mistaking the bitter menace of his tone.

Stansbury leaned across the table as the waiters

cleared the soup plates. "You're not serious, Ralph. The implication is that everyone who disagrees with you is a traitor."

"No, Jim. Not traitors. Not all, anyway. But fools, certainly."

The three women, as if by instinct, suddenly moved to cut off the anti-social argument, each turning to a partner and beginning to talk animatedly. Doyle smiled at the insistent torrent of charmingly mispronounced words Nicole de Matignon was directing in controlled bursts at Cooley who allowed himself to be distracted as Stansbury and the Israeli defense minister suffered the same fate at the hands of Kathy Caldwell, a diplomat's wife for thirty years.

Doyle caught Maria Vicente's eye and winked. Unpacified, she shot a venemous glance at Cooley without missing a conversational beat with the Pentagon foreign affairs chief. On safe ground once again, the group tacitly agreed to keep it there and the rest of the meal moved quickly.

"Coquilles de poisson diverse, sauce Mornay," Nicole de Matignon said, curling her upper lip in distaste. "It is suicide for you gentlemen to eat it. The calorie count for the cheese, eggs, and butter in the sauce is at least five thousand. This dish alone will clog your arteries with cholesterol. Still, it should be superb," she added, digging in heartily.

"What is selle de chevreuil, sauce poirade, Nicole?" Dr. Jordan Cummings asked.

"Venison in a special sauce based on peppercorns, thyme, parsley, bay leaves, carrots, onions and vinegar." She threw up her hands. "Mixed with brown sauce, of course, and the marinade from the venison. My God, *chéri*, to make the damned dish is a career in itself. It comes canned in France," she added staring down speculatively at the saddle of venison which had been placed before her. "I wonder."

Across the table Maria shook her head. "No, Nicole. I happen to know that the venison was a gift from the governor of Arizona. And the president's chef is, after all, a Frenchman."

Stansbury lifted his glass to Nicole de Matignon. "To the chef. God bless him and that marvelous nation of yours that produced him."

Nicole de Matignon picked up the glass of red wine and examined it critically. She had previously characterized a California white wine as bad Montrachet with pretensions.

"Oh, knock it off, Nicole. Even in Paris they now agree that our wines are superb," Kathy Caldwell said, her midwestern-accented French hitting each carefully pronounced syllable like an untalented, but persistent, pianist. The two women were good friends.

Nicole de Matignon grinned. "You forget, *chéri*, that I am not only the French ambassador's wife. I am also the commercial saleswoman of this dress I wear and every other product that France produces. I must even, discreetly to be sure, convey the earthy sensuality for which Frenchwomen are so," here she giggled, "justifiably famous. But the red is excellent. A little thin, perhaps, but quite drinkable. But I know nothing about wine. At home, Jacques and I drink beer. We're Alsatians, you know."

Doyle started to laugh, glancing at Maria Vicente across the table, still seething from her exchange with Cooley. The meal moved with rapid efficiency toward a close. Waiters did not hover over those who dawdled, but moved firmly to retrieve half-filled plates, replacing them with others, the presidential seal always centered on the top. Wine glasses were filled once and beneath

143

the patina of elegance Doyle could feel the creakings of the bureaucratic machine which was the president's kitchen. Overtime for the staff began at eleven-thirty, and orders were to empty the dining room by then.

As the dessert was cleared—Poires Geraldine, named for the guest of honor's wife, an old White House custom—the president rose, tapping his water glass with a fork, and conversation gradually hushed. The ritual of the toasts was about to begin.

"Mr. Prime Minister, honored guests, ladies and gentlemen. It gives me singular pleasure tonight to welcome to Washington, once again, one of our oldest and closest friends, the representative of a country with uniquely close ties of blood and tradition to our own. I have known Yitshak Grosz for more than fifteen years." The president turned and smiled down at his guest. "When we first met I was governor of a large American state, and Yitshak was head of a purchasing mission which had come to this country to buy weapons for its defense." The president's smile widened into a grin. "As some of our French friends here might say, *plus ça change, plus c'est la même chose,* the more things change the more they remain the same." As the startled laughter died down the president ceased to smile.

"However, as Yitshak knows and we all know, things do change. Not friendships, not loyalties, but political situations and the interests of nations. Over the past fifteen years I have watched his great nation, Israel, move from one success to another. From a perilous victory, snatched from the jaws of defeat in 1973, to the impressive military triumph in 1982, we have seen this small nation, heavily outnumbered in men and materiel, repeatedly defeat its enemies, extend its influence and play a role on the world stage out of all proportion to its geographic size or population. But today, at the pinnacle of its military and economic power, our friend and ally is once more confronted with a choice."

Doyle glanced around the room, feeling the tension on all sides. The toast was not following the usual polite pattern of such after-dinner remarks. The president obviously intended to set the scene for the private negotiations the following day with a warning salvo tonight.

"In a sense all statesmen are daily confronted by such choices. But there are times, in Shakespeare's great words, when 'there is a tide in the affairs of men which, taken at the flood, leads on to fortune—omitted, all the voyage of their life is bound in shallows and miseries.' I think one of these times may be approaching for our friends in Israel. I think an opportunity may be about to present itself for one of those rare and precious events in the history of men when an act of generosity reflects not only a nation's greatness of spirit but is also the action which best serves its interests.

"I refer, of course, to the possibility of ending the armed truce in the Middle East and replacing it with a genuine, long-lasting peace. The great burden of administering the occupied areas in Egypt, Saudi Arabia, Lebanon, and Syria has become even heavier during the last year. The restive Arab populations of these nations are demanding, with justice, an end to the Israeli occupation, a return to independence. If their demands are not met, violence will continue and will continue to be met with repression. This vicious cycle has no end except in ever-greater hatred and trouble. The Middle East has been a cancer in the body politic of the world for more than forty years, and the time has come to heal that wound and move to establish a just and peaceful system in the area."

The president picked up a half-filled glass of red wine and turned, raising it to the Israeli prime minister.

"It is with this hope that I raise my glass to Yitshak Grosz and his great people."

Grosz, a short chunky man with a crew cut of bristling gray hair, touched his glass perfunctorily to his lips, and rose, his tanned face a mass of deep lines. At fifty, he looked ten years older. Doyle remembered pictures of the cocky, grinning tank commander who had jumped with a division of Israeli airborne troops into the Saudi oil fields and secured them without the loss of a well within the first two days of the 1982 war. He had then returned to the Sinai front to take command of the tank army which smashed the Egyptian army on the Suez Canal and enveloped Cairo in ten days.

"Mr. President, ladies and gentlemen." Grosz spoke idiomatic American English learned from his American-born mother. His father had migrated from a miserable village in Eastern Poland only months before the German invasion and settled in one of the harshest of the new nation's frontier settlements. "I am here today, as the president so aptly put it, as a supplicant. That seems to be the Israeli prime minister's role vis-à-vis this great nation which has guaranteed our survival in so many desperate times over the past half century. I will not dwell on the number of occasions when one of my predecessors has arrived in Washington, shopping list in hand, with the knowledge that the sympathy of the man in your White House was all that stood between his nation and disaster."

Grosz paused and let his steely gray eyes flicker over the room. "However, ladies and gentlemen, times, as the wise man said, have changed. As I speak tonight Israel is testing its first hydrogen bomb warhead in a deep, sealed shaft in the Sinai desert. Within a matter of months, ballistic missiles with a range of two thousand miles, now armed with fission weapons, will have war-

146

heads of incomparably greater destructiveness. Within two years our missiles will be able to blanket the globe. We will, in a real and not a figurative sense, enter the ranks of world power. So in a sense I am not here tonight as a supplicant, although it is true that my defense minister will present a list of weapons we need from you tomorrow. However, we do not expect them as a gift," here his lined face creased in a sly smile, "since we hold more than enough dollars bought with our oil to pay in hard cash."

Grosz turned to the president, still smiling. "I say these things not in a spirit of boastfulness, but in one of relief. It is never good in a friendship for one friend always to come, hat in hand, begging, while the other, in his greatness of spirit and unbounded generosity, fulfills his needs. Such a relationship inevitably leads to resentment, and I am pleased to be able to terminate it tonight."

Grosz's tough but inately sensitive face hardened as he finished the sentence. "No, I am here, Mr. President, ladies and gentlemen, for a much more serious reason. My nation and I have lived in danger throughout our existence. We do not know the meaning of peace, and, as your president so cogently expressed it, the condition of near-war seems permanent in the Middle East. I wish I could share his optimism that an act of greatness on the part of Israel could restore the region to peace. But I do not share that conviction." Grosz's words beat across the room like the slow strokes of a hammer. "And I do not intend to risk my nation's survival by taking any such risk."

The Israeli paused and sipped water from a crystal glass in front of him. "As a guest I would not normally speak as I am about to, but I know that I am among friends, and among friends one can afford the luxury

147

of frankness. At least one can after one has already eaten." Grosz smiled at the uncomfortable titter which spread through the crowd. "Because I have to say that my country in recent months has become more and more concerned over the evident preoccupation of the United States with its domestic economic problems, and its unwillingness, I dare not say inability, to continue playing its customary role in world affairs. Rumors of unilateral disarmament accompanied by a fortress America complex, a withdrawal from the world scene have come to us in Israel. Always such things are exaggerated, Mr. President," Grosz said, "and I have told my associates that they could not possibly be true. That this great nation, the world's most powerful, will never abdicate its power and responsibilities, leaving in the lurch its allies and friends of so many decades. So, Mr. President, I would like here tonight to express my confidence in your great country and its future as well as the love and gratitude which my own nation and people feel for the United States." Grosz lifted his glass to an outburst of spontaneous applause.

"The son of a bitch," Maria Vicente muttered as they rose from the table and headed for the dining room exit. "The goddamn son of a bitch. He's totally out of line, Steve. That toast was an insolent slap in the face to the president in his own house. How dare he?"

Doyle shrugged. "What did you expect him to say? He's not over here on a social call. The Israelis are worried. They've depended on us since 1948, and despite all their bombs and military success, they're looking at a hostile Soviet Union to their north and a sea of two hundred million Arabs around them just waiting for them to trip. The last thing they want to see is the United States become a second-rate power unable to come to their defense."

148

"Oh God, Steve, will you damned people never learn? Don't you understand that the world has changed? We're not back in the nineteen-fifties. This isn't the Cold War. There isn't any monolithic communist menace any more. We don't need to keep building guns and tanks until the world sinks under their weight."

"Maybe not. But that little socialist Eden you and the boss are pushing isn't going to be worth much if you can't defend it. What about a drink with Bob? He's back from Europe working at a place on Georgia Avenue. It's time you met him."

Maria Vicente looked up at him, her green eyes losing their fire, her oval, almost Oriental face softening. "Yes. I'd like that."

As at all White House dinners under this administration, the crowd left hurriedly, the president and his wife disappearing up the staircase, the Air Force Strings packing their instruments with practiced speed, the last contingent of waiters quickly collecting coffee cups and wadding soiled linen in heaps as the last stragglers left. The traditional after-dinner entertainment and dancing had died in the second Carter administration, not to be revived.

Doyle hailed a taxi and gave a Georgia Avenue address in an area which had, beginning about half a decade before, followed Georgetown and the Capitol Hill area in turning from a black quasi-slum into a mixed neighborhood of soaring real estate values and middle class chic. Young whites without children had moved in, buying the early twentieth-century houses cheaply, ripping off the porches and converting them into pseudo-Georgetown houses. Inevitably, discotheques, leather shops, coffee houses, little French restaurants and the rest of the paraphernalia of the self-conscious

149

middle class had followed. The neighborhood was still dangerous. The islands of newly redone houses were still surrounded by a sea of poverty-stricken, violence-prone blacks resentful of the intrusion. Police cars circled the area like restless dogs, red lights flashing, sirens sounding.

"You're a little conspicuous in your medals and braid," she said.

"They just think I'm a doorman," Doyle said. "Whereas you, on the other hand," he said, letting his eyes slide off the green silk dress barely concealed by the black mink cape.

"I'll just tell them I'm a pro on my night off," she giggled.

The driver had stopped at a large building which looked as if it had once been a warehouse, its windows now covered by plywood panels decorated with abstract designs. The building itself was painted a stark, total black with irregular phosphorescent silver striations splitting the facade. A discreet sign on the door proclaimed it to be the Jelly Roll.

"Is it safe?" Maria Vicente asked doubtfully as a large black doorman in an elegant dungaree suit opened the door.

"Evening, General. Ain't seen you lately."

"Been busy, Cal. Nice crowd?"

"Not bad. The boy sure is bringing 'em in."

Inside the dim confines of the Jelly Roll a five-piece combo of trumpet, tenor sax, clarinet, bass, and piano was into a set of nostalgic nineteen-sixties rock, half a dozen colored spotlights centered on them from around the walls. The room had been stripped to its heavy wooden girders and bare brick walls. A narrow balcony crammed with tables encircled the wall at the second story level and the ground floor was jammed with the same plain wooden tables and rush-backed chairs surrounding a small circular dance floor in front of the band. Streams of waiters came out of the kitchen area to the left of the band and entered on the right. The walls were plastered with framed record covers and posters of all the great popular bands, ranging from stiffly-posed pictures of the early jazz groups playing in New Orleans brothels to the electric suits of the latest stars, the Cancer Clan.

Maria Vicente stared at Doyle as one of the floor managers moved over and greeted him. "My God, Steve, aren't we a little out of our element here?"

"They don't have an age limit," Doyle said as they threaded through the jammed tables to a tiny wooden square just to the left of the bandstand. Beer was the overwhelming drink and Doyle ordered two of the immense steins.

The band finished the set and moved off the platform. The level of noise in the big room rose another notch as the lights came on enough to see a few feet through the marijuana-tinted smog which enveloped the room. The customers ranged from twenty-one, the legal minimum, to thirty-five, almost all dressed in some fanciful version of the blue jean. "Christ, you're the only man here in a tie," Maria Vicente said, shrugging her mink into a smaller, less conspicuous mass behind her.

"Evening, General." A young man with a mane of dark hair hanging down to his shoulders had stopped at the table and extended his hand. "How'd you like our set?"

"Sounded almost like the real thing, Sam," Doyle said, rising and introducing Maria Vicente to the young musician.

"Yeah, I know what you mean. You can listen to the damn records and go over the arrangements, but you always miss something. Spontaneity, I guess. Still, it's fun. We'll be doing our own thing later. Nice to have met you, ma'am," he said, moving off through the crowd, signing an occasional autograph, sipping out of somebody's offered mug.

"Well, I'll be damned." Maria said.

"Only if you sin most grievously," Doyle said, nodding toward the stage.

A stocky young man in blue jeans and ancient T-shirt, which proclaimed "Puerto Bánus All Stars," his feet encased in dirty tennis shoes, had come onstage unannounced and unnoticed, lugging a battered guitar case in one hand and a chair in the other. He unzipped the case, took out a guitar and began to tune it carefully, oblivious to the crowd around him, his blonde head bent over the instrument in total concentration.

Maria Vicente watched in disbelief as the crowd, suddenly aware of him, became quiet. Beer mugs ceased to bang on tables and the waiters on either side of the stage stopped in little clusters. One white spotlight, high on the right, came on and the lights dimmed.

The figure on stage looked up, grinned a quick embarrassed grin, and bent over the instrument. His deceptively stubby fingers moved across the strings in the quick, flickering movement of the classical guitarist, but the sounds were a whispering memory of the West Virginia hills and the Mississippi delta, transmuted somehow from their primitive rhythms into a delicate subtle thing, neither new nor old, transforming the power of the original with the force and virility of a musical technique developed and honed in the stark classicism of Spain.

"My God, how lovely." Maria breathed as the first selection ended and the young guitarist let his hand wander aimlessly over the strings before moving on to

152

the next song, a flamenco so harsh and vital it assaulted the audience like a blow.

For a half hour he played, his calloused fingers moving across the strings with blinding speed and strength, alternating with a feathery touch to call forth the almost inaudible sounds mirroring the despair and death of the spirit. He ended as he began, grinning quickly at the audience, bowing a half bow, zipping up the ancient instrument in the case and carrying the chair off the stage as the band began to straggle back. Applause beat in waves off the brick walls as he disappeared. The band returned and began to play a creditable imitation of the early Wilbur De Paris.

"What kind of place is this? A museum of modern music?" Maria asked.

Doyle shook his head. "That band has four graduates of Juilliard and one from Eastman. They do their own thing mostly. But for kicks they also imitate the great styles of the past here and there. It's the nostalgia bit," Doyle said as the young guitarist approached their table carrying a beer stein. He dragged a chair from a neighboring table and straddled it. "Hi, Dad. Who's your new chick?"

"Hello, Bob," he said, then turned to Maria. "I'd like you to meet my older son. Maria Vicente." The guitarist held out a small square hand, fingers distorted by heavy callouses.

"You play beautifully," Maria murmured glancing from father to son. Except for the square leanness of their faces and a certain similar immobility of feature, there was almost no resemblance. The young man's corn-colored hair curled around a fair face and innocent blue eyes like a halo.

He shrugged. "I cheat a lot. I play eight sets a night here. You do it right, your goddamn fingers drop off like a leper's. But it's a living." He turned to his father. "What's with Jerry? You heard from him lately?"

"He'll be finishing this summer. I think I can get him on with the *Times*, if he wants it. How's your mother?"

The boy shrugged again and took a swig of his beer. "Getting another divorce, I think. That clown she's with is a real dog. But then Mom's taste was never the greatest."

Doyle's head snapped up.

"I meant after you, Dad," the boy said, flashing the same quick, ingratiating smile he used on stage. He rose in one motion, reversing the chair and holding out his hand to Maria Vicente. "Nice to have met you, ma'am. Are we going hunting next weekend?"

Doyle nodded. "I'll pick you up at six on Saturday." The youth shook his father's hand quickly and threaded his way back through the crowd.

"Well, General, you are a mass of surprises."

"He's good, isn't he?"

"Good? He's," Maria groped for the word, "my God, he's the best I've ever heard."

"You've never heard Segovia," Doyle said, tipping back the stein and finishing his beer. "Or a couple of others. But I agree. He's a very talented kid."

"Where did he learn to play like that?"

"One of his stepfathers was in the air force in Spain. When he was about six years old his mother put a guitar in his hands to get him out of her hair. I don't think he ever let it go. He had a superb teacher, of course. A woman. Magda Gonzalez. Have you had enough of this?"

"Not really. But tomorrow's a big day. We're meeting with the congressional budget office. It's going to be a war."

Doyle met her green eyes, remembering their first

night together. It had been an evening of sudden, flaming clashes followed by an awareness of a physical attraction so powerful as to be embarrassing. They had known each other six months, working in close proximity in the exciting early days of the administration, before he had taken her out to dinner. Finally she had looked at him, green eyes both angry and amused. "Look. You want to sleep with me and God knows I've been giving it some thought for a couple of months. But you should know something before we go any further. I operate like a man. I don't want to marry, and I don't want to 'fall in love' with you, whatever that means." They had been standing in front of a small French restaurant in Georgetown on a June night. Around them a swirling mass of laughing youth ebbed and flowed.

"About three months ago," she continued, "I became aware of you as something more than a tin soldier. As somebody said in another context, you gave off a whiff of musk. If I hadn't been so busy, I'd have seduced you before. But I'm seducing you, not you me. And when it's over, and it won't last very long, it'll be me who makes the break. Do you think you can take that kind of relationship, Steve? Because if you can't don't start it. I've had my fill of snivelling weaklings."

It had lasted eighteen months, the first flaming physical need mellowing, affection and companionship growing, until both had begun to panic at the realization of what was happening.

"My place or yours?" Doyle said as they stood in the frigid wind in front of the Jelly Roll.

"Mine."

The jangling telephone pulled him out of a deep, drugged sleep and he felt the weight of Maria across him as she reached for the instrument.

"Hello." She listened for a moment, a lazy grin spreading across her face.

"Yes. He's here, Jim," she said, handing the phone to Doyle and letting her body slip across, cuddling her behind into his crotch.

"Steve?" Jim Stansbury cleared his throat.

"Yes."

"Stansbury here. Sorry to bother you this late." Doyle glanced at his watch. It was four A.M. "However, we have a minor crisis brewing. The president would like you to come right over. I'll have a car there in a few minutes."

"Okay."

Maria turned, twining her legs in his. "What's that all about?"

"He didn't say. Just that I'd better get over there."

"Right now?" she said, smiling and slipping her arms around his neck. "Right now," he said, disengaging himself and staring down at her deliberately provocative pose.

She had been a revelation in the beginning, the carapace of toughness slipping away from her with the same ease with which she had shed the light summer dress in one quick, velvety motion. That first night she had stood before him, legs apart, fists on hip, smiling and totally unselfconscious of her body. He remembered being surprised at how small she was, the faint white stains from her bikini still visible in a white stripe across her small breasts and in counterpoint to the rising mound of pubic hair.

They had come together in a coupling so natural it seemed they had known each other for years. Her hands had moved over his body lightly, touching, stroking, twining themselves in the mat of black hair on his chest. "My God, you are a mass of scar tissue, Steve," she had

156

said, covering the tear in his left shoulder with her lips. Then, in a quick movement, she turned him on his back and moved astride him, leaning forward, black hair haloing her oval face, lifting her body slightly to let him enter, then becoming a part of him as her hips moved gently, almost imperceptibly and her body sucked him inward.

Repeatedly he felt himself brought to the point of exploding within her only to have the tension lessen as her lips lightly brushed his and her body stilled its motion, only to start again in slow, wavelike movements. Then, almost brutally, she had pulled him over on top of her with a demand, "What are you waiting for, General?"

Later she had leaned on her elbow, legs entwined in his and studied him, turning her head to exhale a Gauloise. "You are an odd man, General Doyle. Did you know that?"

"If you are referring to the strange configuration of my member," he said, successfully stifling a yawn, "it is the result of a war wound inflicted on me by a Maori tribesman armed with a poisoned dart gun."

She giggled, running a hand down across his stomach to envelope him in a small square paw. "It seems to have been fatal."

CHAPTER ELEVEN

The black Chrysler from the White House motor pool was waiting for him as he left Maria Vicente's Watergate apartment. A crust of ice covered the windshields of the parked cars, and a cold wind stirred the detritus in the deserted streets.

"Morning, General," the uniformed driver said as he got in.

"Good morning, Sam." The White House drivers doubled as armed bodyguards since a terrorist attack on President Carter's national security advisor in 1980 had very nearly succeeded. A small submachine gun was hooked under the dashboard.

Doyle stared out into the bleak pre-dawn streets, his mind still on the woman curled in the warm bed, the odor of her still on him, the honeyed touch of her skin still a palpable sensation.

The guards passed them through the main gate and he climbed the steps to the White House entrance, rubbing a hand across the day's growth of beard on his face and feeling the ridiculousness of his dress uniform.

A secret service man and the president's night duty secretary guarded the outer office. "Go right in, General. He's expecting you. Would you like a coffee?"

"Black, please."

The president, dressed in a faded cotton bathrobe, pink pajamas protruding from the bottom, sat slumped in one of the flowered easy chairs cradling a large coffee mug embossed with the presidential seal. Harlan Worth, tieless, was on his left, and Jim Stansbury stood before the fireplace smoking a cigar, the picture of unruffled elegance.

"Sorry to interrupt you, Steve," the president said, the ghost of a smile crossing his lips. "Sit down. Harlan's people have finally picked up something specific. I asked Jim to come over because he's got the best feel for how one of these things would be run. And you, Steve, because you know the men involved better than anybody else. I want your judgment. Would you go over what you've got again, Harlan?"

Worth cleared his throat and propped a pair of half glasses on his nose. "First, you should know that we've had Admiral Christman under close surveillance for the last couple of weeks. Agents, telephone taps, electronic gear—the whole bag."

"Did he know this?"

"Yes. No question about it. He didn't seem to care. As you know, he's met with more than thirty high ranking members of the armed forces, key combat commanders and staff men in crucial position. He's also met four times with members of the Police Advisory group, the secret organization set up by a large number of influential police officials in this country about a decade ago to influence Congress and the courts to pass and enforce more punitive laws to control crime. It has since become a hotbed of," Worth paused, at a loss for a word.

"Reactionary fascism," the president interjected. "Go on, Harlan."

"Finally he has seen Ralph Cooley three times. Cooley is president of the Businessmen Concerned for America, another far-right-wing group which was formed in 1979 for the purpose of protecting American values. Its membership includes an impressive number of business executives plus a lot of people who resent the government's interference in their professional lives—doctors, lawyers, engineers, you name it."

"None of this is illegal?" Doyle asked.

Worth looked up. "Meeting with them isn't illegal. And since we didn't know what was being said until tonight, we had no grounds to act."

"And now you have."

"Now we have," Worth said, extracting a thin imitation leather folder from the briefcase at his side. "This document was found in the trunk of a car wrecked on the Beltway last night. The driver, a Soviet intelligence agent attached to the Russian Trade Mission in Washington, was killed. He had just come from a rendezvous with one of Cooley's top administrative aides who has been a Soviet agent for more than two years. Our agents were following him and got this before the highway patrol showed up."

Doyle frowned. "How'd they turn Cooley's aide?"

Worth shrugged contemptuously. "Money, what else? Cooley won't put up with messy financial dealings. This guy had borrowed heavily to gamble in the international currency market. He lost. He was in way over his head. The Soviets bailed him out."

"Why? What did he have that they wanted?"

"Access to the top echelons of American business.

Cooley had ceased to be just a businessman. He's the acknowledged leader of the American industrial complex these days. He's not only more powerful, he's more intelligent than most of his contemporaries and he's gradually built up a personal dominance which makes him the single most powerful man in this country after the president. For the first time in seventy-five years American business has become an organized political force. And Cooley is its leader."

"And this report came from Cooley's aide?"

"Yes. He passed it to the Soviet agent."

"What's in it?"

Worth handed him the document and passed other copies to Stansbury and the president. "I've summarized the contents for the president, but I think you'd better read it. It's not long."

Doyle accepted the document, suddenly feeling very tired. The title on the first page was "Operation Rescue."

This document is a blueprint for the rescue of the republic which has fallen into the hands of men either stupid, traitorous, or both. For more than half a century the principles of individual freedom and initiative on which this nation was founded have undergone a process of subversion until, today, they are about to be replaced by an alien ideology designed to make slaves of us all. Under the system which is being imposed upon us, the state will no longer be our servant but our master. Liberty and freedom will be replaced by bureaucratic tyranny, and self-reliance by dependence. We have ceased to be a nation of individualists and become one of frightened sheep.

During this period we have seen the erosion of

our rights of property, the rise of unbridled crime, the destruction of police power, an end to discipline, the perversion of justice and the decay of our educational system. Under the guise of 'equality' we have been asked to deny the existence of quality. Talent is considered a form of intellectual oppression and diligence regarded as evil incarnate. The eradication of racism and bigotry has been used as an excuse to enshrine mediocrity, weakness and incompetence. Until today, however, this insidious subversion of our values was confined to the internal mechanism of the state. We still remained strong enough to defend ourselves from external enemies and maintain at least a modicum of our traditional liberties. Now, this too is about to be taken from us.

The federal budget for 1987-88, about to be placed before Congress, contains provisions which, if enacted, will leave the United States essentially defenseless before its enemies. Under the guise of combating the economic recession, the defense budget will be gutted, and our capacity to survive as an independent nation will be ended.

The authors of this document have attempted to arrest the course of events by legal means and have been unsuccessful. The present national administration is in the hands of men drunk with power, utterly convinced of the validity of a view of mankind alien to American tradition and culture. This mechanistic view of man, a secular religion composed in equal parts of Marxian dogma, behaviorist theorizing, and pure intellectual arrogance, ignores all spiritual values and holds in contempt the concept of individualism on which this nation was built.

Therefore, given our inability to influence the course of events by legal means, and persuaded that failure to act will result in disaster for the nation, we have reconstituted the Committee of Public Safety of Revolutionary War days to rescue the republic from the present government, re-establish discipline and public order, provide for the defense of the nation, and rejuvenate those qualities of self-reliance, individuality, and belief in God and man which made this country great.

It is not our intention to establish a dictatorial regime. When the present extraordinary economic crisis has been overcome, and the American people have been made aware of the perversions to which our system has been subjected, we will institute free elections. But we feel that an extended period will be needed to purify our institutions and revive the people's faith and belief in those virtues which made America great, before we can take this step.

Doyle looked up from the document. "Is anybody going to take this sort of thing seriously?"

Worth cleared his throat. "It's a very clever document, Steve. Nobody will agree with all of it, but it touches a nerve in almost every disaffected group in the country."

The president nodded. "He's right, Steve. It's a clever appeal to the artisan classes in our society." He tapped the paper in front of him. "They're the ones suffering the most from frustration and an inability to control their environment. They've resented the invasion of blacks, Chicanos, and even women into their factories for decades. They've objected violently to the integration of their schools and neighborhoods. They resent

163

the feeling of helplessness in the face of international competition and lost wars such as Vietnam. Most of all they are depressed by the feeling that the old American hope of making it big, of rising out of the grinding routine of their daily lives, may no longer be possible. That America really isn't, and maybe never was, the land of unlimited opportunity. This is the group, in the hands of powerful manipulators such as Cooley and Christman, who make ideal fascists and always have. Also, they have their hands on a lot of the levers of real power. But skip that flatulent philosophy and turn to page four."

Doyle flipped through the document to a page headed "Action Plan."

"This is the guts of it," the president said.

The takeover of a modern industrialized state by a small military force is, at first glance, impossible. In fact, the experience of recent years indicates that it can be done with relative ease always provided the leaders are willing to exercise exemplary ruthlessness in its execution. The first prerequisite is an iron will, and the second a willingness to spill blood. If these two givens exist, all that is needed to succeed is a small, blindly obedient, highly disciplined military force. The rest is planning.

The Committee of Public Safety has been working on just such a plan for the past month, and it is now complete. Detailed orders are being prepared for transmission to key military and police commanders who have joined us in each region. Similar instructions are being readied for the civilian leaders who will assume power once the physical assets of each region have been secured by the military and paramilitary forces.

Essential to the success of the action is the total control from the first hour of all means of communications—telephone, radio, television, land lines, private communication set-ups—which will deny the central government the ability to contact loyal units. Once in command of communications, we will paralyze the brain and the body will be helpless. Messages to the nation to be transmitted via radio and television are now being prepared. In the first hours, we will attempt to sow confusion and stop any misguided attempts at a popular insurrection against the coup. Later messages will give the impression of overwhelming force having taken command, and convey the uselessness of resistance.

The second most important area which must be controlled from the beginning is transport. Every major airport in the country must be neutralized and all military aviation facilities must be positively in our hands or rendered inoperable. Road and rail transport must be taken over immediately by military or police units to insure that the central government cannot concentrate forces which remain loyal to it.

Immediate control of electricity, water, and gas supplies must be assured. In the event of organized resistance our forces can immediately plunge a community into chaos by cutting these services. Recent examples of widespread failures of the electrical system are instructive. In almost every instance, panic ensued and our civilization, overly dependent on such facilities, came to a virtual halt as essential services ceased to function and people milled around, and the criminal element took over the streets. Cutting gas supplies to homes in midwinter would have a chilling effect on resistance. These actions should be avoided except in extreme emergencies, but given the choice of failing to take control or inflicting chaos, we will choose chaos.

Police power is the basic power mechanism of the state, whatever mushheaded theorists may believe. Thus, it is absolutely essential that we have the tacit support if not the active aid of the forces of public order in key cities and communities. Fortunately, the mentality of most police force members will make them sympathetic to our aims. More important, the Police Advisory Group leaders have seeded our men in key positions across the country. For a period of perhaps forty-eight hours they will be able to retain control of the important state police units and city forces which could hamper our activities. However, resistance will begin to organize at this point as the initial shock and paralysis wears off the political leaders. It is, therefore, essential that the major centers of federal authority be firmly in our hands before such resistance can begin to coalesce.

Our means are limited, but with good planning and organization they should be sufficient. Centerpiece of the physical forces at our disposal is the Eighty-Second Airborne Division at Fort Bragg, North Carolina, and the One Hundred and First Airborne at Fort Benning, Georgia. They have the advantage of high mobility, intense unit loyalty, the best discipline in the army and, most important, officers dedicated to our effort.

Doyle looked up from the folder and reached for the steaming coffee which the president's secretary had placed at his side. "Brooks McLean commands the Eighty-Second and Sam Taliaferro the One Hundred and First."

"They did," the president said grimly. "Within the next few minutes they will be relieved."

Doyle glanced at Jim Stansbury who still leaned against the fireplace, skimming through his copy of the document, and Stansbury nodded imperceptibly as their eyes met. He cleared his throat.

"I'm not sure that's the best course, Mr. President."

"Why the hell not, Jim? They're about to move, aren't they? The thing to do is draw their teeth before they can get it going. Those divisions are their teeth."

"True," Stansbury said. "But who are you going to put in their place? How do you know the replacements aren't in on the conspiracy? And even if they are clean, it's obvious that the rest of the division officers are in their pocket. What could one man do?" Stansbury shook his head. "It looks as if we may have some time," he said tapping the document. "They're not ready yet. But if we warn them with any quick moves, they might jump the gun. There's nothing in here on timing is there, Harlan?"

The FBI director shook his head. "No. But I suspect they're thinking in terms of New Year's Eve, which gives us about a week."

"Why New Year's Eve?" the president asked.

"Most of Washington will be out at some party or other. All the military services are on skeleton staffs. And, maybe more important, police departments are often manned by cops who volunteer to do holiday duty. So they could pack the duty rosters with men loyal to the coup."

Stansbury nodded in agreement. "Worth's right. If I were in their shoes I'd pick a holiday. New Year's Eve is perfect."

"Then what do you recommend?" the president asked.

"First we have to isolate their key men. They've made a serious mistake letting a document as detailed as this get away from them, but they haven't been foolish enough to put any names in it. Still, it shouldn't be hard for Harlan's people and mine to come up with a list. We'll put a watch on everybody coming in and leaving the military bases, nail Cooley with twenty-four hour surveillance, do the same with the top leaders of his businessmen's organization and the leaders of the Police Advisory Group. Within a day or two we should have a fair idea of who the top leadership is. Then we can arrange a sweep to collect all of them. At that point you can move in and change the division commanders and the top hundred or so officers."

The president shook his head dubiously. "You haven't said anything, Steve. What do you think? The Eighty-Second is your old division. Couldn't you just go down and take command tomorrow morning and guarantee it won't move?"

Doyle took a sip of the cooling coffee, wishing it were stronger. "I gave up command two years ago. McLean has transferred every key officer in the division over that period. It puzzled me when he started cleaning house the way he did. It's not normal, particularly since over the years the division has attracted the best officers in the army. Now, he's got it seeded with his men. Nobody's going to take it away from him in a day or a week. Besides," and Doyle tapped the paper, "if you spook this bunch they may move immediately. They're obviously not ready yet and would prefer to wait. But they are a long way down the pike and, if they have to, they could probably kick it off in twenty-four hours. I agree with Jim. We've got to get the leadership first."

"What do you think their chances of succeeding would have been, Steve, if this hadn't turned up?"

Doyle hesitated, meeting each man's eyes. "If the Eighty-Second and One Hundred and First are in their pocket, and it looks as if they are, and if they've really got the type of support among the police and business community that this thing indicates, then I think they might have a fifty-fifty chance of taking control temporarily. How long they could hold it would depend on a lot of other factors."

"What about the rest of the army?" the president asked.

Doyle shrugged. "The Eighty-Second and One Hundred and First are virtually the only divisions we've got that are combat ready. Everything else is in a shambles. About the only other combat force which could make itself felt is the First Marine Division at Camp LeJeune. It's got the transport and self-contained air cover to bloody some people up. But I assume we don't want to get into a civil war situation if we can avoid it."

"And who knows whether the First Marine is reliable?" the president said, half to himself. "Who's the commander?"

"Major General Murray Stein."

"The Marine Corps' first Jewish general?"

"More in the tradition of Patton than Portnoy, sir," Doyle said, grinning at the memory of the squat, medal-bedecked, swagger-stick armed figure of Stein on parade.

"He's a little, ah, theatrical, isn't he?" the president asked.

"Yes. But he's also too intelligent to get involved in anything like this."

The president shook his head. "Cooley isn't exactly a moron and neither is Christman. However, I'm inclined to agree with you. We'd better do as Jim suggested and isolate the leadership. Meantime, Steve, I want you to fly down to LeJeune and sound out Stein. If he seems reliable, inform him of what's happening and tell him I want his division on a war footing immediately. I may bring it here to Washington to protect the city. You'll see, as you read further, that units of the Eighty-Second are expected to parachute in to take the Capitol, the White House, the Pentagon, the police station and both the airports as well as all the public services. They and the One Hundred First will be doing the same thing in New York, Los Angeles, Chicago, and the thirty most important cities in the country."

Doyle had been rapidly scanning the final pages of the report, which ended in mid-sentence on page 22. He glanced up. "There's something missing."

Harlan Worth nodded grimly. "Yes. Obviously Cooley's aide only managed to get a part of it. The actual plan of battle, unit numbers, and the rest were either not available or too dangerous to get at."

The president stood up, ancient bathrobe flopping around his long legs. "All right, gentlemen. You know what you have to do. Obviously, this will have to be kept among the four of us. Nobody else is to know. Your subordinates will simply have to work blind. I'd like to see all of you here at six this evening. By that time, Jim, you and Harlan should have been able to isolate the names of the most important leaders and Steve will know whether we can count on the First Marine division. We'll make plans to break their backs at that time," he said, doubling one slender hand into a fist and pounding it into his palm.

Doyle retrieved a clean shirt he kept in his office for emergencies and made his way to the basement gym of the White House to shower and change. He debated briefly beating himself to a pulp on the Universal Gym which crouched spiderlike in the middle of the small room and reluctantly rejected the idea.

It was seven o'clock when he returned to his office and Sgt. McBain was fiddling with the coffee machine. "Get Andrews on the line and arrange for a plane to take me to Camp LeJeune. Ask them to get a chopper over here in fifteen minutes to pick me up."

The sergeant's eyebrows raised. "Hell, General, they won't send a chopper for you. And I doubt if they'll give you a plane."

Doyle grinned. Buck was right. He was only a major general without a command suffering from delusions of grandeur. He called the White House operations center and talked to the duty officer, a twenty-five-year-old State Department career man with a rank equivalent to captain.

"Sure, General. I can arrange for the chopper and the plane. I'll make a note, of course, that you've got the full authorization of the president."

"You do that, son," Doyle said, suddenly tired.

The leaden mass of the American bureaucracy was beginning to move, but it would be an agonizing process. Nothing could be done without a dozen clearances, and they couldn't go that route. Too many people would have to have explanations, and too many would be tied to the conspirators. Somehow, by tonight, they were going to have to cut through the red tape and set up a special counter-coup staff with extraordinary powers to move. The president would have to invoke his standby emergency powers and something would have to be done to suspend, temporarily at least, habeas corpus and the minefield of legal barriers which, while providing the average citizen with superb protection of his liberties, might well, within the next few days, deprive him of them forever if they were observed.

Doyle turned on the desk switch and the Federal Broadcasting System news logo, an endless tightening circle, flashed on the big color set across the room. Suzanne Wilson, anchoring the morning news, filled the screen with her cool arrogant presence. She had mellowed somewhat since her marriage three years before to President Carter's former advisor for national security affairs. But the blue eyes gazing out of the screen mirrored the steely intelligence with which she handled the news.

"Good morning. This is Suzanne Wilson with the news.

"The Iranian government tonight halted the exodus of more than seven thousand Americans who had begun streaming out of the country following the recent coup. The head of the Iranian junta, General Ghahraman Ghahramani, informed the American Embassy that no more Americans would be permitted to leave, since their skills were essential to the functioning of public services in Iran. He said every effort would be made over the next few days to determine which Americans were essential and which could be given permission to depart. The U.S. government protested the Iranian action in a note delivered to that government's ambassador in Washington today.

"In Vienna yesterday the Jakarta Round trade negotiators announced that any hope of damming the flood of protectionist legislation engulfing the world had virtually disappeared. Although all the members of the conference are in theoretical agreement that further protectionist moves will only exacerbate the worldwide recession, none of their governments is willing to face the political consequences of dismantling the emergency barriers erected during the present crisis.

"Brazil's announcement of its inability to meet its foreign obligations, following defaults by Turkey, Argentina, Poland, and India, contributed to the already existing chaos of the world financial markets. Following the announcement, Germany intervened to shore up the virtually bankrupt Hannover Handelsbank, and in the United States the Federal Reserve announced it would make special credit available to the Federated Bank of California and the Bank of New York to prevent their imminent collapse. Both banks were heavily involved in a recent consortium put together to stave off Brazil's collapse.

"The Horn of Africa threatened to explode once again today as troops of the People's Republic of Tadjoura mobilized to attack Ethiopian forces concentrated south of Lake Abbe. Tadjouran President Omar Abdurrahman Ghalib warned in a radio broadcast that his nation would not tolerate hostile actions on the part of the Ethiopians. In Addis Ababa Lt. General Getahun Gebre-Egzy told a gathering of foreign correspondents that he would not accept the closure of the port of Obok, the former Djibouti, through which the bulk of Ethiopia's foreign trade flows. Gebre-Egzy said that the former French territory of Affars and Issas in which the port is located had been illegally absorbed by Somalia which had then altered the name of the new nation to the United Republic of Tadjoura. Gebre-Egzy went on to say that with the addition of fifty U.S. F-16 fighters and a hundred XM-1 tanks, his army was more than a match for the Soviet-equipped army of Tadjoura. More

173

than a hundred thousand Ethiopian militia had begun the march to the coast, he said, to join the regular army. The Soviet Union's Indian Ocean fleet was converging on Bar el Mandeb strait, apparently with the intention of controlling this vital waterway in the event of hostilities. A spokesman at the Pentagon said the United States naval units based on Diego Garcia were 'somewhere in the Indian Ocean' but refused to clarify his remarks. In Jerusalem, the Israeli government spokesman said his government looked with concern on developments in the Bar el Mandeb strait and warned against the disruption of commerce through the Israeli-controlled Suez Canal.

"The seventh Law of the Sea conference meeting in Gdansk announced a three-month recess today as the industrial nations categorically refused to agree to the demands of the Third World nations for an international corporation with a monopoly on mining all deep sea bed sites. The United States, already conducting experimental extractions within the two hundred mile territorial shelf, announced it would begin commercial production of aluminite and cadmium in the Santa Barbara trench early next year. The Gomar Explorer II, successor to the experimental vessel which raised a sunken Soviet submarine some years ago, will conduct the mining operations.

"The death of Joseph Mengele, former Nazi concentration camp doctor at Auschwitz, was announced in Paraguay. Mengele, believed to be in his late eighties, was the last known surviving war criminal.

"The Grand Prix of Monaco was won yesterday by Sylvia de Muns of Spain. Miss de Muns, driving a Pegaso, was the first woman to win a Grand Prix race since Mary Lemley came in first at the Neuerburgring in the spring of 1983.

"In Taiwan the communist purge of members of the former regime continues. Fourteen former Chiang supporters were reported executed by firing squad at the Fifth Route Army Re-education camp outside the capital. Refugees escaping by fishing boat report a reign of terror among former bureaucrats and army officers. Former Prime Minister Chiang Ching, deposed last summer in a coup led by army officers sympathetic to the mainland regime, is reported still alive under house arrest at a mountain rest home. The mainland leaders, having consolidated their grip on the island after being invited in by the coup leaders, have apparently abandoned their initially cautious tactics and are now intent on gaining total control of the island.

"Unrest continues in the Yugoslav provinces of Slovenia and Croatia today in the face of stepped-up attempts by the Serbian-dominated National Council to enforce new centralizing measures on the nation. Since President Tito's death eighteen months ago, the Serbian faction in the governing body has steadily increased its influence. A bomb exploded outside the Zagreb main post office yesterday, injuring three people, while in Maribor members of a Slovenian separatist movement took over the main radio station briefly to broadcast an appeal for support. Two were killed and one captured in attempting to escape following the broadcast.

"The head of the Stanford University Archeology Department, Chauncey Devereux Callaghan announced today that the box of bones which had been found in a San Francisco bank vault were definitely the remains of the Peking man, missing since the early years of the Second World War. The bones, deposited at the bank by Marine Colonel William Jackson in 1945, had been placed in dead storage ten years ago following Jackson's death and were about to be disposed of when one of the bank officers asked Dr. Callaghan to examine them. No explanation was given as to how Colonel Jackson came into possession of the archeological treasures.

"A soviet nuclear-powered carrier was dead in the water today some two hundred miles from its base at Glandia, the former southwest African port of Windhoek. Two tugs were towing the huge vessel into its base following a failure of its nuclear propulsion system. The Soviet vessel, the Kharkov, was the largest Soviet vessel to use the naval base conceded by the Namibian government two years ago.

"And in Brownsville, Utah, John Wilson, an unemployed bricklayer, was arrested today for bigamy. Wilson has been maintaining two wives for more than twenty years. He has a total of twenty children, eight by one and twelve by the other. The two women, both pregnant, said they were perfectly content with the arrangement.

"And that's the news this morning."

Doyle flicked off the set at the sound of the chopper coming in low across the back lawn. It hovered briefly over the landing pad, then set down gently, its rotors continuing to move. He walked quickly through the White House corridors to the back entrance.

Two hours later the pilot of the small four-passenger jet shook Doyle awake. "Camp LeJeune, General."

Doyle yawned and unstrapped the shoulder safety harness, letting himself down the short ladder onto the tarmac. It was raining, a cold southern rain out of a sullen sky of scudding black clouds. "I'll be back in less than two hours, captain. You'd better keep the tower informed where you are."

The air force officer saluted and turned back to his plane as Doyle hunched over and headed across the runway to a hut which served as tower, cafeteria, and offices for the small subsidiary airstrip on the perimeter of the huge Marine base.

A bored young sergeant glanced up from behind the flight counter and looked him over curiously. "Get me General Stein," he said.

The flight clerk stared at him, jaw in mid-yawn. "Huh?"

Doyle stared at the youth, stifling the reflexes of thirty years of military training. During the flight, he had gone over the sketchy plan of the conspirators and come to the conclusion that the First Marine Division had to figure in their plans in some way. They would be only too well aware that it was the only other combat-ready force immediately available, and they would have certainly made plans to neutralize it. His trip had to be kept as quiet as possible. The flight plan had mentioned only that a "DoD civilian would be arriving at Le-Jeune" and asked the use of the auxiliary runway.

"I'd like to talk to the First Division commander, son. And I want to do it now."

The youth hesitated, sensing the man's authority but held in the grip of the system. "You'll have to identify yourself, sir. I can't put a call through to General Stein just like that."

Doyle hesitated. To identify himself would be to broadcast his arrival across the whole base. As he debated, the door behind him suddenly slammed open, crashing against the tin wall of the quonset hut, and Major General Murray Stein surged in behind it like a miniature tank.

"What the fuck are you doing on my base, Doyle?" Stein blared, planting his five-foot four-inch figure in front of him, his hard belly the size of a basketball straining against camouflage fatigues. His bald head was shaved clean under the billed cap worn low over his eyes.

177

Doyle looked over his shoulder at the two alert young staff officers waiting in the corridor.

"I've got to talk to you privately, Murray," Doyle said.

"Goddamn it. Answer my fucking question. Nobody comes on this fucking base without informing me. I don't give a goddamn if you're the fucking president's personal ass wiper, Doyle. You don't come here onto my turf without telling me first."

Doyle closed the door behind Stein and steered him across the room. "Murray, cut the crap. I'm down here on a personal mission from the president, and I don't want it broadcast. Now get us an office where we can talk, and I'll be out of here within the hour."

"Well, why the fuck didn't you say so instead of standing here with a finger up your ass?" Stein strode over to a door marked "Operations Officer" and ordered its occupant out, waving Doyle to a chair. "What's up, Steve? That asshole in the White House got his balls in a crack?"

Doyle shrugged out of his dress uniform coat and dropped it across an ancient straight-backed chair, glancing around the dilapidated office as he did so. It occurred to him that the American military establishment was taking on the seedy look of an imperial power in its final days, "the dirt of decay having a different smell and consistency from the foul stench of battle," as a French writer on military decadence has put it in another context.

"You don't like him much, do you, Murray?"

"Like him?" The little marine general snorted through his nose as he extracted a slender black Brazilian cigar from his breast pocket, bit off the tip, and spat shreds of tobacco on the floor. "Hell, I've got nothing but contempt for him. Fucking weakminded pansy.

Cut the crap, Doyle. You know what he's doing to us. Cutting our balls off. Turning over the whole fucking world to the sons-of-bitches. Without a fight. You're right, I don't like him much. But you didn't come down here to ask me that. What's up?"

Doyle slumped against the chair, feeling the weariness of a night without sleep well up in him. "Any possibility of coffee in this spit-and-polish base of yours?"

Stein grinned. "Corporal," he bellowed through the closed door. "Two black coffees. Now quit stalling, Steve," he said, for the first time using a normal tone of voice, his brown face dropping the mask of the tough Marine general. "What are you here for?"

Doyle would have preferred more time to feel Stein out, but he didn't have it. The ghetto intelligence in front of him, sharpened by a lifetime of clawing against discrimination, of compensating for being a Jewish semi-midget in a profession of WASP giants, had been burnished to too high a gloss to play games. He had to gamble that Stein was an outsider, too unstable and unreliable to be in on the coup.

"You know what's been going on since Christman and the others got fired last month?"

Stein stared down at the gray ash forming on the tip of the long cigar. "Some. He's been traveling around the country visiting units, making some sort of pitch to keep the president from cutting the defense budget."

"Did he see you?"

"Me?" Stein smiled, his brown eyes hardening against the hurt. "You know better than that, Steve. Christman come crawling to the kike general? You gotta be kidding. No, he didn't come. But he sent some of his boys. That drunken friend of yours."

"Sam Carlyle?"

"Yeah. The Virginia lush."

179

Doyle warmed his hands on the coffee cup and felt the exhaustion seeping through his body. "What did he want?"

Stein shrugged. "How the hell do I know? He pussy-footed around for an hour or so feeling me out, but he never really came to the point. It all sounded kind of halfassed to me. Is that why you are down here? The president worried about a cabal of officers opposing him on the Hill?"

"Something like that."

Stein was amused. "And you're supposed to con me out of joining?"

Doyle stared into his coffee before meeting Stein's steady look. "No, Murray. That's not why I am here. I want to know whether you can take the Eighty-Second Airborne out of action if you have to."

CHAPTER TWELVE

Doyle was conscious of a hollow feeling compounded in equal parts by hunger, fatigue, and the beginnings of despair. It was almost noon. The meeting had been going on for an hour, but they were getting nowhere. Option after option had been taken up and discarded. Stansbury had suggested the immediate arrest of all the plotters, the declaration of martial law, and a nationwide broadcast by the president describing what was happening. Worth objected.

"It can't be done, Jim. We don't have the legal basis. My agents would refuse to move, even if I ordered them to. Since that trial back in 1979 when the New York special agent in charge was convicted of authorizing break-ins on the orders of the president, nobody in my outfit is going to take an illegal order. You know damn well most of my men are lawyers. They're not going out on a series of nationwide arrests of prominent figures without ironclad justification."

"Then use my men, Mr. President," Stansbury said.

"That's illegal, Jim. Besides they wouldn't be able to

do it quickly enough to have any effect. It would take at least a week to deploy them."

"We could try the Criminal Investigation Division at the Pentagon," Doyle said. "But it's sure to be infiltrated. They'd know within the hour what we are planning."

The president shook his head. "No. I don't want anything to spook the Pentagon. Not yet. We've got some time. As long as they don't know that we're aware of the coup, we can be reasonably sure they won't move. Once they find out their cover is blown, they might move up the timetable before we could develop a counter." He looked at the three men, their faces worn with tension and fatigue. "You understand, I don't think they have a chance of a snowball in hell of bringing this off. The country simply would not permit it. But what they could do is set back my program for months if not years. The trials would tear the country apart and polarize it even more. This has got to be avoided. We've not only got to stop this thing, we've got to stop it without violence and without scars."

"I think it's already too late for that, Mr. President," Stansbury said. "I doubt if you can put a damper on it. Reports from my people and Harlan's are continuing to flood in. It's bigger than we thought. And it's been going on longer. The real driving force behind it doesn't seem to be Christman but Cooley and that association of businessmen he dominates. Most of the planning has come from an ad hoc staff working out of the association's offices. They've got a network of contacts with military officers and police groups around the country which must have taken years to develop. It's all been very cleverly done under the guise of study groups, seminars, and cross-disciplinary meetings bringing together leaders from different specialties. Cooley used them to proselytize. And he's done well. We've got a thoroughly frustrated society. The intellectuals and the upper class are impatient. And the people out of work are sullen and angry. Many of them think the system just won't work any more. It's too cumbersome, too complicated, too ridden with sectarian quibbles. It's a classic situation in which people look for a leader."

"Goddammit, they've got one," the president exploded. "My program has the most revolutionary proposals ever presented by a leader of this nation. What more do they want?"

"They see your program as taking power from them, Mr. President, and giving it to a central government bureaucracy," Stansbury said gently. "In retrospect, it might have been wiser to co-opt some of these people and bring them into your administration."

"Instead of antagonizing them?" the president said, his chilly blue eyes fixing on Stansbury. "Well, Jim, we both know it wouldn't have worked, and even if it had been possible, I would not have done it. People such as Cooley would have demanded compromises which would have watered down my proposals to such an extent that they would have been useless." He shook his head. "No. There was no other way, and it's still going to work. They cannot possibly have enough support to overthrow this government. The people will rally behind me."

"That still leaves us with the problem of how to draw their teeth," the FBI director said.

"I know. And I think I really have only one choice. I'll go to the people. I'll expose the whole dreary business in a nationwide broadcast tomorrow at eight P.M. I'll name names and call on the people of the nation to support me. Meanwhile, I want an extraordinary meeting of union leaders convened here tomorrow afternoon.

I'll call on them to paralyze the country if these fools should move. The Teamsters, rail brotherhoods, communication workers, government unions, they will all support me. Acting in concert they could bring the nation to a halt and any coup d'état along with it."

Stansbury looked at Doyle. "Will it work, Steve?"

"The unions can block roads and blank out normal communication channels, but the airborne divisions are self-contained. They've got their own logistics setup. They were designed to operate in isolation for limited periods. You close down a major airport, and they'll simply take over a stretch of superhighway, set up a landing strip for their STOL planes and operate from there. The helicopter squadrons can leap over obstructions." He shook his head. "I wouldn't depend on unions being of much use in stopping it."

"You're against the broadcast?" the president asked, his voice colored by irritation and impatience.

"No. I think you've got to go to the people. It may bring Christman and Cooley and the others to their senses. But right now I think you ought to give the order for the First Marine Division to move to Washington en masse. Let them bivouac on the Mall and the White House grounds. Saturate the city with them. Take over the Pentagon. The courts might eventually say it was illegal, but you're commander in chief of the armed forces, and that gives you dictatorial powers over their movements. Stein has his division under control. Oh, undoubtedly, Christman has infiltrated his staff, and they would be warned. But before they could get the airborne troops moving, you'd have the First Marine emplaced and combat-ready. I doubt if they're prepared to see the armed forces tear each other apart. After all, they see themselves as patriots. The object of the operation is to make the United States secure against the communist menace. An internal civil war would assure our destruction."

The president stood up and moved across to the windows overlooking the immense expanse of lawn behind the White House. "It would be an admission of internal dissent which could paralyze the remaining years of my presidency. The spectacle of a president beseiged behind a barricade of troops on the lawn of his own house." He shook his head. "No. There simply has to be a better way." He turned back. "Harlan, gather a hundred of your best agents, men you trust implicitly. You do the same, Jim. Get me the chief justice over here. I'll have him issue warrants. I think we are going to make some quick arrests. I'll meet with these men in the auditorium of the Justice Department tomorrow morning and point out the need for what they are being asked to do. Meanwhile, Harlan, I want a detailed action plan to locate and arrest all the key members of the conspiracy so we can make an immediate and massive roundup."

"Mr. President, I'd like permission to bring in a company of Stein's men for your personal protection while this is going on," Doyle said.

The president frowned. "You don't think the secret service is capable of protecting me?"

"No. Not against modern weapons and trained troops."

The president shrugged. "Very well. But I want them out of sight. You can put them someplace where they can be rapidly deployed by helicopter. But you may not bivouac them on my lawn." He smiled as he spoke. "You'd only spook the tourists."

The president's secretary knocked and followed the sound into the room. "Mr. President, there is an urgent message for Mr. Worth."

The FBI director took the yellow telex message and read it quickly.

"Let's have it, Harlan," the president said, watching his face.

"They've slipped the lead."

"What?"

"Cooley, Christman, and the others. They've lost their tails."

"Good God, man, what the hell do you mean? How could they?"

Worth shrugged. "It wasn't difficult. Cooley and Christman simply went to the roof of the Federal Steel Corporation building, took a high-speed helicopter and were gone. The others used some fairly simple but effective techniques to lose tails. There's no way to stay with a man who knows the ropes and knows he's being followed."

The president nodded. "Then we'd better move fast. They must know that we've discovered something." He turned to Doyle. "Steve, get Stein. Ask him how long it will take to mobilize the First Division and get it moving to Washington. Get me my press secretary. We'll have to do the broadcast tonight. There's no way out. And ask the chief justice to get over here as quickly as possible."

"Hurry yo ass up and wait, man. This here army is fucked up, I tell you, man. I mean fucked up."

"Where we goin'?"

"How the fuck do I know? They got evah C-5 in the fuckin' country sitting on this here field, man. We gonna exercise. Yes, suh. We gonna fight them fuckin' Reds till they ass splinters."

"Ain't got no artillery, tanks neither 'cept them little bitty ones. What kind of fuckin' exercise is that, man?

186

Them Reds, they got tanks big as houses. I ain't even exercisin' on 'em without no tanks."

"Shit, man. Exercise ain't real. It's just fucking your hand, man. Don't worry none."

"Shut up back there."

"Fuck you honky, goddamn sergeant."

"He ain't a honky. He's black."

"Worst fucking kind, man. When we going?"

"Sundown, I hear the loot say. He don't know where. Said we got a mission."

"Fuck his honky ass."

"I hear we goin' to Chicago."

"Naw. That pussy I got over in the general's office, she done told me it's New York and Washington. We gonna pretend like we taking over the towns. Gimme a drag that joint, you hog."

"Shit, that good, man. Ain't nothing like grass 'cept maybe pussy."

"How the hell you know? You ain't even smelt it for weeks."

"Yeah, man, but I got a good memory."

"Gimme the fuckin' joint."

"Quit the fucking smoking back there or I'll hang your asses out to dry."

"I shoot that sumbitch in the back, we ever git in action. I frag that shithead. My daddy said they did that in 'Nam. Shot the motherfuckers in the back, they get mean. Had a bunch of real tame officers, man."

"Shit, you couldn't hit him if'n he was in your fucking pocket, man. Gimme the goddamn joint."

"We got half the fuckin' division here, man. I ain't never seen no exercise like this."

"Other half's over on the other field, man. The whole fuckin' shootin' match. Them goddam cooks gonna have theirselves a time with our women while we gone."

187

"Yours maybe. She can't go an hour without some of it."

"Shut your fucking mouth, nigger. You want your mouth busted?"

"Goddamn it, quiet back there or I'll have your asses once this thing is over."

"I shoot me that sumbitch we ever get in a war."

"Shit, man, shoot him now. We got live ammunition."

"Yeah. How come we got live rounds? What these motherfuckers think they doin'? You get yo' ass shot using live rounds. Shitasses like you, man, they ought not to be 'lowed out with no fucking live rounds."

"You dumb nigger. You don't know shit. We gonna take over the towns and shoot them fuckin' honky cops. How you like that, motherfuckah?"

"Yeah. I like that. Get me a motherfuckin' honky cop. Yeah."

"All right, haul ass. We're moving out. On your feet. And get rid of the fucking cigarettes. There's a couple of billion fucking gallons of gas in these goddamn planes."

"Goddamn it, Jake, what the hell is going on? We've got twenty thousand men ready to board aircraft down here headed out for thirty different cities, and we still haven't got any orders."

"Cool it, Harry. The orders are on their way. It's all part of the exercise. You know we've been planning it for months. This is a crucial test, Harry. We've got to know if that division is ready. It's all we've got left to move with quickly in an emergency and it's got to be perfect."

"I still don't see what the fuck this operation has got to do with being combat-ready. We pretend we're taking over the thirty biggest cities in America. What's that got to do with combat?"

"Cool it, Harry. What if we had to move into Venezuela or Canada some day? It would be the same exercise. Only you'd have a map of Caracas or Montreal instead of San Francisco and Chicago."

"Yeah, okay. But I tell you, Jake, you assholes up in the Pentagon better know what you're doing. I'm chief of staff of this goddamn division and I'm here to tell you turning twenty thousand of these assholes loose with live rounds is inviting disaster. And I've told the general that."

"How's the mobilization going, Harry?"

"What the hell do you mean, how is it going? Perfect. The third brigade took four hours to form up on the runway because of a traffic jam. All our communications gear went to the wrong airfield. Thrity-five hopheads in signals got into a mini race riot when an infantryman raped one of their telex operators in the back of a truck. You want more? Goddamn women in combat situations anyway."

"Are you going to be able to move on time?"

"Sure, Jake. We'll move. But listen, Jake."

"Yeah?"

"You sure this business is kosher? I got a bad feeling about it. Something's wrong. I can't put my finger on it, but something's wrong. I've been hearing some peculiar things lately."

"Harry, you are the best fucking logistics man in the army. You're nervous about the operation. Get 'em off the runway into the air, and your job's done. Go home and get drunk and wait for that star to be delivered when it's all over."

"Fuck you, Jake."

* * *

Doyle stared at the map of the United States covering an entire wall in the White House war room, a steel-reinforced concrete bunker four stories underground constructed during the second Carter administration after it had become obvious that the new Soviet mirved laser-guided Raskolnikov missiles launched from Gorskov-class submarines could score direct hits on the White House with less than three minutes warning. The bunker was totally self-contained, capable of being automatically sealed and fed with recycled oxygen for a period of three months. Bunks for thirty staff members lined the narrow access corridors to storage areas for food and water. An underground passageway led to an escape hatch near the Washington Monument in case it proved impossible to exit through the debris of the White House. Similar bunkers had been built at strategic points around the country to ensure the survival of key members of the industrial and military establishments who would be essential to reconstruction following an all-out nuclear war.

The Continental Fighter Defense Command—CFDC—bases appeared on the plastic grid covering the map. Armed mostly with F-15J and F-16F fighters, they were designed to defend the United States from the Soviet Union's fleet of Backfire and Lynx bombers. With the failure of SALT VI in 1984, the Soviet Lynx, an Intercontinental bomber with a speed of Mach 3, had gone into full production. Three hundred of them were now in the Soviet arsenal. Doyle turned to the captain in charge of the war room. "Can you vector C-5s from Fort Bragg and Fort Benning to these target cities and give me an intercept from the fighter commands?"

"Yes, sir." He moved to a small computer console and quickly entered symbols for the thirty cities and special targets scattered across the United States followed by a string of mathematical symbols. In minutes the air control map was flooded with a series of lines showing the progress of thirty theoretical C-5 transports and the optimum intersection point by the fighters.

"Suppose the transports tried evasive action? Electronic jamming?"

The captain shook his head, grinning. "No way, General. Those fighters would be on them like tigers no matter what they tried. The present state of the art gives the defense almost total electronic control."

"You're on standby, not operational orders, aren't you?"

"Yes, sir."

"How long would it take you to become operational?"

The captain hesitated, shrugged. "About five seconds."

"You mean you could assume control of the whole fighter network in five seconds, superseding the Pentagon?"

"Yes, sir. Provided I had the proper command to do so, sir," he added hastily.

"What's that?"

"An order from the joint chiefs of staff or personally from the president, sir."

Doyle took the small elevator to the corridor facing the president's office. The antique clock dating from Andrew Jackson's time began to chime seven P.M. He moved to one of the windows overlooking the White House lawn. A thin film of snow covered the grass and the Christmas lights reflected off it in a kaleidoscope of colors. A choral group stood in front of the Pennsylvania entrance, the strains of "Adeste Fideles" filtering softly through the double windows installed in 1978 during the first great push to conserve fuel.

191

Maria Vicente came up beside him and slipped an arm through his, resting her head on his shoulder. "Are you going to take me to dinner?"

"I was just thinking I don't even have a Christmas present for you."

"Maybe we can think of something," she said, grinning at him with mock wantonness.

"I'm going to have to be here for a while, Maria. Something is going on."

"You don't mean the damn fools are really going to do it? They couldn't be so stupid, Steve."

"They might. Christman, Cooley, and the others we know are in on it have slipped their tails, gone underground. It doesn't look good. I've got to see the president now. Will I see you later?"

She grinned. "If you feel up to it. In a literal sense, that is."

Doyle took her in his arms, feeling her tense under his hands, remembering the velvet feel of her body. "I'll try to be there by midnight."

"Don't do anything stupid, Steve. Generals aren't supposed to be heroes."

"I doubt if there will be any violence. All this is being done in the rarefied atmosphere of high policy and statesmanship."

"You mean it's some sort of elaborate bluff to influence the president?"

Doyle hesitated. "Something like that. They just can't be stupid enough to try a coup."

"Steve, I hope you're right." She kissed him quickly and disappeared down the corridor.

Sergeant McBain was reading a comic book, his size thirteen shoes scarring the paint on the gray metal desk in Doyle's outer office. He came to his feet at half attention. "Evenin', General."

"Hello, Buck. Have those marines come in yet?"

"Landed at that private field out in Virginia half an hour ago, General. Civilian trucks are bringing them in to a bivouac area behind the Smithsonian. They'll set up tents and stay out of sight as much as possible."

"What about food?"

"They're bringing a portable field kitchen. Trust the gyrenes. They won't go without vittles."

"Have we got communication?"

Buck gestured toward the walkie talkie and Doyle picked it up, flicking the transmit switch. "Major Haines, General Doyle. Come in please."

The marine major's voice came through in a crackle of static. "Major Haines reporting, sir."

"Haines, what are your orders?"

"We're to move to bivouac area Bravo, set up camp and be prepared to move on your orders on ten minutes notice."

"What's your complement and armament, Major?"

"One hundred and seventy men armed with M20s. Three light machine gun teams. Four ninety-millimeter recoilles rifles. Two light mortar teams, sir."

"All right, major. I'll let you know if we need you."

Doyle cut off the radio and turned to the big sergeant. "Get me General Stein, Buck."

Buck dialed Camp LeJeune on the special military telephone, patiently working his way through the military switchboard and handing over the phone.

"Stein?"

"No, sir. General Stein is not available, sir."

"What the hell do you mean he's not available? This is General Doyle, the president's military aide. Get him on the phone."

"I'm sorry, General." The crisp young voice came

across the distance as impersonally as an ice cube. "The general is not on the base."

Doyle exploded. "Then get him on his radio, goddamn it. This is urgent. Tell him to call General Doyle at the White House. Did you get that?"

"Yes, sir."

"Who are you, anyway?"

"Captain Clark, sir. His personal aide."

"Then why aren't you with him?" Stein never moved without his retinue of brilliant young officers. Doyle felt a sudden unease. Something was wrong. No young aide, knowing Stein, would freeze out a general calling from the White House.

The young officer hesitated. "He decided to go alone, sir."

"Who's his second in command? General Means? Put him on."

"Sorry, sir. General Means is not available."

Doyle was about to shout into the phone when the line went dead.

"Tell the switchboard not to take any more White House calls," Brigadier General Thomas Means told the young aide and turned back to Stein.

"Listen to me, Murray. We haven't got much time. I've got to know where you sent Haines."

Stein tilted his huge leather armchair back against the wall and lit a thick Montechristo. "Fuck you, Tom. You're a goddamn traitor and you're going to wind up with your back against a wall. You and these three thugs of yours," he said gesturing toward the young marine officers armed with snubnosed submachine guns equipped with silencers who leaned against the walls of his office covering the windows and door.

Brigadier General Thomas Means, second in command of the First Marine Division, shook his head. He was a little over six feet, fifty years old, with a graying crew cut and a face and body the consistency of cured leather.

"Murray, it's all over. The Eighty-Second and One Hundred and First Airborne Divisions are dispersing across the country right now. We've got people in every key spot. Nothing can stop us. You really should have joined us."

"Nobody asked me," Stein said.

Means shook his head. "We knew you, Murray. You wouldn't have come in. Too much of that weak-minded liberal shit in your head. Anyway, it's too late now. Where's Haines? He can't hurt us, but he can cause trouble. I want him out of the way. We know he's somewhere in the Washington area, and you've got to give us his location."

Stein grinned suddenly. "You're in trouble, aren't you, Tom? You walk in here with three submachine guns, and that's about all you've got. Out there," he waved toward the door, "it's all mine. And I think I'm going to take it back." As he spoke, Stein shot out of his chair and strode across the room. Means motioned to one of the young officers. As Stein reached the door the gun made a sound like a muted typewriter and the stocky figure slammed forward from the weight of half a dozen .38 caliber bullets smashing in a neat circle in the middle of his back. He crumpled to his knees leaning against the door, head skewed like a broken doll.

"All right, let's move," Means said. "We'll have to let headquarters know that a marine detachment is loose somewhere in Washington. Clark, get Stein's body out of here. Put out an order that he's had a heart attack and that I'm in temporary command. Parker," he said turning to the young captain who had shot down Stein,

"Call a meeting of the regimental commanders and their deputies in my office. We'll hold them in the command center while our people take over. Get everybody we've got moving. This goddamn division has to be immobilized for at least twenty-four hours."

The president nodded curtly as Doyle entered the Oval Office. Stansbury, Harlan Worth, and half a dozen assistants were scattered around the room. Washington Police Chief Jefferson Tubman towered over the others. A former star basketball player, his six feet six inches had filled out to impressive bulk in middle age. "All right, gentlemen," the president said, "you know why you're here. We have evidence that a group of former military leaders in combination with reactionary business groups are about to attempt a coup d'état to take over the country. They appear to have gotten control of certain military units and to have subverted police officials around the nation. We're here tonight to plan countermeasures. We'll start with you, Steve. What's the status of the First Marine Division?"

"I contacted Stein earlier today and the advance unit we requested is in place at the Smithsonian. But I think that's too far away, Mr. President. They ought to be on White House grounds."

The president shook his head impatiently. "What about the division itself? When will it be able to move?"

"Stein told me he can move some units out for Washington within six hours. To get the whole division here will take forty-eight provided we can get him the transport he needs. I'll need an order from you to get the air force moving."

"You've got it. How will you deploy it once it's here?"

"We'll emplace them around all the airfields and approach roads to the city. Cover the White House, Capitol, Pentagon, and all the public service and communications centers. About half the division will encamp on the Mall as a reserve force. I should tell you I'm having trouble reaching Stein."

The president waved his hand impatiently. "Use White House communication. He's probably out in the field getting his unit together. You're in overall command of the military measures. Set up a headquarters unit here in the White House. Now, Harlan, have you located Christman and Cooley?"

The FBI chief shook his head. "They've vanished. We think into some army or air force base. There's not a trace of them anywhere. The other former joint chiefs and all the top leaders of the conspiracy whom we've been able to identify have also gone underground. We've got wiretaps on every phone which could give us a lead, but nothing has surfaced yet."

"Stansbury?" The president turned to the elegant figure of the intelligence director.

"We have a report that Christman entered Fort Bragg early this morning. I'm trying to check it out."

"That means they may be planning to move more quickly than we thought."

"Either that or they're panicking, which could work out to the same thing."

"What do you think, Steve?"

"They know the plan is burned. If they're smart they'll move as quickly as they can. But it's Christmas Eve for them, too. They'll be having the same problem we are. Everybody's out at some party getting smashed."

The president's secretary slipped in, circled the room and handed him a folded note. He read it and glanced up at the others. "This resolves our doubts, gentlemen. I asked the head of the Federal Aviation Administration to have his controllers check any unusual military air activity. This is his reply. Approximately twenty-five C-5s just took off from Fort Benning and another twenty are about to leave Fort Bragg. That's twenty thousand men, gentlemen. Headed for the most important targets in the country."

Worth wiped his face with a handkerchief and cleared his throat. "You can order them back to their bases, Mr. President. Go down to your command center and take over. They'll obey you. Most of the men flying those planes are not in the conspiracy, and the ones on them aren't either."

"What about it, Steve?"

"It's worth a try."

"Then let's go." As the president lifted himself out of his chair, a muffled explosion jarred the room.

"Jesus, what's that?"

"I'll take a look." Doyle moved quickly through the president's outer office, past startled secretaries, toward the front of the White House. Looking out through the double windows at the snow-covered lawn, he could see the muzzle bursts of automatic rifles and machine guns as dark figures moved rapidly in attack formation across the lawn. Two secret service guards lay crumpled in front of the White House Main entrance and the small guardpost at the main gate, blasted by a satchel charge, lurched crazily off center.

Doyle turned and came up against the slender figure of the president. "My God, Steve, what are they doing?"

"Killing your guards. The coup just started. That's a special forces commando out there. You've got to get out of here. We can go down to the control room, get orders out to stop these transports and then get you out the emergency escape hatch. I'll send a car there. You can be in the marine guard encampment within five minutes."

The president hesitated, staring out at the lawn where the firing had ceased except for a lone holdout somewhere near the old State Department building. Troops were forming up in front of the main entrance. An officer was barking quick commands.

"No, goddamnit, Steve, I won't do it." The president's thin face was white with rage. "I will not scuttle out of the White House like a frightened crab, running off into the night to save my skin from a group of fascist thugs. I'm going to talk to those men. I believe they're simply following orders, not really knowing what they're doing. They may even think it's some sort of exercise."

"Don't do it, Mr. President," Harlan Worth said, stepping between him and the door. "It's crazy."

The president brushed past him and opened the door of the White House, pushing hard to dislodge the body of one of the secret service agents crumpled against it. Doyle followed him out into the light of the entrance chandelier and onto the marble steps. Colored patterns from the White House Christmas tree reflected off the president's white shirt as he stood coatless in the cold night. "What are you men doing here? Who is in command?"

Major Mason Pruitt spun around at the sound of the president's voice, an exultant grin still on his face. For an almost imperceptible instant he hesitated, then saluted. "I am, Mr. President. I wish to inform you that you are under arrest."

"Under arrest? By whose order, young man?" The president's voice was steely. "I am the commander in chief of the United States Armed Forces, as well as president of the country. Just who has the power to arrest me?"

"The Committee for the Preservation of the Republic, sir," Pruitt said. "Now I must ask you and General Doyle to move inside while my men secure the grounds and set up a perimeter." Pruitt moved toward them, the small submachine gun, a toy in his big hands, pointing at them with negligent command.

"I'll be damned if I move inside," the president said, eyes sweeping across the two dozen soldiers standing at attention in front of him with the practiced eye of a politician. "Do you men know what you are doing? Have you any idea of the enormity of the crime you have just committed? Do you know that all of you can be tried and executed for high treason for taking part in this exercise and following this man's orders?"

Pruitt moved up the steps at a run until he was three paces from the president. "That's enough, Mr. President. You are not permitted to make a speech. Move inside please."

"Did you men hear that? This officer is telling the president of the United States he can't talk on the porch of his own house?" The president turned on Pruitt, chilly blue eyes blazing. "By whose authority, young man? Who chose to order the elected head of this government to be silent?" He turned back to the men, now becoming visibly uneasy on the lawn as Pruitt backed down a step before the rage and force of the man on the steps.

The president, sensing the moment of indecision, pressed his advantage. "Do any of you know what you are doing? Did anybody tell you? You're professional soldiers doing your duty, following the commands of your officers. I understand that. But I'm your president, your commander in chief, and I'm telling you that the men commanding you are criminals using you for their own ends to overthrow your government and I am now ordering you—"

Pruitt stepped forward to within three feet of the white-faced man on the steps, muzzle of the submachine gun steady. "Move inside, Mr. President." His voice was flat, inflectionless.

"I'll be damned if I will. You men there. Arrest this man—" The words died as a stream of twenty-two caliber bullets stitched tiny black holes in a circular pattern on his chest, and he slumped backwards, falling like a broken doll over the body of one of his secret service men. "All right men," Pruitt's voice lifted in a snarl of command, "set up the perimeter. Secure all entrances and exits. You, Edmonds, Burke, pick him up and carry him inside. General, after you," Pruitt said motioning toward the door.

Doyle moved inside as two of the soldiers slung their submachine guns and picked up the president's body. Worth and Stansbury met him inside the door. "God, they killed him," Worth said, shaking his head in disbelief. "What do we do now?"

Doyle moved past him heading for the elevator. "I'm going to try to stop those transports, then get hold of the vice-president. He has to be sworn in so he can take command. Both of you should try to mobilize all your men and keep them on standby. Tell Tubman to do the same with the police. I'll get orders to all of you as quickly as possible."

Worth gestured toward the lawn. "What? Against fully armed troops? What the hell do you expect my FBI men or the cops to do with their damned .357 magnums and a few old-fashioned submachine guns?"

"Harlan, everything is in chaos right now. They're using men who don't know anything. If we can retain some control, some counterforce, there's a chance we can turn it around. Have the attorney general contact all the state governors. Get on the phone around the country to police chiefs and heads of the highway patrol. They can't have subverted all of them. Tell them to mobilize and head for a rendezvous point in the state capitals. We'll get orders to them as soon as possible."

"Where will you be?" Stansbury asked.

"Depends on how quickly I can locate Vice-President Harrington. We've got to have a legal focal point to rally to. I'm going to try to get the First Marine moving toward Washington now. And stop those goddamn airborne troops from taking over the country if I can."

Through the window he saw Pruitt turn toward the White House entrance. "You'd better come with me. We can get out through the emergency bunker exit."

The three men moved through a crowd of White House employees as Worth and Stansbury shot out quick orders to their men who had gathered in the White House to disperse and try to reach their offices. Doyle inserted his key in the small bunker elevator and the three men descended four floors into the steel and concrete command post. The guard in the corridor checked their passes and motioned them onward.

"Sergeant, the president has just been shot upstairs. I want that elevator immobilized immediately. Can you do that? I don't want anybody coming in here."

The guard hesitated. "Sir, I take my orders from Major Czermak."

"Then get him out here."

"Yes sir." The guard pressed a red emergency button to the left of the elevator and almost instantly four armed men erupted out of a small guardroom at the end of the concrete corridor. The duty officer came out of the central command room at a run. "What the fuck is going on, sergeant?" he asked, stopping in mid-sentence at the sight of Doyle and the others. He saluted automatically. "Sorry, General, I thought somebody had leaned against the button."

"The president's been shot. He's dead. A coup d'état is taking place. I want this elevator immobilized at this level immediately. Seal off the area as if we were under attack."

The major glanced quickly at the other men and snapped an order to the sergeant in charge of the watch who moved to a steel box, opened it with a key and flipped one of the fuses.

"I'm not under your orders, General," the major said, face stiff. "The elevator is immobilized, but I've got to contact the office of the joint chiefs immediately for instructions. You understand, sir. I can't seal off the area indefinitely on your orders."

"Listen. There is nobody in the Pentagon who can give you an order. It's being taken over by rebellious elements, traitors. Your duty is now to your country." Doyle glanced around the impassive faces of the guards.

"We're wasting time. Let's go. Harlan, you and Jim had better get the hell out of here while you can. Major, have one of your men take them to the emergency exit point."

The officer snapped an order and led Doyle to the command center. The three computer operators looked up and returned to their machines. "Forty-five C-5s are out there with orders to take over thirty prime targets around the country as part of this coup. They've got to be stopped. Get me the head of the Air Defense Command."

"Sir, I'm not under your command." The officer's voice was stubborn now. "My orders are to turn over this command center to the president personally. I'm very sorry, sir, but you have no standing in this command post."

"All right, try the Pentagon. See if you can get the watch officer."

The major nodded to one of the operators and a voice came over a small loudspeaker. "Pentagon command center."

Doyle took a small mike from the operator. "This is General Doyle, the president's military aide. Put me through to the duty commander."

Within seconds a decisive voice came on the line. "General Carlyle here."

"Sam, Steve Doyle at the White House."

"Hello, Steve. What's up?"

"You mean you don't know?"

"Know what?"

"They've just killed the president."

"Oh, Jesus. That wasn't part of the plan. Who did it, Steve?"

"The commando that took over the White House."

"That goddamn trigger-happy Pruitt." Carlyle's aristocratic voice was bitter. "Well, it's too late now. We're committed. I suggest you surrender, Steve. It's all over."

"Sam, don't be a fool. You're going to have a civil war with him dead. You've got to stop those planes."

"No way. They're all airborne. Some of them approaching target. It's too bad he's dead, but in a way it makes it easier. Is Czermak there?"

The young officer took the mike from Doyle. "Czermak, sir."

"Arrest General Doyle and turn him over to Major Pruitt. Once you've done that, clear your command area and push the destruct button. I want that command center out of operation within five minutes. Do you understand, Czermak?"

"Yes, sir."

The young officer turned, face set, undoing the flap on his holstered .45. He slipped out the weapon, checked the clip, pulled the slide to set a cartridge in the slot, reversed the weapon and handed it butt first to Doyle. "You've taken over the center by force, General," he said, a touch of a smile on his face. "Who do you want to talk to?" The three enlisted men on the computers watched the scene in disbelief.

Doyle took the automatic and set the safety. "Get me General Stein at the First Marine Division in LeJeune."

The young officer nodded to one of the computer specialists whose hands flicked across the control panel. "Pick up the green phone, General."

"General Means here."

"Tom, this is Steve Doyle in the White House. Where the hell is Stein? I've been trying to reach him all evening."

"Dead, Steve. Some clowns shot him down in his office about an hour ago. I've got things under control now. What the hell is going on? The Pentagon seems to have gone crazy."

"There's an attempted coup, Tom. The president's dead. I need every man you've got up here as soon as you can move them. How long will it take to get a regiment on the way?"

"Four or five hours. Maybe less. Listen, Steve, before he died, Stein told me about Haines and his combat group. Where are they? I want to get in contact."

Doyle stared down at the phone, feeling a slight chill along the nape of his neck.

"Steve? You still there? I need to contact Haines. Where have you got him bivouacked?"

Doyle replaced the receiver on the cradle. "Get me

the Continental Air Defense Command. General Jameson."

Once again the young computer specialist flicked his fingers over the control panel and motioned toward the bile green telephone. "General Jameson?"

"That's right."

"This is General Doyle, the president's aide. I'm in the White House control center."

The lazy voice at the other end of the line came back. "What can we do for you, General?"

"The president's been shot. A coup d'état is under way. We need your help, General."

"Yeah, boy, I reckon you do at that. What the hell you been drinkin'?"

"General, this is no joke. The White House has been taken over by a commando team from Special Forces. There are forty-five C-5s on their way to thirty top targets across the country. Check your air controllers if you don't believe me. I'll wait in the command center."

"All right, son. I'll do just that."

Doyle would remember the next ninety seconds as among the longest of his life. Half a minute into it a White House phone jangled and Major Czermak grabbed it, listened briefly and handed it to Doyle.

"General? Pruitt here. Get that fucking elevator operating or we're dropping gas grenades down the pipe. You got thirty seconds."

Doyle grinned. "Nice try, Mason. The atomic shield has been moved into place. You couldn't blast your way in with coastal artillery."

"Oh, shit." Pruitt hesitated. "Listen, General, I'll make you a deal. For old times sake. We've won. You know that. The president's dead. Those two divisions are going to have the country locked up within a few hours. You open up that tin can down there and surrender, and I think I can get you on the inside of this thing. Save your ass."

"No dice, Mason. You haven't got anything locked up. This isn't Paraguay. It's going to take one hell of a lot more than twenty thousand troops to keep this country under control. By this time tomorrow you'll all be hunted fugitives." The buzz of the green phone interrupted them, and Doyle hung up the White House line.

"Yes."

"General Jameson here. That you, Doyle?"

"Yes."

"Sure is something funny going on. That I gotta admit. For one thing nobody is answering his phone. What?" Doyle head Jameson partially cover the mouthpiece of his phone as a jumble of voices came through. "Doyle?"

"I'm still here."

"A combat team just took over Kelly Field in Mobile. Truman Air Defense control in St. Louis is also gone. I'm told that the forty-five C-5s you talked about are in the air and moving on targets. Also, an order has gone out to shut down every civilian airport in the country. International flights before the point of no return are being turned back. What the fuck is going on?"

"I told you, General. A coup d'état. I haven't got much time. I'm in the president's command bunker, but they're going to shut down its communications within minutes. Listen, General, you've got to stop those transports."

"And just how do you expect me to do that, Doyle?"

"Send up your fighters. Have them fire warning salvos. Talk them down on the nearest field. Tell them orders have been cancelled, any goddamn thing to keep them from their targets."

"And if that don't work?"

Doyle hesitated. "Shoot them down, General. We've got no other choice."

"You know what you're saying, Doyle? There's five hundred men on every one on them planes. You want me to kill twenty thousand of the best troops we've got?"

"General, it's either that or turn the country over to these assholes. Which do you want to do?"

"How do I know you are telling me the truth?"

"They're taking over your airfields, aren't they? It may already be too late to do anything. Anyway, you must know what's going on. Didn't Christman contact you? Didn't they try to bring you in?"

"Not Christman." The air force general's voice sounded suddenly tired. "But I was contacted. I thought they were a bunch of damn fools and told them so. Never thought they'd have the balls to go ahead with it. Should have reported them."

Doyle realized he was gripping the phone so tightly his knuckles were white with strain. "What are you going to do, General?"

"If they won't turn back, we'll shoot 'em down, son."

Doyle hung up, realizing as he glanced at the faces of the four soldiers that they had heard the conversation through an open mike on the computer console.

"Jesus Christ," one of the computer specialists said, almost in a whisper.

"I'm leaving, Czermak. Once I'm gone, follow orders. Destruct the command center and get your men out through the emergency exit."

"What do we do then?"

"Go get drunk, son." Doyle said moving off toward the end of the passageway where a mile-long miniature railway would deposit him at the emergency exit near the base of the Washington monument.

* * *

Vice-President Joshua Harrington was not in a position which befitted his office. He was flat on his back being screwed out of his mind by his twenty-two-year-old secretary. He hadn't meant to come over tonight, but his wife's annual Christmas Eve party for the Grand Dames of the Middle South had given him a golden opportunity and he had gone out the side door of the old navy mansion, given his secret service detail the slip, and picked up a taxi on Massachussetts Avenue.

He'd called first. That was the deal they had. And she'd said sure, come on up. And here he was. Involuntarily he arched his back as her warm, wet loins stroked him, contracting around him in rhythmic spasms. Christ, not yet. She liked to go on and on. Her hands were twisted in the mat of hair on his chest, gray now, but still thick as a bathmat, as his wife had once said in disgust.

Her nails were digging into him now, not drawing blood, but scratching in a way that made him feel twenty again. "Come on, baby," she said in that husky voice. "You got all night?"

And he exploded inside her, feeling as if his life itself was draining away in the thin semen of late middle age. "You are something else."

She grinned, sitting up astride him, hands balled into fists on her hips. "That, Mr. Vice-President, is what we used to call a shit-eating grin."

"How about a beer, honey?"

"Sure thing. She slid off him and walked across the bedroom, taut hips bouncing, grabbing a crumpled terry towel robe and flinging it over her shoulders as she moved.

He turned on the miniature bedside television set and watched as a test pattern filled the screen. Puzzled, he flipped channels and came up each time with the same neat geometric design. "What's going on with the television?" he called through the door.

"Try the radio. Maybe there's a blackout or something."

The girl appeared, pouring a glass of beer carefully down the slanted side of a chilled glass. He hated burying his nose in a head of beer, and she'd quickly realized it.

Harrington was about to touch the radio button when the test pattern dissolved and the Federal Broadcasting Company news desk came into focus. An unfamiliar face filled the screen, reading somewhat nervously from a single sheet of paper.

"Good evening, ladies and gentlemen. I have an announcement to make. The Committee for the Preservation of the Republic, an organization of patriotic Americans, both civilian and military, has taken over the government of the United States. The president is dead. All major cities of the country have been taken over by military forces loyal to the committee. The army, navy and air force are under the committee's control. The police forces and state patrols of all large states are obeying our orders. The committee urges the citizenry not to panic. Stay in your homes. Continue to act normally. The situation will be clarified periodically by members of the committee who will speak to you at the regular news broadcast times."

"It's some sort of joke," Harrington said, falling back on the bed. "Like that thing Orson Welles did when I was a kid. The War of the Worlds."

The girl handed him the beer and Harrington gulped it quickly, grateful for the dry, bitter cold of the Pilsner. He handed the glass to the girl and reached for the phone, dialing the White House confidential number.

210

The operator came on immediately. "White House. May I help you?"

"I'd like to speak to the president. This is Vice-President Harrington."

"Just a minute, sir."

"Mr. Vice-President?"

"Yes. Who's this?"

"I think you'd better get over to the White House right away, sir. A very serious situation has arisen. If you'll tell me where you are, I'll have you picked up."

Harrington dropped the phone back on its cradle and met the girl's eyes. "Something's wrong. They never answer that phone with 'White House.' It's a direct line to the president's office." He dialed again.

"Vice-President's residence. May I help you?"

"This is the vice-president. I'd like to talk to Mrs. Harrington."

His wife's raspy voice came over the receiver almost immediately. "Joshua? Where the fuck are you? Do you know that this house is overrun with soldiers? They're ruining the goddamn carpets and they've scared the shit out of my guests. Will you get your ass out that whore's bed and get over here?"

Harrington heard sounds of a brief struggle. "Mr. Vice-President?"

"Yes."

"This is the commander of your special guard. We were sent here to protect you. Let me know where you are, sir, so I can get a detail over there to keep you under surveillance."

"I hear they shot the president, son."

There was a moment's hesitation on the line. "Just let us know where you are, sir, and we'll protect you."

"Yeah. Thanks very much, son," Harrington said replacing the phone. "It's true. There's been a goddamn

211

takeover. Those fools. Those goddamn, miserable stupid fools."

"Who?" The girl had crawled back into bed and moved her body against his for warmth.

Harrington remembered his conversation with Christman at the Capitol. "Just a bunch of damned fools, honey," he said, getting out of bed heavily, feeling the weight of his sixty-four years.

"What are you going to do?"

"Find somebody who will swear me in as president and take the goddamn country back."

CHAPTER THIRTEEN

The emergency exit from the White House bunker was a small, tasteful stone building located near the base of the Washington Monument. A young military guard sat in the windowless building facing the elevator doors. "Good evening, sir," he said, rising and saluting as Doyle came out.

"Good evening. Have Mr. Worth and Mr. Stansbury left?"

"Yes, sir. Mr. Stansbury called for his car, sir. May I secure a vehicle for you?"

"No, thanks, I'll get a taxi. Meantime let me have a look at your White House telephone directory."

Doyle flipped through the book, bound in blue matt plastic decorated with the presidential seal. He dialed quickly, facing the elevator, wondering how much time he had.

"Vice-President's residence."

"I'd like to speak to him, please. This is General Doyle at the White House."

A new, crisp young voice came on.

"General Doyle, Vice-President Harrington is under protective custody. Where are you, sir? I'd like to have a detail take you under its protection, sir."

Doyle was about to hang up when he heard Mrs. Harrington's raspy voice come over the receiver from a distance. "You lying little piss ant. What do you mean he's under custody? He's out with his whore—" Her voice stopped abruptly as a hand covered the phone's mouthpiece.

"General? Are you still there, General?"

Doyle hung up thoughtfully and began thumbing through the directory, stopping at the name of the vice-president's press secretary. He dialled quickly.

"Hello."

"Matt?"

"Yes, who's this?"

"Doyle."

"Doyle?"

"From the president's office."

"Oh, hello, Steve. What's up?"

"Listen, Matt. I've got to get hold of the vice-president. It's urgent."

"Call him at home, Steve. You want his confidential number?"

"I've got it. He's not there."

"Oh. What makes you think I know where he is?" The voice was cautious now, dripping chilly formality.

"Cut the crap, Matt. He's got a girl. One of his secretaries. Everybody knows it."

"Yeah? Well, if everybody knows it, call them."

"Listen, Matt," Doyle said hurriedly, trying to keep the man on the line. "I've got to get him. Now. We've got to swear him in."

"What?" The voice of the vice-president's press secretary shot up a squeaky octave.

"The president's been killed. Some sort of military coup d'état is in process. I've got to get hold of Harrington, get him sworn in somehow and find out what he wants to do."

"Where are you now, Steve?"

Doyle told him.

"Listen. I'm at the Watergate. I'll pick you up in five minutes. Okay?"

"Yes. But it had better not be much more."

Doyle returned the young soldier's salute and moved out of the small building into the dimly lit street. The uncomfortable bulk of the .45 automatic tucked in his belt bit into his stomach. A bow and arrow, he thought, would be about as useful. Snow was falling more heavily now, and traffic had slowed to a glacial pace as drivers felt their way across the slick streets. The Christmas trees ringing the base of the monument looked in the distance like sugar confections as the blanket of snow covered their branches and dimmed the colors.

Matt Skille, the vice-president's press spokesman, arrived some seven minutes later, steering his BMW to the curb and flipping open the door. "Christ, Doyle, where's your coat?"

"I left in a hurry, Matt."

"Yeah. Tell me what happened."

Doyle ran down what he knew rapidly as Skille turned toward the northwest, driving with assurance through the slowed traffic.

"Jesus. So they really did it."

"You knew about it?" Doyle asked, voice sharp.

Skille waved a long slender hand. "I didn't know anything. But rumors have been circulating. The same ones you must have heard," he said, glancing over at Doyle. "The boss had a couple of visits from Christman and Cooley. He thought they were full of shit. What do

215

we do now, Steve? They can't possibly pull it off, can they?"

"With the president dead, it makes things very tough, Matt," Doyle said, gripping the door handle as Skille, a former Minneapolis newsman, put the car into a controlled skid and took a turn onto Connecticut Avenue. "Also, it looks as if they've got hold of the Pentagon's communication and command setup. They're issuing the orders. It's a professional army and has been for twenty years. It obeys orders. Somehow we'll have to short-circuit that command set-up, get to people directly."

"That's going to be a little tough if they've taken over all the public communications media."

Doyle nodded. "I know."

Skille brought the car to a halt in the driveway of a renovated apartment building just off DuPont Circle. "This is it. He's in Apt. 420 on the fourth floor," Skille said as he slid out of the seat.

As they approached the apartment entrance, a compact young man stepped out of the shadows. "Mr. Skille."

"Oh, hello, Craine. This is General Doyle."

"Yes, sir. I recognize him. Excuse me, sir. The vice-president's upstairs. He tried to give us the slip, but we followed along."

Skille smiled. "Okay. How many?"

"Four of us, sir. But, sir, we've just heard on the radio that the president has been killed. It can't be true?"

"Yes. It is true, Craine. You're guarding the new president. And there are people who are interested in killing him. We're going up. Be ready to move out immediately. Meantime dig in and don't let anybody up there."

Sue O'Brien opened the door, holding the short terry towel robe together with her left hand. Skille and Doyle brushed past her into a small living room. Harrington looked up from tying a shoelace.

"Hello, Matt, Doyle. What the hell is going on?"

Doyle gave him a rapid summary of the situation as the vice-president shrugged into a crumpled white shirt stained with lipstick and began to loop an old-fashioned wide tie which must have dated from the mid-nineteen seventies. It was part of the image of antique, careless elegance he cultivated.

"The First Marine Division is one of the keys to the situation then?"

"It could be. But Stein's unavailable and it looks as if Means is in on the coup."

"Is there any way we can be sure? Have you got some other way of contacting the division?"

"Major Haines has a radio at his bivouac at the Smithsonian. He's been told to shut it down and take orders only from me. We could try to use that channel."

Harrington nodded. "Okay. But first I've got to get myself sworn in. Matt, get hold of the chief justice. Ask him if he can come over here right away. Can you reach that marine detachment by phone?"

Doyle nodded. "They're patched into a direct line from that museum."

"All right. Tell that commander I want him to try to get hold of a loyal senior officer at that base. Tell him to call me here. Meantime what about the local police force?"

"The chief was at the White House when the president was killed. I doubt if Jeff was in on it. I asked Worth to get everybody mobilized and ready to move."

"He's that big black? The ex-basketball player?"

"Yes. Jefferson Tubman."

Matt Skille broke in, holding his hand over the phone. "The chief justice is on his way over, sir. I'd

217

better let your guards know," he said, leaving the apartment.

"We need a secure command post, Doyle. Someplace where they won't be able to locate me. Got any ideas?"

"We'll have to try to make it to that marine bivouac at the Smithsonian and work from there."

"Okay. We'll move as soon as I'm sworn in."

"Two Galaxies in the scope, Joe. Range fifty miles and closing."

"See if you can raise him."

"Big Mother, this is Continental Defense Command Squadron Ten. Do you read me, Big Mother? Come in."

"Squadron Ten, this is Big Mother. We read you. What's your pleasure?"

"What's your heading, Big Mother?"

"Our mission is confidential, Squadron Ten. We're under orders not to divulge."

"Big Mother, our orders are that you abort your mission. Repeat, abort mission, Big Mother. Confirm."

"What the fuck do you mean, abort? We're not under Defense Command Control. I'll abort when Benning tells me to and not before. You guys off your rocker or something?"

"What's the range, Joe?"

"Thirty and closing."

"Big Mother. This is Squadron Ten. Miles Air Force base is a hundred miles ahead of you. My orders are to put you down there."

"Ten, you flipped or something? This mission is going to Houston as ordered. Now clear my airspace, shithead."

"Big Mother, my orders are to force you down at

218

Miles if you do not comply. If I can't force you down, I'll shoot you out of the air. Come in, Big Mother."

"You crazy son of a bitch, you realize I got five hundred airborne troops on this bird? You're out of your goddamn gourd."

"Big Mother, I repeat. My orders are to force you down or total you. Come in."

"Listen, mister. I got orders direct from the general. You're not getting me to put this bird down. So if you got the guts to burn five hundred men, you go right ahead."

"I'm going to hit your left outer engine, Big Mother. You might still be able to ditch her if it doesn't take your wing off."

"Oh shit, the fucking bird's on fire. I'm putting it down on the road, Jim. The motherfucker iced us."

White Knight, this is Vassal Two. White Knight, this is Vassal Two. Do you read me?"

"Read you loud and clear, Vassal Two."

"White Knight, there is something wrong with our map. The place marked as the city waterworks is a swimming pool and lake in the middle of something called Piedmont Park."

"Your map is correct, Vassal Two. Surround the objective and report when secured."

"But Colonel—"

"Goddamn it, Captain, I'm White Knight. You've broken security. Do it again and I'll have your balls."

"Sorry, sir—er, White Knight. But it can't be the waterworks. There's nobody around but a bunch of hookers."

"Goddamn it, Vassal Two. Are you questioning my staff maps? Secure the objective, goddamn you."

"Yes, sir."

219

"Okay, Harry, get the men deployed. Colonel says it's the objective."

"Captain, that's a lot of crap. One of my men is from Atlanta. He says the waterworks is up on the other side of town. This is a swimming pool."

"Yeah. Well you tell it to that fucking bird colonel if you want to. As far as I'm concerned he just declared it the waterworks."

"What about the hookers?"

"How the fuck do I know what about the hookers? What the hell are they doing in the park anyway?"

"The kid from Atlanta says it's kind of a rendezvous point. Guys come in and pick 'em up here."

"In this fucking weather?"

"Yeah, well, Captain, people screw in all kinds of weather."

There were six of them at the ceremony: the girl, who had changed into a cream-colored pants suit, Harrington, Doyle, Skille, a secret service man and the chief justice, a big man in a dinner jacket, face slightly flushed from eggnog and most of a bottle of burgundy.

"I forgot the oath, Josh. But the exact wording isn't important. Just put your hand on the Bible and swear after me. I, Joshua Harrington, do solemnly swear that I will uphold the duties and responsibilities as President of the United States vested in me by the Constitution, so help me God."

Harrington repeated the words and shook hands with the chief justice. "I hope I get the opportunity, Homer."

"So do I, Josh. So do I. I've been waiting for them to show up at my place ever since I heard the news. But I guess they don't think the law counts for much as long as you've got a gun in your hand."

As the chief justice spoke the chatter of a machine

pistol ripped through the night answered by the heavier burps of an automatic carbine. The agent raced for the window, vaulting a chair, looking down into the street below. "Jesus, there must be a full platoon out there. You'd better get out of here, sir. We won't be able to hold them for long."

Harrington nodded. "There's a back way. Down to the cellar and out into the alley that gives off onto Connecticut." He grinned, slipping an arm around the girl. "I figured I might have to beat a hasty retreat out of here sometime, and how right I was. Loan us your car, honey. I'll call you when I get the chance. This ought to add a little excitement to that doctoral thesis you're writing."

The girl fumbled through a massive knit bag and handed over a set of keys. "I'll stall them as long as I can," she said.

They moved down the hall to the fire stairs as the firing increased in intensity. "Christ, I ought to be down there with them," the agent said, half turning.

"Son, you get your ass down the stairs first and clear a path for us," Harrington said. "You're not here to prove you've got balls but to keep me from getting killed." As they reached the cellar, Harrington motioned to a red door behind the furnace. "It gives out onto an alley where Sue parks her car. You think they may have fanned out to cover the rear?"

Doyle shrugged and drew the heavy automatic out of his belt, slotting a cartridge in. "I'll go first and draw any fire," he said to the agent. "You cover me as quick as you can."

"Yes, sir," the agent said, arming the small Israeli Uzi machine pistol.

Doyle slammed against the roll bar and moved into the alley in a crouch, running, feeling the sour taste of

221

fear well up in his throat. The soldier at the end of the street lifted his M-20 and fired a burst just as Doyle hit the deck, rolling behind a parked car. The agent had stepped into the street behind him, his little machine pistol burping in rachitic bursts. The soldier crumpled and Doyle came to his feet.

"Quick, where the hell is her car?"

Harrington was already running down the alley toward a small Japanese sedan, fumbling at the door. He flipped Doyle the keys and piled in the back seat as the agent knelt in the alley facing back. "I'll hold them, sir. You'd better get moving."

Doyle stared at the dashboard in momentary panic, searching for a key slot until Skille ripped the keys out of his hand and started the little car with a vicious twist. "Shit," the president said, "I hope one of us chauffeur-driven big wheels still knows how to drive."

Doyle slipped the little car in gear as the agent's gun began to chatter behind them, and they skidded down the alley into a deserted Connecticut Avenue. "They'll be on the radio. We'll be cut off from downtown before I can make the Smithsonian."

"Any suggestions, Matt?" the president asked.

"Yeah. The subway. They'll be expecting us in a car. I doubt if they'll try to cover the underground."

Doyle nodded. "It's a chance." He turned the little car around Dupont Circle and brought it to a stop across from the subway entrance. In the distance the wail of police sirens cut through the night. "They're using the police, which makes it even tougher. Tubman must have lost control."

The three men descended into the almost-deserted subway, bought tickets and walked along the platform, empty except for a sleeping drunk. "Where do we get

222

off?" Harrington asked. "I haven't been on this thing since they opened the line."

"The Treasury Department is the closest station. We can probably get a taxi over to the Smithsonian from there."

"Then what?" Harrington asked.

"I'm not sure. Maybe get a helicopter to take you out and get you down to LeJeune if we can recapture control of the First Marine."

"And try to take the capital by force? Shit, Doyle, that would mean civil war."

"What other alternatives are there?"

The roar of the train interrupted Harrington's reply. The three men boarded the last car, empty except for three black men in colorful suits and wide-brimmed hats passing a bottle back and forth.

One looked over at them and winked at his friends. "Hey, you honkies. How 'bout a li'l drink? We celebratin' Christmas."

Harrington shook his head. "Thanks. We've already got a load on."

The black, tall and skinny, got up and staggered down the car, holding a flat pint bottle in a paper sack. "Sheet, man. You can't never get nuff of this stuff. It's like pussy, man. More you gets, more you wants." He stuffed the bottle in Harrington's face. "Drink up, honky. We celebratin' the virgin birth." He finished the sentence with a long, high, giggling laugh.

Harrington pushed the bottle away, and the black suddenly ceased to laugh, his face contorting into a scowl. "You too fuckin' good to drink with us, that it, honky? Well, fuck yo' ass," he snarled, suddenly turning and slamming the half-filled bottle the length of the car. It smashed against a seat stanchion, brown liquid sloshing across the carpeted floor of the subway car. In the same motion the skinny man slipped his hand into a coat pocket and came out with a switchblade knife.

"Well, now, honky. You too good to drink with us, maybe you ain't too good to contribute a little bread for us to drink with, huh. Les' jes see the color yo' money and don't fuck me around 'cause I'm bad, hear? Real bad."

His two companions had risen and joined him now. Matt Skille shrank back against the subway wall, jaw hanging loose in terror. Harrington started to rise as the black brought the tip of the knife within a hair of his left eye. "You set, honkie, or you gonna have a glass eye."

Doyle moved slightly, aligning his body at an angle to the black holding the knife, and snapped his right hand upward, the edge catching the man's Adam's apple and crushing his larynx with a sound like ripe fruit splattering on pavement. The man staggered back, dropping the knife and gripping his crushed throat with both hands, eyes bulging. The other two began to move in on Doyle, one with a knife, the other with a shiny piece of chromium pipe.

Harrington stood up, grinning, his big ex-fullback's body tensing with pleasure. "Well, goddamn, Doyle, let's whip us some ass." The two men stopped and exchanged glances as the subway train slowed to a stop.

"You better pick up your friend and get him to a hospital. He'll be dead in about five minutes if you don't," Doyle said softly, gesturing toward the crumpled figure fighting for breath on the floor of the train.

"You honky sumbitch," the black with the knife said, backing toward the door. "We gonna cut yo asses." He turned and ran, followed by his companion.

"What are we going to do with that?" Harrington asked, gesturing toward the dying man.

"Nothing," Doyle said, ignoring the feebly struggling figure on the floor. "We haven't got much time, Mr. President. We're going to have to move fast or they will close off all our options."

Harrington nodded, leaning against the acceleration of the subway train. "I know. What I need is a national forum. But that's obviously out of the question. They've taken over all the radio and television networks. There isn't any way to reach the people directly."

Matt Skille cleared his throat, trying to avoid looking at the dying man who had now almost ceased to struggle. "Maybe we could make a deal?"

"A deal?" Harrington looked at him. "What kind of a deal, Matt?"

"Well, they are going to need legitimacy. I mean a lot of people aren't going to like it, their killing the president. The way things stand now, it's all illegal. But if you agreed to front for them, like be a figurehead, they could cloak the whole thing in a sort of pseudo-legality."

"And you want me to do that?"

Skille shook his head. "No. But you could pretend to. Until you could get some sort of national audience and also find out who is loyal and who isn't."

Harrington turned to Doyle. "What do you think, General?"

"Might work. They've got to be pretty uptight right now. This is a country of almost two hundred and fifty million people. They've got less than twenty thousand men to run it. They might jump at the offer."

Harrington nodded. "Yes. They might. But there's one big problem with doing it. Unless we move almost immediately, they'll have time to consolidate. Once people accept that I'm with them, they'll cease to resist."

"What about a joint session of Congress?" Skille said.

"You address a joint session and the country on television."

Harrington stared at him. "Christ, it would be perfect. What makes you think they'd go for that?"

The train pulled into the Treasury station and the three men left quickly, stepping over the now quiet body, Skille's short figure taking two steps to the president's one as they moved quickly toward the escalator.

"There wouldn't be any danger from their standpoint. They'd have a copy of the speech beforehand. You'd just have to take the risk and chance it once you got on the air. I don't think they would have the nerve to cut you off in front of two hundred and fifty million Americans."

"We could infiltrate some of Harlan's men and maybe some marines into the House chamber to protect you. They won't be coordinated enough to stop the broadcast in time to block your message," Doyle said.

"Sounds risky as hell. A lot could go wrong," Harrington said. "Still, it's the only chance I can see right now. How do we go about it?"

"First we get you over to the Smithsonian and stick you in the middle of the marine detachment. Then Matt and I will try to locate their command post. It's probably in the Pentagon or the White House. We'll go over to make the deal."

Harrington nodded. "Okay. Let's try it." They had emerged into a deserted Pennsylvania Avenue only a few hundred yards from the White House. A silent crowd had gathered, filling the sidewalks, pressing up against barriers blocking off the broad boulevard and manned by impassive airborne troopers.

A police cruiser, red light flashing in a heartbeat tempo, suddenly made a U-turn and pulled up to the curb beside them. Doyle groped inside his jacket for the butt of the gun as the giant figure of the Washington police chief, Jefferson Tubman, emerged.

"Mr. Vice-President. Been looking all over for you. You want to get inside?"

"Hello, Jeff. Whose side are you on?"

"The side of the people, Mr. Vice-President. They've taken over my headquarters, and I've transferred command to a mobile radio van. There's a civil war on inside the police force. About half the men are with me and the other half with a group that's cooperating with the coup. You want to get in? It's not safe standing here on the street."

The three men crowded into the cruiser's back seat. "Take us to the Smithsonian, Jeff. There are some loyal marines there. Then I want to see if you can locate the men who are running this thing. Doyle and Skille here want to talk to them."

Tubman nodded. "They're operating out of the White House, using that command center in the basement."

"It was supposed to be blown up."

"Yeah. But that guy who killed the president—what's his name?"

"Pruitt."

"Yeah. Well he got some men over to the exit building right after you got out. Killed the guard and went down in the passageway and wiped them all out. That's what I hear. Anyway, they're running things from there. They're still fighting over in the Pentagon. I heard it's a real mess over there. The security guards been blowing the hell out of things."

Doyle shook his head. "Things are coming apart a little for them. They must not have countermanded the standing Pentagon destruct orders in case of trouble. Communications must be a shambles."

"So much the better," Harrington said grimly as the police cruiser swung into the driveway and came to a stop before a marine machine gun post.

Doyle got out. "Where's your commander, sergeant?"

Major Haines emerged from behind the ancient brick building which had once housed the entire museum. "General Doyle?" Haines saluted.

"Yes. Major, we've got the president with us."

"The president? I thought he had been killed."

"He was. Vice-President Harrington has been sworn in. He's now the president. He'll be in your charge," Doyle said, introducing the new president to the crew-cut young marine officer, now at rigid attention. "Have you contacted the division?"

"Yes, sir. General Stein is dead. General Means has taken over command. But there is a lot of confusion. He had a meeting of all field grade officers and above and tried to arrest most of them. There was a firefight in the main mess hall." The young marine sounded as if he didn't believe what he was saying. "It looks as if about half the officers may be dead, sir. The communications center doesn't answer."

"All right son. Keep trying to raise somebody. And don't reveal your whereabouts." Doyle turned to the president. "I guess we better get going."

Harrington nodded. "Good luck. You're going to need it."

Chief Tubman's driver wheeled his car out into the main traffic of Adams Drive and flicked on the flashing red light. Tubman was on the radio. "Hello, Hut. Come in, Hut."

A static-stained voice came back. "What's up, Chief?"

"Hut, I'm gonna be busy for a while. Maybe for a good while. You are in command until I get back to you. We are in a war, Hut. But we are legal, hear? Those other motherfuckers are acting against the law and against the president. You keep trying to round them up and turn them around."

The voice came back. "Okay, Jeff. But, listen. We gotta clean out headquarters. All the off-duty guys are going in there and coming out on their side. If I can collect about fifty men, I think we could take it back. They've withdrawn the army unit that took it over originally."

Tubman glanced at Doyle, eyes arched in a question.

"Tell him to give it a try," Doyle said. "They're probably stretched as thin as hell right now trying to cover all options. Your deputy may be right. They won't be expecting a counterattack."

"Hut, give it a shot. But don't get killed. You are in command until you hear from me."

The car swung up Fifteenth Street and stopped at a barricade. Doyle leaned out and snapped a command at the young lieutenant facing him through the window. "I've got a message from President Harrington. Let us through."

"President Harrington. Jesus," he said, standing irresolute. "I've got to check it out, sir," he said, bringing the walkie talkie to his mouth. After a minute he snapped to attention and motioned for the barricade to be moved. The car moved along between single lines of troops, turned left behind the Treasury building, cut right into Executive Avenue and entered the east wing driveway.

As the car came to a stop, Admiral William Christman, in uniform, descended the steps. "Hello, Doyle, Matt. We've been looking for you all over town."

Doyle saluted the big man. "We've got a message from President Harrington, Admiral."

Christman smiled faintly as he led them into the White House. "President Harrington? I thought he had to be sworn in before he became president."

"He has been, Admiral. By the chief justice."

Christman nodded. "Yes. That would be like Josh. Everything legal before he drops the load on you. Come on in." He led them into the Oval Office, which had been converted into a general staff command post. Half a dozen card tables crammed with phones and communications equipment filled the big office.

Ralph Cooley sat behind the president's desk, talking into a phone. "Yes, goddamn it, Mac, I'm telling you to get your ass over to the governor's mansion and get that son of a bitch to see reason. We hear he's mobilizing the national guard. We've only got five hundred men in St. Louis. He'll blow them away if you don't stop him. What? How the fuck do I know how to stop him? He took the fucking bribe, didn't he? Take a photostat of the check over and rub it under his goddamn thieving nose, but stop him from mobilizing the guard. That shithead thinks he's Napoleon or something."

Cooley nodded grimly to Doyle and Skille, listened another few seconds and hung up. "Okay, where is he?"

"In a safe place," Skille said. "We're here as his emissaries."

"You're here as my prisoners, Skille. And Harrington will be too, as soon as you tell me where he is. Now spit it out."

"It won't work, Ralph," Doyle said. "He moved as soon as we left him. We don't have a clue where he is right now. Our people are expecting us out of here within half an hour in Tubman's car. If we don't show, they'll know it's no deal."

"And then what?" Cooley said, leaning back in the president's chair, his face splitting in a grin. "We con-

trol the country, Doyle. Thirty cities are in our hands."
A young army officer motioned frantically for Christman to take a phone.

"Christman here. What? What the hell did you kill him for? Goddamn trigger-happy sons-of-bitches. All right. He's dead and the headquarters are secured. Are the fighters returning to base? Okay."

Christman hung up, his craggy face gray with fatigue. "They killed Jameson."

Cooley shrugged. "Have they got the Continental Air Defense Command and headquarters secured?"

"Yes," Christman said. "Jameson and his staff stood them off with sidearms for twenty minutes. But they've finally taken over. The fighters are coming back in." Christman turned grimly to Doyle. "There are three thousand dead airborne troops out there because of you. The fighters got six C-5s. I will personally order your execution when this is over."

Cooley held up a big hand. "Take it easy, Bill. What does Josh want? Why did he send you?"

Skille cleared his throat and raised his voice to make himself heard over the noise in the big room. "He wants to avoid a civil war if he can help it, Ralph. He thinks what you've done will tear the country apart unless we reach some sort of compromise." Skille nodded to the phone. "That governor out in Missouri is only one of many who aren't going to take this lying down. There will be blood in the streets, and it could lead to a real civil war. God knows what our enemies overseas will do when they see us tearing ourselves apart."

"Not if he just surrenders to us now," Cooley said.

"He won't do that. If you force him to, he'll fight."

"With what?" Christman interjected.

"The First Marine Division," Doyle said.

"Stein's dead. Means is in command," Christman said. "He's our man."

"Have you talked to him lately?" Doyle asked.

Christman snapped out a command to one of the communicators and turned back.

"Okay," Cooley said. "Let's hear what Josh proposes. I don't think there's a chance we'll go along, but it can't hurt to listen."

Skille took a breath, his pale, thin face tense with strain. "It's fairly simple. You've made your point. The president is dead. His policies are going to die with him and that's what interests you. Josh proposes to announce to the nation that the patriotic purposes of your action have been achieved and that, in the name of legality, you're turning the country back to him."

Cooley grinned. "Just like that? And what do we get out of it?"

"Full pardons. Josh promises that there will be no recriminations or prosecutions."

"Full pardons, Well, I'll be goddamned. Hear that, Bill? That's beautiful. Here we take over the fucking country, control all the sources of power and communications, and he's got nothing. Absolutely nothing, and he offers us pardons."

"Admiral Christman." The communicator looked puzzled. "I cannot reach Camp LeJeune. Nobody's answering."

"Have you tried Means's office?"

"Yes, sir. The radio doesn't answer, and I get a busy signal from the telephone switchboard."

"What about downstairs? They've got a special line from the command center, haven't they?"

"Yes, sir, but it was knocked out in the fighting. They're still trying to get the special channel operational."

Christman turned to Doyle. "So Means couldn't bring it off? I didn't think he would. Most of the marines were Stein's handpicked men. There is still nothing you can do with one division. Especially since they don't have any air transport."

"It's a full combat division, Admiral," Doyle said. "And it's concentrated in small detachments. The president will be able to rally other units from LeJeune. It won't take him long. If we're not careful we're going to have a civil war on our hands. The armed forces will be turned into a shambles and leave the country defenseless before the very forces you're so afraid of."

"The nukes haven't been touched," Cooley said. "They are our insurance, not a bunch of dogfaces. No foreign power would move against us as long as our nuclear deterrent is intact."

Doyle shrugged. "I hope you're right."

Cooley was drumming on the president's big desk with the long ivory letter opener which had been a present from the president of Uganda. "Maybe we ought to have a meeting with the committee, Bill. The deal he's offering is useless to us. But there might be a role for Josh in this after all."

Christman turned to the young communicator who was still trying to raise Camp LeJeune. "How long will it take to get the committee together on a conference line?"

"Five minutes, sir."

"Get started."

"We are a committee of twelve. Within five minutes we'll have a conference call through uniting a majority." He smiled. "We operate on democratic lines. I'll present Josh's proposal to them. And also one I'm developing in my own mind. So if you'll be good enough to wait in the outer office until we're finished I'll call you."

233

* * *

"Jesus Christ, Jake, you ought to see it. There's hundreds of them smeared across the road like ketchup. He must of tried to put it down on the interstate. Looks like he hit maybe ten cars before he plowed into the goddamn semi. Jesus."

"I can't hear you too good, Hank. Static is terrible. We're contacting every funeral home within a hundred miles. The governor is calling out the national guard to give you a hand. I've got cars beginning to block off access to the interstate at both ends. We'll route along State 304 but you're gonna have a big pileup at both ends of the crash site for an hour or so from the cars that have already got through."

"Yeah. They're backed up for a mile now, more coming every minute. I'll rip up the divider and get 'em headed toward the road block as soon as I can find some farmer with a 'dozer big enough to do it. Hold it."

"Hank, get a fucking lane open for the ambulances and hearses. We're gonna have every undertaker in the state here within an hour. How many men have you got on the scene, Hank?"

"About fifteen so far. We've emptied every state patrol barracks in this sector and the others are mobilizing. Also, I've got about half a dozen of the sheriff's men and some of the constables from these little towns."

"You know what happened? I mean how come he came down there?"

"No. But somebody at the airport here says one of the commercial flights in the same area saw a fighter plane firing at him."

"Jesus Christ. You think maybe we're in a war?"

"Hell, Jake, how could an enemy fighter get over East Tennessee? Naw. I think he had engine trouble or something or maybe the pilot was drunk. Oh, Christ."

"What's the matter? The fucking static is terrible."

"Nothing. They just brought a head in without a body. Listen, Jake, I gotta get this goddamn mess of shit organized. Tell the national guard not to come tromping in here with tanks or anything. We got bodies spread out on either side of the road for a couple of miles."

"They got the fire under control?"

"Yeah. They're laying 'em out on the highway. Looks like pieces of steak charred on a grill."

"Jesus."

"Yeah. You know what, Jake?"

"What?"

"They all look like they're praying. The burned ones. Doc says their ligaments in the elbows tightened with the fire, and they're laying their hands up in the air like they was praying."

CHAPTER FOURTEEN

General Tom Means surveyed the main mess hall of the First Brigade. Every field grade officer and above who could be located was there. He cleared his throat and tapped the microphone. "Everybody hear me?"

A murmur of assent floated through the building. As he started to speak one of his aides moved through the crowd to his side. "We've secured all the armories except the military police barracks. The commander has refused to hand over his weapons. He says he wants a personal order from either his colonel or from you."

"Where's the commander?"

The young officer surveyed the crowd. "Colonel McNeil. Over there by the coffee machine with the guy from the Judge Advocate General's office. The one with the walkie talkie."

Means nodded. "All right. Are the exits secured?"

"Yes, sir. We've only got about fifteen men. But it ought to be enough. Nobody else is armed," the young officer said, surveying the mass of men in the mess hall.

"All right, gentlemen. I think we can start. Some of you may have an idea of what's going on. Others not. So I'll explain. As most of you know, the armed services and a good many civilians in the country have been greatly disturbed by the actions of the present administration in the field of national defense. The cut in our budget and the consequent reduction in armaments and manpower has been drastic. The present budget will mean a cut of almost thirty percent in our effective defense forces and this in a world which becomes more dangerous every day.

"In order to counter this, an organization was formed some months ago. It is composed of some of the highest ranking military men in the country, headed by Admiral William Christman, and some of the best known of the nation's civilians. It's called the Committee for the Preservation of the Republic. Tonight, about two hours ago, this committee assumed effective power in the nation under the command of Mr. Ralph Cooley, chairman of the board of the Federated Steel Corporation, and Admiral Christman."

Means stopped at the sudden hum of conversation which began throughout the room, letting it subside.

"The Eighty-Second and One Hundred and First Airborne Divisions have dispersed across the country and are now in effective control of the thirty largest cities. Virtually every military installation in the nation is under the committee's command. Of all the first line commanders in the armed forces contacted by the committee, only General Stein refused to participate. As a result he has been put under arrest and I am now in command of the division. I realize that there are some among you who will not be in agreement with what we've done. I respect your scruples and on the part of the committee I have been authorized to offer you retirement immediately at a pension commensurate with your present rank and length of service."

He paused. It was the crucial moment. If there was no protest, they would all follow him. That was the military mind.

"General." The voice came from the back of the mess hall, but it carried as if amplified in the enclosed space.

"It's the goddamn lawyer from the JAG office."

Means nodded in the direction of the speaker. "Get somebody to collar that military police commander. He's giving orders by radio."

The young officer nodded and began to shoulder his way through the crowd.

"Yes, Colonel," Means said, turning back and looking across the crowded room.

"General. What you are proposing is treason. Any man in this room who takes part in a military uprising is subject to a general court-martial and risks the death penalty if convicted. You're asking these men to participate in an armed uprising against their president and their country in violation of the oath they took when they became officers."

"The president is dead," Means said. "The only effective government of the country is the Committee for the Preservation of the Republic. I'm not here tonight to debate with you. I'm in command of this division. All I want from you is an answer."

The young officer had reached the commander of the military police and held out his hand for the walkie talkie. Means watched without being able to understand their angry voices. Suddenly, outside the mess hall, a submachine gun chattered, then another. The body of the young marine officer collapsed through one of the mess hall doors, his green camouflage tunic soaked with blood.

"Christ, let's get the fuck out of here," one of the officers in front of him shouted.

Cooley leaned back in the big leather chair donated to the president by the Veterans of Foreign Wars. "Okay, Skille. The committee is willing to consider Harrington's proposition. We'll give him a safe conduct to come over to negotiate."

"Safe conduct?" Skille stared at him and laughed hysterically. "You mean your word of honor?"

Cooley grinned. "That's right. Mine and Bill Christman's. If we can't agree, he'll be free to go."

Doyle interrupted Skille's protest. "We'll accept Admiral Christman's word. Go get him, Matt."

Colonel Juan Cuervo surveyed the city map with satisfaction. Five hundred thousand people were out there drinking everything from skull-buster to eggnog made with the finest French brandy, celebrating Christmas Eve with all the religious fervor of an Alcoholics Anonymous convention in a distillery. And not more than a dozen realized that he and his five hundred men had taken command of the city without firing a shot. It just showed what good planning and meticulous staff work could do.

The police station had been a little hairy. He'd had maybe two dozen of the lieutenants and sergeants with him, but the chief and most of the senior brass had refused the committee's advances. So he'd had to take over. It hadn't really been all that difficult. He'd encircled the building with a company. His inside men had immobilized communications for about five minutes before he gave the order to storm the building. The cops had just stood there with their mouths hanging open when they came busting in. Once they had the radio room working for them, it was all over. The word had gone out that martial law had been declared and the police were to take orders from the army.

The chief had been taken at his home and was being held incommunicado along with four of his top captains. The others had finally agreed to go along. The fire department had been even easier. A new chief, their man, had been brought in two weeks before and he'd simply called his men and given the right orders.

At the waterworks and the gas and light company there hadn't been a hitch. Twenty men had moved in and taken over. The guards, armed with revolvers and shotguns, had surrendered immediately when they saw his men's firepower.

The three television stations had refused to go off the air at first. But they'd put a stop to that. Good staff work was the key again. They'd cut the power. Same with the radio stations. His men were bringing in the night news staffs and the news editor of the morning paper for a conference. It made it easier that the biggest television station and both the morning and afternoon papers were owned by the same company. Its president was in on the operation. Within a couple of hours they should have at least one station back on the air to transmit orders to the populace and the morning papers' first editions would carry similar instructions.

He'd get his star for this operation. No question about that. Especially since so many simple-minded assholes at the Pentagon had refused to go along.

Suzanne Wilson glanced up from the mass of copy on the anchor desk of the Federal Broadcasting Company studio in Washington and frowned. Outside the glassed-in enclosure of the newsroom a dozen heavily armed paratroopers had taken up their stations. A young captain was arguing with the program's producer, Milton Bagen. As she watched, the officer shrugged his shoulders at the gesticulating Bagen and made a quick, chopping motion with his arm. Two of his men moved to the glass door, always locked a few minutes before the broadcast, and methodically demolished it with their rifle butts. The captain reached through, flipped the lock and entered.

"I'd like your attention, please," he said, young face glistening with a film of perspiration. "The government of the United States has been taken over by a group of patriotic citizens organized as the Committee for the Preservation of the Republic. The army, navy, and air force are cooperating with this committee. All organs of government have been secured by us, and resistance is futile. My men and I have orders to take over this network and close it down temporarily. You are to remain where you are under my orders until one of our media specialists can get here and take charge."

"It's some goddamn Christmas Eve joke," one of the newswriters, already a little tight, said, beginning to laugh. "It's that goddamn soap peddler executive producer's idea of a joke. Hey, kid, lemme see your toy gun." The writer stood up and reached for the submachine gun. As he did so, a paratrooper stepped forward with an automatic carbine at port arms and slammed the butt into his head, the metal edge ripping a wide gash at the hairline, draping the writer across a typewriter like a broken doll.

Ralph Cooley was standing behind the presidential desk when they came into the Oval Office. Big, muscular arms bulged where he had rolled his sleeves up above the elbow. Coffee stained the expensive silk tie extending over his bulging belly. He motioned them toward the circular coffee table made from one slice of giant redwood. "Hello, Josh. Glad you could come," he said, grinning. "Let's get some coffee and see where we are."

Harrington moved across the room and took the large overstuffed chair customarily reserved for the president, cutting Cooley off. The fat man grinned and dropped on the sofa. "I've discussed the problem of the vice-presidency with my associates, Josh, and they have decided to give me carte blanche in dealing with you."

"The presidency, Cooley. The presidency. You keep forgetting that the chief justice has sworn me in and that I am legally president of this country, whereas you and your associates are criminal usurpers."

"Maybe so, Josh. But we've got the guns, and the ones with the guns usually run things. So I suggest we get down off this lofty legal plane into the mud of reality. We control the country. You control nothing. So the question is what have you got to negotiate with?"

"Legitimacy," Harrington said. "Legality. The confidence of the electorate. You're without a shred of any of these. How the hell do you expect to control two hundred and fifty million people without it? They'll rise up and massacre you."

"Soviet revolutionary theory indicates that a small band of ruthless men can overpower an amorphous mass if they possess the intelligence and the will. We have both, as I think we've proved. There are some bodies lying around out there. And more across the country. If there is resistance there will be a hell of a lot more. It won't take people long to get the message."

"Christ, Cooley. You're a little crazy. How'd you get Bill Christman to go along with something as nutty as this is?"

"Go along?" Cooley threw back his massive head and laughed, a roar coming out of the meaty folds of his throat.

"Hell, he was eager. So were the others. You aren't living in the real world, Josh. That bloodless intellectual automaton who was president had lost all sympathy. People are scared, Josh. They are without jobs, money, and confidence. And they are terrified we will soon be defenseless in the face of our enemies. That's what this is all about. I assure you that once we are able to explain the situation to the nation," he glanced at his watch, "in about an hour, we'll have an enthusiastic populace behind us. Make no mistake about it."

"So you don't need me?"

"No, Josh, we don't need you. However, we're interested in bringing this off with the least loss of life and the least bitterness possible. We'd like to hold the country together, not tear it apart. And you could play a part in this."

"How?"

"By backing the coup. By making a public statement supporting us and our aims."

"Why would I do that?" Harrington said, controlling his surprise.

Cooley grinned. "Because you don't have any choice, Josh. That's why."

"And what's in it for him?" Matt Skille broke in. It was too good to be true. They were taking the bait on their own.

"In it?" Cooley looked puzzled. Then he laughed again, spilled a few more drops of coffee on his tie. "Sorry, gentlemen, I was making the common mistake of attributing to my opponents the same noble motives which drive me. But, of course, there would have to be something in it for you, Josh. What did you have in mind?"

The president shot a venomous glance at his aide, who cringed. "Cooley, you're not a fool. And if you didn't need me you wouldn't be sitting here talking when you've got a country to run. So let's cut the crap. I don't condone what you've done, and I don't agree with your motives. But it's done, and we've got to save the country. We can't afford a civil war. Our enemies would be on us like jackals if we began to fight among ourselves."

"Exactly our sentiments, Josh. What do you propose?"

"I propose that you turn the country over to me. Retire from the field. Send all the units back to their barracks. Go home. In return, I will give you my word that there will be no prosecutions, no punishment. Nothing. A complete pardon for everybody."

Cooley stared at him, momentarily unable to speak. "Well, I'll just be damned. One thing I've got to hand you, Harrington. You've got the balls of a brass monkey. Just hand it over? Like that? And go home? Mister, you have just got to be kidding."

Harrington shook his head. "Think what your alternative is going to be. Within twelve hours, people are going to wake up and find a bunch of superannuated businessmen and tin soldiers running their country. And they're not going to like it. There are a hundred million guns registered in this country and God knows how many more illegal ones. You're going to find yourself with a country in arms at your throat. There will be a spontaneous national rebellion against you and it will overwhelm you. You'll wind up hanging by your heels like Mussolini."

"Highly romantic, Josh. There may be a few fools

who'll take to the woods. But it's Christmas Eve and cold as a well-digger's ass out there. They'll come on home soon enough. As for rebellion, there aren't many people with the stomach for it. That's one thing we found out over the past few months." He shook his head. "No. You're dreaming, Josh." He paused, sipping from a coffee mug embossed with the presidential seal. "However, we would like to have you on our side. We might even be willing to go so far as to let you become president in name in order to avoid any problems."

"You mean to be figurehead?" Harrington's voice was deep with sarcasm.

"In effect. You'd be one of the group running the country. We're not politicians and we're going to need men like you, certainly in the beginning. It would have the advantage of holding the cabinet together and keeping the administration functioning. We recognize the danger that things may come apart in the beginning, although we're banking on the professional bureaucracy to keep them running normally. They won't risk their pensions," he said drily. "Still, if we could maintain the fiction of continuing government legitimacy it would be a big help. Each cabinet officer would have one of our men at his elbow calling the shots, of course."

"Like in the communist countries where the party men really run things," Skille said bitterly.

"That's right," Cooley said. "Not a bad analogy at all. What about it, Josh? It's the patriotic thing to do."

Harrington glanced across at Doyle, who nodded.

Cooley watched the exchange with a smile. "Well, General Doyle. Our handsome proletarian national hero. You seem to occupy a position of trust with our new president. And I also get the feeling that you aren't totally at one with the committee's aims, am I right?"

Doyle shrugged. "I'm a soldier, Mr. Cooley. I follow orders."

"Admirable attitude, General. I am now about to give you one. I want that marine detachment you ordered up here from LeJeune located and immobilized. Do you understand?" As he spoke, the sounds of small arms fire penetrated the Oval Office windows.

"Never mind the marines, Ralph," Harrington said. "I think we just might have us a deal."

Cooley stared at him, his blue eyes like light-colored ball bearings in the suety mound of his face. "You mean that, Josh? You'll accept the role of a figurehead?"

"Not entirely. I recognize you've got the power. But I don't think you can run the country. I'm going to have to be more than a puppet. But I suspect that our aims are not that far apart. You want a strong national defense and the protection of the free enterprise system, I assume. Well, I can buy both of those."

"Good, Josh, I was hoping you'd agree to something like this," Cooley said, his hoarse voice warm with emotion and relief. "You know, I think you might wind up being president after all when this is all over. Not right away, but once we've got the system restructured in such a way that we can be sure that no more kooks like this last one are going to come to power."

Harrington cleared his throat. "I think we ought to get this out to the people as soon as possible, to avoid any chaos or misunderstanding. You might not believe in a revolution in the streets but I'm not so sure. Also we want the Soviets and the Chinese to know that we're not helpless."

Cooley nodded. "Question is what's the best method of doing it?"

"Television," Matt Skille said. "The president ought to go on television. The sooner the better."

Cooley nodded. "Yes. That probably is the best way. Normal programming should begin again tomorrow morning. We could probably arrange for a broadcast about mid-day on Christmas. That would get you a maximum audience."

Harrington shook his head. "No. I don't think that will do it."

"It's not ideal," Cooley agreed. "We need something more dramatic."

"What we need is a joint session of Congress. I'll go before them and explain what's happened. And I think the members of this junta ought to be with me."

"Committee, Josh. Committee. We're not some banana republic in Central America," Cooley said, voice sharp with irritation.

"Committee then. I think its members ought to be there with me. I'll explain what happened, who is responsible, and that I have agreed to head a new provisional government until new elections can be called. Then I'll ask Congress to pass a law by acclamation giving us powers to govern by decree for a year."

Cooley stared at him, a slow grin spreading across his fat face. "Well, now, Josh. That's a goddamn creative idea. I must admit it hadn't occurred to any of us how we were going to handle Congress. You know, you might just earn your pay after all."

A young paratrooper captain came into the Oval Office unannounced. "Mr. Cooley, Admiral Christman would like to see you in the war room."

"What's up, son?"

"The governor of Illinois is mobilizing the national guard. He's given our people in Chicago six hours to surrender. The police there have barricaded themselves

247

in their headquarters building. Looks as if we're going to have to blast them out."

Doyle moved down the White House driveway, heels crunching into the hardening snow, waiting for somebody to stop him. He had slipped out a side door of the Oval Office when Cooley left and strolled past the guards out the front door. There was virtually no security control as messengers and officers raced in and out of the makeshift command posts in a scene of total confusion.

The hook was in. The plan should work, but it was going to take split-second timing. He walked through the gate, returning the salutes of the airborne troops. The general's stars were enough to get him through the barricades shutting off Pennsylvania Avenue.

He headed for the Smithsonian, lengthening his stride as he passed the lounging troops in front of the Treasury building.

He had gone over the chances of a surprise attack on the White House by the marine company but had rejected it immediately. There were close to five hundred airborne troops encircling the mansion grounds. Half a dozen light tanks and some recoilless artillery pieces were already emplaced along with a dozen light machine gun teams. The marines would have been slaughtered by superior fire power before they got beyond the fence. They would have to go with the original plan. Which gave them maybe one chance in three. Doyle hailed a taxi as he passed the rear of the Treasury building.

"Jesus, some Christmas Eve, huh, General?" the driver, a sallow-faced man in a heavy parka, said as he climbed in.

"Smithsonian Main Building. Yeah. Pretty cold."

"Cold? Shit, I'm talking about the coup." He pronounced it coop. "You in on it, General?"

"No."

"That's good. 'Cause the ones who are are gonna get their asses shot off."

"I hope you are right," Doyle muttered.

"Huh? Oh yeah. Well, they can't get away with it. The country's not gonna put up with it. The boys and me, we wuz talkin'. Something don't happen by tomorrow, we're gonna get out the old rifles and start potting us some soldiers. You better get out of that uniform, General, if you're not in on it. It ain't gonna be healthy to be walking around in one."

"Not everybody in the army is in on the coup," Doyle said, suddenly very weary.

"Yeah. Well, ain't gonna have time to go and ask, polite like. Here you go, General. Place looks deserted. That's three-fifty."

Doyle fumbled for the money, scanning the building. He had told Haines to get everybody under cover and keep them there. The guard post had disappeared and all vehicles were out of sight.

"Better remember what I told you, General. Get rid of the uniform and keep your head down."

The marine was behind him, forty-five jammed in his ear, as he turned the corner. "I'd like to see Major Haines."

"Over here, sir." The major appeared and waved the sentry back to his post. "I've got everything under cover."

Doyle nodded, moving with the marine into a small tent with a primus stove, a folding cot, and a rickety card table which served as his command post. "Listen, Haines. They've bought it."

The major whistled. "You mean they're going to let him address Congress?"

"Yes. Air force planes are heading out to pick up the members right now. The address is scheduled for noon tomorrow. You sure you know what to do?"

Haines nodded. "I've been working on the logistics ever since you left. Four of my officers are reconnoitering the Capitol grounds right now. They report that there are less than twenty men on guard. The relief goes on at six A.M. We should be able to bring it off with no problem. There's so much confusion nobody knows what's going on. You could get away with almost anything."

"What about LeJeune?"

"There's been some fighting. Colonel Wilson, who's an artillery man, seems to be in command. You want me to try to raise him?"

"Yes."

Haines led him to the communication tent where a young sergeant sat at a compact radio transmitter receiver.

"What's going on, son?" Doyle asked.

"They definitely killed General Means, sir. Him and about ten other officers. There was some sort of battle in the mess hall between the military police and the general."

"Who's in command?"

"A bird colonel, sir. Name's Wilson. Should I get him?"

The marine turned back to the radio and in a few seconds a harsh voice came over.

"What the fuck do you want, Haines? I'm busy, goddamn you. We just had a mutiny down here. Stein and Means are dead."

Doyle took the microphone and identified himself.

250

"Colonel, how long would it take you to get the 5000 men in trucks and on their way? Fully armed, live ammo."

"Well, General, with luck about four hours. Another eight to get there."

"Then move out. Get them going piecemeal. You'll get specific orders en route. Stay in radio contact with this command post."

"On whose authority, General?"

"The same one you used to execute General Means. I'm President Harrington's special representative. You better start moving, Colonel."

"I'm going to be at this number," Doyle said, handing the major a card with Maria Vicente's telephone number. "It'll be my command post. We've got to split up so we can't all go into the bag at once. If you have any problem call me there. I've got to get moving. Matt Skille will be calling me there any minute. Have you got any non-military transport?"

Haines smiled. "The boys liberated a couple of museum cars."

"Let me have one."

Doyle drove through the almost deserted streets of the capital, its brilliant Christmas decorations winking through the snow which had once again begun to fall in a heavy, crystal blanket. There were no patrols on the streets although an occasional police car passed, its red light blinking. If the plan was working, Police Chief Tubman would have begun to withdraw his loyal men from the streets and concentrate them for tomorrow's operation. The town was, to all intents and purposes, in the hands of the insurgents.

He parked in front of the massive Watergate complex and identified himself to the armed guard patrolling the entrance. Maria's voice came over the intercom, heavy with sleep.

"General Doyle? Well, tell General Doyle he's a little late for dinner and that he can bugger off."

Doyle took the phone from the guard. "Maria. Listen, this is serious. I've got to see you."

"Yes. Well, General, it's serious when you stand me up on Christmas Eve without even the grace to call. In words of one syllable, Steve, screw off."

"The president's dead," Doyle said into the phone, glancing at his watch. Skille's call would be due any minute. He might not get more than one chance.

"What?"

"He's dead. Haven't you been listening to the news?"

"There wasn't any. Something is fouled up at the TV stations. All I get is a test pattern."

"Maria, will you for Christ's sake tell this guy to let me up?"

She met him at the door. "If you're pulling some sort of sophomoric joke, Steve," she said, holding an ancient blue robe tight around her.

Doyle moved past her into the apartment. "Has Skille called?"

"Skille." Her eyes were heavy with sleep.

"The vice-president's PR man."

"That gutless creep. No. Should he have?"

"Any minute. Josh Harrington is president."

"Josh Harrington? That coarse reactionary hillbilly? Oh, no. Steve, you weren't kidding?"

"No." He told her briefly what had happened and what they were planning.

"It won't work, Steve. They'll have the Capitol packed with their own men. You'll never get away with it."

"It's the only chance we've got. We have to take it

away from them before they get themselves organized. Right now everything is confused. Nobody knows where anybody stands. A lot of people will be waiting to jump one way or another tomorrow at noon, depending on who they think is going to win." The telephone chimed and Steve moved for it quickly.

"Yes."

"Steve? Matt."

"How'd you get a phone?"

"I'm in my office. The damned fools. They control the switchboard but nobody realized we almost all have direct lines. But they will soon. It's chaos here right now, Steve, but that goddamn Cooley is no dummy. He's getting it under control fast. We've got to move quickly. Otherwise he's going to lock off every option we've got. You better warn LeJeune. They're concentrating a couple of combat teams: Sometime tomorrow they'll move in to neutralize the First Division."

"They'll be too late, Matt. Where's Harrington?"

"Upstairs trying to calm down the president's wife. She's in hysterics. I'm writing his speech. Two of them. One for Cooley to look at and one that he'll actually give. They've mobilized the air force to bring in Congress. There ought to be about three hundred and fifty congressmen and maybe three-quarters of the Senate. It's going to work, Steve." Skille's voice was cracking with excitement.

"Okay. Haines knows what he's got to do. With a little help from the chief's men and some of Harlan's FBI he may be able to pull it off. Also, five thousand men of the First Marine will begin moving in a few hours."

"I've got to get off, Steve," Skille said, hurriedly hanging up.

Maria Vicente put her head in her hands and began

to weep. Doyle moved to her side and slipped an arm around her shoulders, pulling her toward him. "Oh, Jesus, Steve. They can't have killed him. All he was trying to do was help people. Why did they have to kill him?"

"It was an accident."

Her head snapped up. "An accident? You mean the way it was done was an accident. But nobody in that bunch would have hesitated, would they, Steve? I mean that soldier who killed him knew he was doing what they wanted him to do?"

Doyle shrugged.

"Who are they, Steve? What kind of monsters would do it?"

Doyle rubbed a hand across his jaw, feeling the wire-like stubble of his beard, suddenly very tired. "They're not monsters, Maria. They're ordinary men. Most of them anyway. They undoubtedly think what they're doing is for the good of their country. I doubt if many of them have much personal ambition. Cooley, maybe. But not the military and probably not the businessmen and police and the others who are in on it. They saw your saintly president tearing the country apart, disarming it in the face of its enemies, and turning it toward socialism."

"Oh, for God's sake, Steve," Maria said impatiently, digging her knuckles into her eyes and drying her tears. "That's total bullshit."

Doyle shrugged, fatigue and the sudden let-up of tension leaving him drained of energy and will. "You wouldn't have a beer and a sandwich by any chance? And maybe a razor."

"Jesus, Steve, forgive me." She put her arms around his neck and rubbed her cheek against the stubble on his chin. "I might even think of something else for the warrior home from the wars."

*　*　*

Major Mason Pruitt stood at attention in front of the big presidential desk first used by President Chester A. Arthur. It had been made from the timbers of a British ship of the line, the *Courageous*, which foundered off Cape Hatteras at the end of the War of 1812.

"Pruitt, you've caused us one hell of a problem. You know that?"

The officer shrugged, meeting Cooley's gaze. "If I hadn't killed him, he might have turned those dogfaces on me. He was the president. Out there talking to a bunch of blacks and Chicanos who didn't know what the hell they were supposed to be doing. I didn't have any choice. You better be damn glad I burned him. Otherwise we'd all be in the slammer or dead."

Cooley nodded. "All right, Pruitt. I accept that. You may well not have had any choice. But I'm about to give you another assignment, and this time I want that gun of yours not only out of sight but out of action."

The officer said nothing, standing silently in the big office, now crammed with desks and communications equipment, heavy cables coiled across the floor in webs.

"Tomorrow at twelve noon Vice-President Harrington," Cooley stopped and corrected himself, "sorry, President Harrington, is going to address a joint session of Congress. He's going to tell them that he accepts our action and that he has joined us."

Pruitt frowned. "How do you know he won't double-cross you?"

Cooley's voice hardened. "Major, I know he won't doublecross me because I've got control. You understand? Harrington has agreed to be our puppet. Now, I want this to look genuine. Get over to the Capitol and check the ground. Figure out how many of your men you'll need to keep things in hand. An absolute minimum. We own the city now. The police are ours. Our men are in every key installation. There is no point in packing the Capitol with soldiers. We want an image as normal as possible. This program is going all over the United States on every television channel. It'll be the biggest audience since they showed the unexpurgated version of *Hair* in 1980. Now, Pruitt, I want you there but I want it done with discretion. No goddamn overwhelming presence. Just enough to do the job."

"Yes, sir." The soldier's voice was edged with sarcasm.

"And you use violence only under direct orders from me or Admiral Christman. Is that clear?" Cooley watched him leave, a compact mass of muscle and menace. Men like Pruitt were essential, of course. Without their amoral violence no operation like this would succeed. But once it was over they had to be caged or eliminated. Cooley made a cryptic note on a looseleaf note pad.

"Governor of Illinois on the line, sir," one of the communicators said.

"Hello, Bob. Cooley here. Listen, Bob, what's this I hear about you mobilizing the guard to move on our people in Chicago?"

Cooley listened briefly.

"Listen to me, Bob. Everything you say may be right. We may well be a bunch of murderous traitors. But you'd better take a hard look at the power situation before you take us on. We've got the entire armed services behind us. You understand that? Those pitiful weekend soldiers of yours are going up against some of the best trained troops in the world. Do you really want to be responsible for their slaughter?"

Cooley listened again.

"All right, Bob. You're right. At the moment we've

256

got less than a thousand men in Chicago. But we can put twenty in within a few hours if you force us to. As for planes, what have you got? Twenty old trainers? They'd last about five minutes against a squadron of F-16Is. Now get it straight, Bob. You'll never get to Chicago. We'll blow your men right off the highway."

Cooley listened, meaty face congested with irritation.

"You're not thinking, Bob. Illinois isn't guerrilla country to begin with. It wouldn't take long to winkle your men out of wherever they hole up. Get your head straight. It won't work. Especially not after noon tomorrow when Harrington goes on TV."

Cooley smiled now. "Yeah. That's right, Bob. He's decided to come with us. Keep the country from coming apart. Now, can I count on you not to do anything foolish?"

Cooley frowned. "He's asleep. I'll have him talk to you tomorrow just after the speech. Can we count on you until then?" Cooley listened and grinned. "Okay. That'll do it. Two P.M. tomorrow. You won't regret it."

Cooley hung up as one of the communicators called out. "Sir. The Denver police have refused to surrender. They're barricaded in their headquarters. I've got Colonel Nelson here on the line."

"Where's Christman?"

The big admiral came in and took the phone from the communicator. "Nelson? What's going on?" He listened for half a minute, glanced at Cooley and spoke into the phone. "Use your recoilless rifles. Blow a hole in it and dig them out. We can't have a battle going on in the center of the city all night. Get it done, Nelson. Don't fool around."

"It's getting a little out of hand, Bill," Cooley said, lighting a short black Montecristo, biting off the end.

Christman shrugged, his face gray with tension and

257

fatigue. "No military operation is ever clean and clear, Ralph. Killing people is a messy business, and one you can't control like those factories of yours. So far we've lost remarkably few people. With Harrington willing to make that broadcast, we should consolidate sometime tomorrow. Whatever happened to Steve Doyle? I thought you had him here?"

"We did. He just walked out. With those general's stars nobody thought to stop him," Cooley said. "But what can he do? He's by himself. Harrington is in our hands."

"He's a dangerous man, Cooley. I want him out of action," Christman said.

"Then put somebody on it."

"I've got other things on my mind. How many planes did that maniac in the Air Defense command shoot down?"

"Six."

"Six. Sweet mother of Jesus," Cooley breathed. "Three thousand men dead for nothing."

"We've managed to get other units airborne. All the targets are being hit. We should have everything under control by morning. According to plan."

"Within a few hours it won't matter. We'll have our people in command of every combat unit in the armed forces. What about the governors? Have you gotten through?"

Cooley consulted a list. "About half still to go. But with Josh agreeing to go along with us, they won't be a problem. Anyway, what can they do? Start a civil war? Once that speech of his has gone out over radio and television, we're in."

"You'd better be right, Ralph," Christman said. "Without him I'm not sure we can bring it off. The country's too damned big. There are too many threads of power we haven't been able to tie up."

Cooley stood up, agile despite his bulk, and moved around the table. "We couldn't do anything else, Bill. If we hadn't moved he would have taken our country away from us. Don't weaken now."

CHAPTER FIFTEEN

Maria shook him gently.

Doyle came awake the way his grandfather had taught him: unmoving, eyes closed, waiting until consciousness was complete. Maria was lying beside him propped on an elbow, the strap of her slip down over her arm, revealing one small breast.

"Rather provocative staging, that," he said in a mock British accent.

"Yes, Chauncey, the gardener says the same thing," Maria mimicked back.

Doyle grinned and slipped an arm around her waist, pulling her down on top of him, feeling the hard tip of her breast against his chest. "What time is it?"

"Seven-thirty. When do you have to be there?"

"Harrington is scheduled to speak at noon. Haines and Chief Tubman will already have their men in place. There's nothing much to do but wait," he said, letting his hand move down across the smooth silk to the small of her back.

"Stop it," Maria said automatically, moving her body

to insert one of her legs between his. "What do you think will happen?"

"I don't know. It's a long shot. They're still terribly disorganized. Nobody knows anybody else or who is in command. I'm banking on that. Confusion is our biggest asset."

"You're worried about that man who used to work for you, aren't you?"

"Pruitt? Yes. He's an animal. He can smell danger. But they'll have to put him on a leash. And he probably won't go up to the Capitol before the president leaves the White House. By then it will be too late."

"What if it doesn't work?"

Doyle's hand had now reached the smoothly rounded curve of her behind which twitched involuntarily at his touch.

"A woman's buttocks, General, are not an erogenous zone. They're composed of layers of fat with virtually no sensitive nerve endings."

Doyle moved quickly, locking her legs between his, pulling her quickly to the right and as she reacted by drawing back, turning her smoothly on her back. "What is it that black leader said about the position of women in his movement? Prone?"

Maria giggled. "And a cry rose out of the crowd: 'Is that the movement's ideological position or the speaker's personal preference?' " Her arms encircled his neck. "Goddamn it, General, I'm getting used to you. I'd take badly to your winding up on a marble slab."

She reacted instantly to the touch of his hand, opening her legs and murmuring, "To hell with this love-making. Let's fuck."

The snow had stopped falling, leaving a two-inch layer on the Capitol grounds. Spotlights highlighted the building and reflected off its windows, and somewhere in the darkness a military radio crackled. The Five Hundred Forty-First Ranger combat team which had taken over the building without firing a shot the night before from a stunned Capitol police force was mustered in front of the massive building. At an order they broke ranks at a trot and moved toward the line of trucks pulled up in the parking spaces reserved for members of the Senate.

As they moved out, fifty city policemen armed with riot guns entered the building, spreading out through its maze of corridors. Four dressed in heavy blue overcoats took up guard duty at the main entrance. It was four A.M.

Major Mason Pruitt watched the changeover, frowning. The cops were useless, but he'd have his own men in place before noon. He climbed into his jeep and moved off into the darkness.

In the shadows of the Supreme Court Building across First Street, Washington Police Chief Jefferson Tubman and Marine Major George Haines watched the scene. As Pruitt's jeep disappeared down the hill, Haines raised an arm vertically and dropped it. Shadowy figures moved quickly from concealment at each end of the huge building and converged on the main entrance. One policeman turned as a camouflaged figure appeared at a dead run and lifted the riot gun in a quick clumsy gesture. The marine's gun butt caught him on the jaw as he sought to free a gloved hand and sent him flying in a limp heap, his cap rolling grotesquely in the snow. The other three surrendered without a move and their places were taken by four other policemen as the marines entered the building, covering each other, keeping to the walls and spreading out.

Police cars now began to converge on the big building as Chief Tubman spoke into a hand mike. Within minutes the parking lot had disgorged more than a hundred men in blue police uniforms, most of them black.

A quick spatter of gunfire came from within the building and died quickly at the answering burp of the marines' automatic weapons. A voice came through the small radio attached to webbing on the marine major's chest. "Capitol building secured, sir."

"Any casualties?"

"Negative. Two hostiles dead, four wounded. We're bringing them out. You can send in the replacement police any time, Major."

Haines nodded to Tubman, who moved across First Street and led his men into the building. The police cars moved out singly, breaking off in different directions as they left the grounds, and within minutes the area was deserted except for the four policemen at the Capitol entrance, beating their hands and stamping their feet.

Cooley slept, his big head on top of a pile of papers on the massive desk. Around him the room was quiet except for the chatter of half a dozen telex machines. Paper cups bearing the dregs of coffee covered the tables and ashtrays overflowed with butts. A brown stain spread across the center of the great seal of the presidency on the rug which covered the Oval Office floor. The beefy mass of a communications sergeant was sprawled on the light yellow sofa.

A telephone operator's head snapped up as the line came alive. "Mr. Cooley." He left his chair and shook the big man. "It's California. Admiral Kelly in San Francisco."

"Admiral? Cooley here. What's the situation? I've

been trying to get you all night. Arrested? Arrested by whom? Okay. Put him on.

"Admiral Chisholm, this is Ralph Cooley. You know who I am? Good. Now listen, Admiral, a group of patriotic citizens headed by me and Admiral Christman have taken over the government of the United States during the night. The takeover is temporary until we can have new elections. The president is dead. The vice-president was sworn in last night. He is with us. Is that all clear, Admiral?"

Cooley listened, his heavy face a mask.

"Very well, Admiral. If that's your decision. However, I have a very good reason to believe that you are going to regret it deeply. President Harrington will speak to the nation at noon today. I suggest you listen to him before taking any action.

"Get Christman," Cooley said. As he spoke the big naval officer came through the door.

"I just talked to Kelly. He's being held prisoner at the headquarters of the Nuclear Submarine Command in San Francisco. Some sort of an officers' committee has taken command, headed by Harry Chisholm."

Christman nodded. "Youngest rear admiral in the navy. The new wave. One of the ex-president's fair-haired boys. What did he say?"

"He said he has thirty Triton submarines armed with 480 mirved atomic missiles and he is giving us twelve hours to surrender and turn the country back to the proper authorities."

The trucks came to a stop in front of the gleaming new central police station at Eighteenth and K, spilling out fifty marines in combat gear, led by a huge black policeman. They moved quickly through the unguarded glass doors and spread out.

"Nobody move," the young lieutenant barked to the half-dozen policemen behind the gleaming formica-topped reception counter. One of his men vaulted the counter and motioned the three switchboard operators away from the phones. Outside, police cars began to pull up behind the trucks, disgorging dozens of mostly black police officers.

"What now, chief?" the young officer asked Tubman.

"Second floor. The control room for radio cars. Guts of the whole operation. Let's go." They moved up the stairs two at a time, the massive ex-basketball player moving out ahead of the young marines. At the landing he stopped briefly, surveying the city's police control center through a long plate glass window.

"You gonna have to shoot your way in, son. There's an anti-terrorist lock on the door and the glass is bullet-proof."

The young lieutenant motioned to one of his men who slung the short A-12 anti-rocket launcher off his shoulder as his companion slipped a charge into the breech. "Back up. It'll blow hard."

The rocket smashed into the lock mechanism of the door, dissolving into a white-hot sheet of flame, spewing debris over the cowering attackers. "Okay, go." The young lieutenant led his men through the opening, shoving back the remnants of the door with his gun butt just as one of the control operators raised his .38 in a two-handed grip and shot him through the forehead. A young marine cut the policeman down with a short burst of his M-20.

Tubman's deep booming voice cut through the smoke and noise. "No sense in fighting. We got a hundred men with automatic weapons. Tell 'em to quit, Harry, and there will be no prosecutions."

A beefy policeman rose from the floor, brushing flecks of debris off his uniform. "Okay, men. Do as he says. The army will be here within minutes anyway. You haven't got a chance, Jeff. I got through to Christman just before you blew the door. They're on their way."

As the big man spoke, the marines moved through the control center methodically demolishing equipment, wiring grenades to blow up the heavy radio gear, and ripping out wiring.

"What the fuck are they doing?" the big cop said, reaching out as if to stop them.

"Your people are deaf, dumb, and blind now, Harry. And they got no commander. Come on, we gettin' out of here. Let Christman have the damned place. See what he can do with it."

"Christ, Jeff, you're turning the city over to the criminals. When they find out we can't direct patrol cars they'll go ape."

"That's right, Harry. Something you should have thought about earlier.

The looting started shortly after nine A.M., first in the ghettos surrounding the central city as the residents realized that no police patrols were in the streets, then moving toward the downtown area like a forest fire gone wild. Christmas sightseers from the outlying areas driving through the city slums were blocked by overturned cars blazing at intersections and the chaos increased as they abandoned their cars and tried to escape on foot.

Four Labor Department secretaries on their way to a Georgetown party attempted to break through a barricade on Georgia Avenue. They were pulled from their car and repeatedly and publicly raped in an alley as

266

hundreds of spectators laughed and cheered. Isolated police cars were overturned and burned, their occupants disarmed and beaten unmercifully. Liquor stores were the first targets of the looters, then food and furniture.

By ten-thirty central Washington was a mass of roaming mobs. Woodward and Lothrop was the first of the big department stores to go as bricks through its windows were soon followed by a surging horde of laughing people. Garfinckel's private police force shot five looters before being overwhelmed and torn apart by an enraged mob. Within minutes the crowd had broken into and begun to strip every store in the central city. An eerie silence engulfed the upper stories of the office buildings, deserted on Christmas day except for a rare frightened face appearing briefly at a window.

The Washington subway system was overwhelmed within the first half hour as passengers surged down the escalators burdened with loot and fought for places. The computerized routing system came apart at eleven A.M., automatic brakes were activated and every train in the system came to a halt in the darkened tunnels. Panic spread as passengers poured out onto the rails. Rape, robbery and death in the half-deserted cars became a commonplace as knife-and-gun-wielding thugs moved among them.

The traffic light system had been blown when the police control center was destroyed, and the city became a massive traffic jam. Ambulances attempting to bring out the injured took to the sidewalks until these too became hopelessly jammed with cars attempting to extricate themselves.

Youths moved along the stalled cars, ripping out radios and other valuables before sprinkling gas among them until the streets became a raging inferno of exploding gas tanks and blazing hulks.

In the White House Ralph Cooley and President Harrington watched the carnage on television as network helicopters criss-crossed the city documenting the anarchy and destruction. "God damn it, man, get some troops out there. You've got to re-establish control. They'll burn the city down."

"We don't have the troops, Josh," Cooley said. "Christman is trying to get men in here, but they are all committed. The Illinois National Guard is moving on Chicago. Arkansas, Montana, Georgia, and half a dozen others are poised to move. We have to use the men we have to block them."

"There are half a million combat troops in the fucking army, Ralph. Are you telling me you can't find enough to control the capital?"

"Once you go on the air and tell them you're with us, we can get operational control of all the armed services. Right now about all we have from most units is a promise of neutrality. We've only got two divisions and three combat teams under our direct orders, Josh, and they are all in action." He handed the big politician a sheaf of papers. "Here's your speech. We're going to have to send you up to the Capitol in a helicopter. Pennsylvania Avenue is blocked and nobody can get through at ground level."

Harrington stared at the papers. "I've got my own speech, Ralph. I sent you a copy last night."

"Yeah," Cooley said, lighting a cigar. "I know you did, Josh. But we thought this would be better. I'm sending Christman and the other joint chiefs who resigned last month up with you to the session. They're the representatives of the provisional government. Now, Josh, I don't have to tell you what will happen if you try to pull anything. We expect you to read this speech word for word, as written. If not," he turned to the red-headed officer beside him, "Major Pruitt will cut you off. You understand? This is no time for game playing."

Harrington nodded, stuffing the sheets in his jacket pocket. "Then let's get going. There's going to be nothing left of this town but cinders if we don't do something and do it fast."

"What the fuck do you mean they're going to pool it? You tell that son of a bitch he's pooling nothing. First goddamn coup d'état in United States history and the dumb bastard thinks he can pool it? Listen, Seymour, you get our camera in there or I'll have your ass on toast, you hear? And what's more I want Suzanne in there live. This is the biggest story the Federal Broadcasting System ever covered, and goddamn it I want it blanketed." Gary Stein, executive producer of the Federal Broadcasting System's evening news, hung up the phone and grabbed another.

"Jake? You got the footage of the Kennedy funeral? Johnson's? Nixon's? Yes, you bet your ass I want all of them. Every goddamn slice you've got of a president's death and funeral. Especially the ones who were assassinated. What have we got on Lincoln? What? Listen, wise ass, I know there wasn't any television then. Get me stills or paintings, you motherfucker.

"Suzanne," Stein said, hanging up and snatching for another phone. "Get up to the helo pad. I want you over there now. We gotta get on live with commentary before the main event."

Suzanne Wilson looked up, an island of icy calm in the midst of the newsroom chaos. She had been an anchorperson for four years now, sharing the duties with a shifting series of men until she had become the senior spokesperson for the network, famed for her acid wit and chilly good looks. "You're forgetting the censor,"

269

she said, gesturing toward a middle-aged figure in a vested suit going over a script at a table near Stein's.

"Fuck him. Get over there. I'll handle the censor."

The figure looked up from the script. "You'll handle nothing, Stein," syndicated columnist Kip Dean said, rising. "I'll go with Suzanne. Meantime, you will run none of this crap you've been giving me. No news other than an announcement every ten minutes that the president will speak at noon. You understand?" He turned to the young army officer who lounged near the water fountain talking to one of the pretty young female producers who handled the weather. "Captain Justice here will make sure that nothing else comes out, Stein. If it does he has orders to kill you and destroy your transmission facilities."

"Oh shit. The biggest news story of the century and we can't cover it."

"Precisely," the man said. "And once we establish control there will be a great deal more you won't cover, my friend. Shall we go, Suzanne?"

As they moved to the elevator, Suzanne Wilson turned to him. "You cannot possibly bring it off, Kip. You realize that?"

"My dear, we have brought it off. The president is dead. The armed forces are ours. So are most of the police. Josh Harrington is going to announce the formation of a new provisional government. Who is going to resist?"

"And what's your role going to be? Are you going to continue writing that column of yours under censorship? Who will you criticize if your people are in power?"

"No, my dear. I am going to be the first Minister of Information, a job I will use to shut off the disgusting morass of pornographic filth, leftist lies, and pervasive degeneracy which has overwhelmed the country over the last three decades. I will be the Cato of the new regime."

"Oh, Jesus Christ," Suzanne Wilson said in disgust. "Are you going to forbid screwing too?"

"Only with animals, my dear. Only with animals. Even if they are consenting."

Doyle reached the street in front of the Watergate apartments at nine A.M. The building was outside the main area of rioting, but he could see the billows of smoke rising from the central city and hear the occasional popping of small arms. He moved down Virginia Avenue, avoiding small groups of aimless young blacks, transferring the heavy automatic to a side pocket. Constitution Avenue was deserted except for occasional cars which had managed to extract themselves from the paralyzed streets in the central city.

On his left, the White House was ringed with troops and armored vehicles. Doyle cut across to Fourteenth Street and moved quickly to Independence Avenue. The Smithsonian was quiet as he turned onto a back path to the marine bivouac, answering the quiet challenge of a sentry. In the control tent a tall black captain rose and saluted, grinning.

"How's it going, Captain?"

"Fine, General. Just fine. All our boys are in place. We're just waiting for action now."

"Can you contact Haines?"

He nodded, barking a few words into a miniaturized walkie talkie before handing it to Doyle. "Haines? Doyle."

"Yes sir?"

"Any problems?"

"Not so far. We're out of sight. The police are handling things. The place is packed with people. Congressmen, senators, staff, and about a division of newsmen. If anything starts here a hell of a lot of people are going to get hurt. I've got my men wired up, so I can move them at will."

"I'm coming up. Stay out of sight and let the police handle it unless there is bad trouble. Pruitt and some of his rangers are sure to be coming up with Harrington. Keep out of their way. Don't get into a confrontation. Get the cops to locate them and keep them under surveillance. Sooner or later you'll have to take them out."

"They're your men, aren't they, General?"

"I used to command the unit."

"We'll hurt as few as possible, General."

"Don't be goddamn fool, Haines. They won't surrender. You'll have to kill or disable them all."

"Yes, sir."

Doyle walked up the deserted Mall past the already-fading Christmas decorations. Instinctively the rioters and looters seemed to avoid the open spaces, and he moved unchallenged past an occasional armed jeep to the Capitol building. The police at the main entrance passed him through a throng of newsmen waving credentials and screaming to get in.

"Where's Haines?" Doyle asked the black police captain in charge of the detail.

"Still in that room off the House floor. What's going to happen, General?"

"We're going to take the country back," Doyle said, heading for the House chamber.

The big presidential helicopter settled on the back lawn of the White House, its rotors feathered, engine muted. Cooley, in shirt sleeves despite the biting cold, held out his hand to Harrington. "Josh, you won't regret it. Together we'll get this country moving again. I give you my solemn word that we'll hold elections within two years. There just wasn't any other way to stop the fanatical son of a bitch. You must realize that now."

Harrington turned and ran toward the helicopter, his big body retaining the lithe grace of his football years.

Cooley faced the red-headed army officer at his side. "Pruitt, I want you on him like a burr. If he attempts to escape, stop him. If he deviates from that speech we wrote, arrest him. You understand."

Pruitt grinned. "Sure. What if he won't go along with it?"

Cooley stared at the big man climbing the steps of the helicopter. "Then use your judgment."

Pruitt lifted a hand lazily and ten of his men moved out toward a second helicopter, idling a hundred yards further on. He raced to the president's bird and lifted himself aboard at the last second as the skids picked up.

Harrington looked up from the sheaf of papers in his hands, eyebrows raised.

"Orders, sir. Mr. Cooley wants to make sure you're protected until the secret service is reconstituted."

"You're the man who shot the president, aren't you, son?" Harrington asked.

Pruitt nodded. "He didn't follow orders."

"And so long as I follow orders you won't shoot me?" Harrington asked, turning back to the speech Cooley had handed him.

Doyle glanced at his watch. It was eleven-fifty-five and the well of the House was filling up, senators moving into the section set aside for them, special seats for members of the cabinet and Supreme Court in the front row, House members scattering out along the remaining

273

seats of the hemicycle. A horde of newsmen had flooded into the press and visitors' galleries, among them a scattering of blue police uniforms. On the floor of the chamber plainclothes detectives and FBI men mingled with the congressmen.

Doyle slipped the miniaturized walkie talkie out of his pocket. "Haines?"

"Sir?"

"Are your men in place?"

"Yes, sir. As soon as the speech starts they'll move into the galleries and cover the exits to the chamber. They'll burn anybody who interferes."

As he spoke the doors behind and to the left of Doyle opened and Josh Harrington entered. Tall and lithe despite his bulk, he bounded up the steps to the podium and shook hands with the speaker and majority leader seated on the dais behind the speaker's platform. In the auditorium and galleries everyone rose, standing for a moment in respectful silence until Harrington reached into his coat pocket, extracted a pair of heavy black-framed glasses and spread out the crumpled pages of his speech in front of him.

"My fellow Americans. I am here today on a sad and tragic mission. Our president is dead, and the nation is being ripped asunder by internal strife the like of which has not been seen since the Civil War. The capital city is being looted and burned beyond the walls of this building, and across the country our fellow citizens are preparing to go to war with each other."

Harrington looked up from the papers in front of him and removed his glasses. "These are the first words of a speech written by Ralph Cooley and the members of the military cabal which has taken over the country in an illegal and abominable coup d'état. Sitting below me," Harrington pointed toward the four former chairmen of the joint chiefs of staff placed slightly apart from the cabinet, "are four of them. Military men whose lives were supposedly devoted to the defense of their country but who have savagely and traitorously betrayed it and murdered their president."

Admiral William Christman stared up at the man on the podium, face tight with rage and despair, as Harrington continued. "One of them I count among my personal friends. A hero of three wars, a man of courage and personal honesty beyond question, a man honored by his nation. But today this man is a traitor and I denounce him and his companions as such," Harrington said, jabbing a thick finger in the direction of the four military officers. Christman had started to rise when he saw the young marine kneeling four feet in front of him levelling a submachine gun. He and a dozen others had slipped into the chamber as the speech began and taken up positions guarding all aisles and exits.

"Haines?" Doyle spoke into the walkie talkie.

"Sir?"

"Has anybody located Pruitt?"

"No sir. He came off the helo with the president and disappeared. There was a lot of confusion. A big cargo bird with troops was trailing the presidential copter but it faded off at the last minute."

Doyle swore into the mike. "Try to find him, Haines."

Harrington's big voice was filling the chamber now, deepening in timber and taking on confidence. "They have told you, these men who shot your president down in cold blood on Christmas Eve, that their motives were patriotic. That your president, the man you elected to lead this nation, was either a traitor or a fool, and that their actions were designed to save us from disaster."

Harrington leaned forward on the lectern, big hands white with the pressure of gripping the dark wood. "I tell you today that they lied. They rebelled against the legitimate government of this nation out of greed and personal ambition, not patriotism. They killed out of fear of a man whom they knew they could not control. And across the country today small bands of their deluded followers are leading men in battle against their legally elected government.

"I wish to tell them all: lay down your arms and surrender. For if you do not you will be hunted like animals through the streets and destroyed. Here and now, I say to the citizens of this nation: take arms against the traitors who do not surrender. Kill them where you find them. Take back your cities and towns. Do not give up."

Doyle watched the fascination mixed with fear and horror on the faces of the audience. Harrington had paused, eyes sweeping the House chamber. "That is my message to the nation today. But before you put it into effect, I wish to temper it with mercy. Among the men who are rebelling against their government are many of good will. Men more confused than evil. So I propose here and now to offer, to any who will step forward at this time and surrender, a full pension and immunity from prosecution by the law. This offer will be valid for a period of six hours. If by then the rebellion has not ceased and power returned to its lawfuly elected officials, then I wish, with the consent of this chamber, to declare the perpetrators of this rebellion outlaws subject to summary execution by the citizenry."

Suddenly the chamber was on its feet, a swelling mass of applause rising from it as cheers drowned out Harrington's voice.

"The stupid shit," Doyle heard Pruitt's low voice behind him. "Don't move, General. This thing I'm holding can cut your spine in two with one burp." As he spoke, the marines in the House chamber began to withdraw from the big auditorium, the youth in front of the former joint chiefs coming to his feet in a crouch and moving backward toward the exit behind the podium.

"Haines," Doyle said, bringing the mike to his mouth.

"Put it down, General," Pruitt said. "Major Haines had a little accident. Those miniature walkie talkies of his backfired. We came in through the roof from the bird and took him out. I'm giving the commands now. His men think they are obeying his orders. Now don't do anything to disabuse them of that idea."

"You're a bit too late, Pruitt," Doyle said. "Harrington's already done the damage. All over the country people are going to begin to hunt you down."

"Words, General. You know that. We've got the horses. All he's got is words. And he won't have them much longer."

"What are you going to do?"

"Do? Hell, General. I'm going to do what I'm told, just like always. And my orders are to shut him up. One way or another."

Doyle glanced around the chamber. Haines's men had disappeared and in their places Pruitt's rangers had taken up position, the snubnosed, silenced Heckler and Koch .220 submachine guns he had obtained for them controlling the assembly. Against them, Tubman's lightly armed police wouldn't have a chance. Pruitt raised his arm, tensing to give the signal to move, when a young pock-marked ranger appeared at his side. "Major."

"Yeah. What the fuck is it?"

"That marine radio we took."

"What about it?"

"They're sending messages. It looks like the whole fucking First Marine Division is on the Beltway heading here. They're diverting units all over town. A full battalion is heading for the capital. They're tryin' to reach that major you totalled."

Pruitt jabbed Doyle in the kidneys. "Did you call in the First Marines?"

Doyle nodded. "They'll have ten thousand men in the capital within an hour. That outnumbers Cooley's forces by about five to one. Plus which they've got heavy armament. It'll be a slaughter if the army doesn't surrender."

"Shit," Pruitt said, staring up at Harrington who continued to speak.

"I know there are many among you who disagree with the late president. On occasion I did myself. He was not a lovable man, but he was an honest one. Honest and dedicated. And to kill him in the name of patriotism was monstrous. We have in this society mechanisms for dissent and checks and balances to protect the rights of minorities. These men did not have to rebel to be heard. They rebelled because they knew that the nation was behind the president, and that their only chance of success was armed action against the nation.

"They must and will be stopped. But to do so will require immediate, continuing decisive action. In order to quash this rebellion, I come before you today to request special powers for a limited period to reestablish law and order in the nation. These are not normal times and normal means will not suffice. I, therefore, ask that you vote me extraordinary special powers to rule the nation by decree, suspending the Bill of Rights and constitutional safeguards, until this rebellion is under control. I ask you to trust me and to go back to your home districts to help stamp out this treason and heal the wounds it has opened."

Harrington paused and stared around the big room and up at the hushed galleries. "Those in favor?" he asked, voice low, almost inaudible.

The legislators rose and a wave of assent exploded over him followed by spontaneous applause. Harrington lifted his arms in a massive V, accepting the acclamation.

"What are you going to do, Pruitt? Shoot him?"

Pruitt grinned, his scarred, intelligent, brutal face breaking up in a mass of upturned lines. "Well, General, that wouldn't be smart, would it? No. I think I'll bank me some credit." He moved out in front of the podium, facing the only four men in the room who had not stood to acclaim the president. Doyle realized too late what he was about to do.

"Pruitt, no," he said, leaping forward as the machine gun jittered soundlessly and the four joint chiefs crumpled in their seats, a neat line of small holes stitched across their bemedalled chests.

"That ought to end your rebellion if nothing else does," Pruitt said, lifting a closed fist and motioning for his men to follow.

The silent execution of the four officers had passed almost unnoticed in the bedlam which engulfed the House chamber. Hundreds of senators and congressmen had stormed down the aisle to pound Harrington on the back and shake his hand. A small force of uniformed police led by Chief Tubman gradually gathered around him and pushed through the crowd.

One of Harrington's massive hands gripped Doyle's arm. "What's going on, General?"

"We're home free, Mr. President," Doyle said. "The

First Marine Division is taking over the capital. They should be in the White House by now."

"They are," Tubman interrupted. "The troops up here were listening to the president's speech, and when the marine units came in sight they surrendered. Same thing is happening all over town. Even my cops are coming home," he added drily.

"All right," Harrington said. "Let's get up there. We've got a lot to do. Doyle, you are in command of all loyal military units. I want a rundown of what the situation is as soon as possible. Get the rebels to surrender where possible, but where it isn't, I want them taken out and quick. Matt," he said turning to his press officer. "I want to meet with the press in an hour or so at the White House. National television if it can be laid on. Tubman, I'd appreciate it if you could assign some men to me for the moment." His eyes scanned the crowd.

"Where is that murderous ranger major? The one who killed the president and just shot down Christman?"

"Pulled his men out of the Capitol and left. Just in time too. These marines just found out he killed their commander."

"Hunt him down, Doyle. Bill Christman was a misguided man, a traitor. But he was my friend and he didn't deserve to die that way."

"Yes, sir."

"Matt, get the cabinet together. I want to meet with them all immediately. And the chief justice. We're going to have to legalize this state of emergency some way. Also I want to see the Board of Economic Counselors right after the cabinet meeting. All right, gentlemen, let's move."

CHAPTER SIXTEEN

"Good evening. This is Suzanne Wilson with the evening news.

"As of this moment last night's attempted coup d'état which resulted in the death of the president seems to have been totally suppressed. President Joshua Harrington's decisive action in rallying Congress and the nation behind him at noon today effectively broke the back of the revolt, and its leaders are either in custody or fugitives. Large numbers of those who participated in the uprising have taken advantage of the president's generous offer of amnesty and turned themselves in.

"In many instances junior officers who were unaware of what was happening have arrested their seniors and taken command of their units. Only in Denver and St. Louis are detachments of troops holding out. In Denver some three hundred rangers of the Eighty-Second Parachute Division and an undetermined number of city policemen have been surrounded in the city hall by units of the state national guard and an aroused armed citizenry.

281

"In St. Louis, more than a thousand police and troops have retreated to the dock area and are pinned with their backs to the Mississippi river. Their commander has repeatedly refused requests for his surrender and has promised to fight to the death.

"In most other cities all major coup units have surrendered to national guardsmen. Police officers who took part in the uprising have accepted the amnesty and been reintegrated into their commands.

"Here in Washington, President Harrington met with the press in the early afternoon following his first cabinet meeting. He confirmed the entire present alignment of the cabinet and asked that the nation remain calm in this emergency. After reiterating his offer of amnesty for all participants of the coup attempt, President Harrington introduced one of the leaders of the uprising, Ralph Cooley, president of Federated Steel Corporation. Cooley, who had himself accepted the terms of the amnesty, called on all members of the conspiracy to surrender immediately to competent authorities, assuring them that they would not be prosecuted.

"The press questioned the president closely as to his plans and as to the wisdom of the amnesty offer. Here are excerpts from the press conference."

"Mr. President, George Segal of Crown Broadcasting System. Do we understand correctly that anyone who participated in this criminal rebellion can escape punishment simply by surrendering before six o'clock this evening?"

"Yes, George. That is correct. My first responsibility is to restore order and get this country back under control, not to take revenge. Our national safety is at stake. A civil war among members of the armed forces would leave us helpless in the face of our external enemies. It

282

would be a temptation perhaps too great for them to resist. I have, therefore, taken the only course which I feel can guarantee our survival. There must be an immediate and total coming together of all forces in defense of the nation."

"Does that include the special forces major who murdered the president and shot down the former joint chiefs in Congress today?"

"It includes any and all participants in this criminal uprising. I wish to stress, however, that my action is in no way intended to approve of their actions. I take it as a matter of practical necessity. We cannot defend this nation if there is a fratricidal war going on among members of the armed forces. Yes, Dick."

"Dick Mariani, Federal Broadcasting System. Mr. President, you have asked for and been voted emergency powers to deal with this uprising. The Bill of Rights has been suspended and you will govern by decree. Congress has been sent home. All this is unconstitutional, Mr. President. There are no provisions for such an unprecedented usurpation of power by the presidency. Will the Suprene Court not overthrow all this?"

"That's a good question, Dick, and I can only say that exceptional situations require exceptional methods. Congress is the voice of the people. It has voted me the powers I felt I needed for an indefinite period. I have discussed the matter with the chief justice, who agrees with me that there is no other course to take. We'll get around to legalizing everything in good time."

"Wilson Bradley, New York *Times*. You say the emergency powers were granted you for an unlimited period, Mr. President?"

"That's correct. And now, gentlemen, if you'll forgive me."

Suzanne Wilson's cool image returned to the screen. "That was President Harrington outlining the situation and the measures he has taken. Since his press conference at three P.M. today, he has received a flood of messages of support from the nation's governors, national guard commanders, mayors, and members of the armed services. The back of the rebellion seems to have been decisively broken.

"Here in Washington, in an incident the details of which are not clear, the assassin of the president, Special Forces Major Mason Pruitt, was shot while apparently attempting to surrender. Pruitt and a dozen of his men had held off repeated assaults by First Marine Division troops on their position in the old Post Office tower. Then, shortly before the six o'clock amnesty deadline, Pruitt attempted to surrender. Members of the marine siege force apparently misunderstood his intentions and shot him down. The remainder of Pruitt's men fought to the death. Marine casualties were more than forty dead.

"The White House has announced that Major General Steven Doyle has been appointed chairman of the joint chiefs of staff with temporary line command of all units of the armed forces. General Doyle has called a meeting of all senior army, air force, navy and marine commanders in order, as he put it to an FBC reporter, to re-establish military control. Names of the other new joint chiefs will be announced shortly, he said."

"Well, Cooley, you fucked it up royally," Harrington said, staring across his desk at the unshaven, dirty, sweat-stained figure of the industrialist.

"Hadn't been for you, Josh, we would have brought it off," the big man said wearily. "We had it all under

284

control until you started talking. Bill always said we couldn't trust you."

"Ralph, I want the names of everybody who was in this with you. Both officers and businessmen."

"Fuck you," Cooley said, yawning. "Get your great FBI to find them for you. I won't."

"Ralph," the president leaned across his big desk. "I need your help. What I said out there on television was no joke. The Soviets began mobilizing this morning. The Chinese followed. Germany is on red alert. The whole world is in a state of intense anxiety. We've got to act responsibly over the next few days. I can't afford to have other outbreaks happening behind my back. You're a patriot, man. You didn't pull this fool stunt for personal aggrandizement. You thought it was genuinely in the country's interest. I accept your motives. Well, now that you've lost you've got to act like a man."

Cooley nodded his head wearily. "We'll cooperate, Josh. But in our own way. No names, because I don't trust you and with good reason. Despite the amnesty, you had Pruitt destroyed like a mad dog. I'll communicate with my people and tell them to back you. I'll bring the most important down here for a conference. All on condition that you keep your promise of no punitive measures. And I want it in writing. Otherwise, no deal."

"I'm going to need your help, Ralph," Harrington said. "This country has been divided over the past two years by policies which were largely unacceptable to a majority of the ruling elites. I am going to change that. You may find that what you were seeking is not so far from what I want." Harrington rose and extended his hand to the fat man.

Doyle rubbed the stubble on his cheeks and yawned. He could smell the stale sweat congealed under his

285

arms. He hadn't changed clothes in almost forty-eight hours. His mouth had the furry consistency which comes from total exhaustion or a massive hangover. The last holdouts in Denver and St. Louis had surrendered at midnight. Casualty figures were beginning to drift in. Including the 3,000 men who died in the six C-5s shot down by the Air Defense Command, the two airborne divisions had lost some five thousand men. Civilian casualties totalled about a thousand. The First Marine had lost more than two hundred.

The senior officers who led the coup or tacitly participated in it had been relieved of command and sent to their homes under house arrest. Interrogation of the junior officers who had taken part was proceeding to determine which had been knowingly involved and which had simply been following orders. The president's promise of no punishments would be carried out, but every officer who had been a willing participant would be retired or forced to resign immediately. It would, Doyle thought wryly, solve the problem of forced cutbacks. More than half of the active service general officers were implicated in one way or another. Among them were some of the forces' most talented commanders. Six were known suicides.

The red phone on his desk chimed. "Yes."

"General, this is Colonel Harrelson, combat intelligence center. Satellite photos show the Soviets are beginning to stand down. Our monitoring of their internal radio communications indicates that they are returning to normal first grade alert from a war footing."

"What about their nukes?"

"Silos have been secured, sir. Guidance crews are back to normal mode."

"The Chinese?"

"We've informed them of our satellite information on

286

the Soviets, sir. Their mobilization was in answer to the Soviets', not to our," the officer hesitated, "problems. We expect them to be standing down shortly sir."

"Fine. Thanks, Harrelson."

Doyle punched another button. "Strategic Air Command."

"This is Doyle. Get me General Sutton."

"Sutton here."

"Spike? Doyle. Intelligence tells me the Soviets are standing down. The Chinese should be following shortly. I've talked to the German chief of staff. He'll go back to normal mode when we do. Have your people secure the missiles and get our planes down. I don't want any goddamn accidents now that we've got this thing under control."

"Okay, Steve. We'll be down in an hour."

"Let the Soviets and the Germans know you're starting. I'll handle the Chinese. Use the Pentagon hotline."

Doyle hung up and glanced at his watch. It was four A.M., his third day with virtually no sleep. The president had called a cabinet meeting for eight A.M. "Buck," he called through the open door to the outer office now packed with radio gear wired to the Pentagon communications center. "Get me a clean uniform and wake me at seven." Doyle put his head down on the desk and slept.

Maria Vicente began to proofread the final draft of the president's Provisional Economic Plan at about the time Doyle's head dropped to his desk. A team of thirty Treasury Department and Office of Management and Budget economists had begun work the previous afternoon at five P.M. using guidelines laid down by the Board of Economic Counselors after a meeting with the president.

"Congress," Istvan Esterhazy had pointed out to the economic team, "is no longer a factor in the equation, ladies and gentlemen. We are free to come up with a program which will put the country back on its feet without regard to the partisan political forces which have made management of the economy so difficult to date. In addition, for the moment at least, we can ignore constitutional restraints. What we want over the next twelve hours is the broad outline of a pure economic policy which will guide this country from the brink of ruin to a solid socio-economic base. It's a precious opportunity. Dr. Vicente will coordinate your efforts. I don't need to tell you that this is a unique situation. Don't botch it. Dr. Vicente will give each of the teams the president's broad guidelines. We want, before morning, a wages and prices policy, an investment program, a social welfare outline, the broad parameter of tax reform and proposals for public employment. All of you have done an enormous amount of work on just these problems for the former administration. In doing so you made compromises, cut corners and trimmed your sails to the political winds. What we want now is a program that will work, regardless of its socio-political implications. At some point tomorrow the president will take it to the country. He may even call for a referendum." Esterhazy paused. "In a very real sense the ideas you come up with tonight will be those which govern this nation over the next decade. I expect the best you've got."

Doyle glanced around the cabinet room and took the outer row seat behind the president indicated by an usher. In addition to the Cabinet, the Supreme Court, the Board of Economic Counselors, the director of the Intelligence Advisory Group and FBI, and Doyle as acting chairman of the joint chiefs of staff, were present. Maria Vicente, dark smudges of fatigue marking her eyes, winked at him from her seat next to Esterhazy. They rose as Harrington entered the room and walked to his place at the center of the table, exchanging greetings with old friends.

"Good morning, ladies and gentlemen. I apologize for the ungodly hour, but I'm sure you all understand the urgency of this meeting. We have got to regain the country's confidence. Out there today is a shaken nation, uncertain of itself and distrusting of its leaders. We've got to give them something they can get a grip on. And we've got to start pulling this great nation out of the morass into which it has fallen. I asked Istvan Esterhazy and his people to come up with a provisional economic program last night, one which takes no consideration of political factors, because I think we have an opportunity, tragic though its genesis is, to make some dramatic and essential changes in the country which simply would not have been possible under the normal democratic process."

Harrington paused and glanced around the table. "I see some shocked looks, and I confess what I am about to do is not going to sit well with a lot of people. Nonetheless, it must be done. This is no time to allow ourselves to be blocked by tradition and its perhaps outmoded forms. We have an opportunity. If we accept it with good faith and in the knowledge that we are serving our fellow countrymen, people will, I am positive, understand and approve. It is for that reason that I plan to call for a referendum on the broad outline of this socioeconomic plan which you have before you. In its essence, it is what the president wanted with a few more teeth. I want the people to vote on it directly. With their massive approval, and I am sure it will be forthcoming, we can move with decisiveness to get the nation moving forward again.

"You all have before you a summary of the plan. A more detailed outline will be available later today. Even that will be only an outline. It will take several weeks to work it out in detail. There will be changes. It's not locked in concrete. I will now read you the broad outline which is, of necessity, couched in somewhat simplistic terms.

"One. All wages, profits, and prices will be controlled. A Wage Profit and Price Control Board is herewith established with the power of criminal sanctions to administer all wages, profit and prices for an indefinite period.

"Two. All capital investment in excess of five hundred thousand dollars annually must be approved by the Investment Control Board which is herewith established."

Harrington looked up. "This is a key provision. Lack of rational creative capital investment has been one of the prime causes of this depression from which we are suffering. The board will redirect capital investment into productive channels and decide what proportion of each company's profit will be invested and which distributed as dividends. There won't be many dividends, ladies and gentlemen.

"Three. Operations of the stock exchanges are temporarily suspended. The Securities and Exchange commission will proceed to set up a commission to evaluate the intrinsic value of all stocks and bonds. In emergency situations stockholders can borrow against this established value of their stocks."

Harrington absorbed the gasp which rose around the table. "Ladies and gentlemen, this is a temporary measure. I'll be frank with you. Stock markets are an outmoded economic mechanism which haven't worked except as a vehicle for speculators for more than half a century. Their ability to form capital is negligible as is their vaunted stabilizing role. I intend to do away with them following a period of transition. Stock prices and returns will be set by government commission and the public will be able to invest. But the commission will control prices. Speculation will cease.

"Four. Strikes and lockouts are prohibited. A Labor Management Arbitration Board is herewith established to adjudicate labor-management disputes."

Again Harrington looked up from the blue imitation leather folder in front of him. "We simply cannot afford the economic waste of strikes in a period of crisis such as the one we are going through. The unions are going to have to understand and swallow this. Once things are more normal, we can discuss some less rigid system. However, I must be frank. Strikes are economic vandalism and some other method of settling disputes must be found.

"Five. The tax system will be fundamentally reformed. All special exemptions will be voided. Income in excess of fifty thousand dollars per year will be taxed at one hundred percent. Inheritance taxes will confiscate all inheritances in excess of five hundred thousand dollars."

Harrington looked around the table and grinned. "I just cost myself two hundred thousand dollars a year, so nobody should scream too loud. Also, this is the provision which will get us sixty percent of the votes in the referendum.

"Six. Control of the media will be established for a limited period. This measure is taken to prevent the publication of false and misleading information during the emergency period."

"Good God, Josh, you can't be serious," the chief justice exploded, rising from his chair, his thin, lined face suffused with astonishment. "You can't do any of this, Josh. The economic portions are unconstitutional, but this is monstrous."

"Can't? That's not a word in my vocabulary right now. I've got to do it. If I don't, those jackals in the press will be all over us before we can get this thing going. It is, in many ways, the key to the whole program. We need a breathing space, and I intend to have it."

"I won't allow it, Josh. I won't permit it," the chief justice said.

"And how will you stop it?" Harrington asked.

The chief justice stared back. "I will resign and go to the people."

"Accepted," Harrington said, turning to the official note taker. "Please enter in the record that the chief justice has tendered his resignation and that it has been accepted. Since you are no longer here in an official capacity, Homer, I suggest that it is appropriate that you leave." Harrington motioned to the head usher who escorted the chief justice out of the room.

"If there are any others who can't stomach what we are about to do, I suggest they leave now," Harrington said.

Three cabinet officers and one member of the Board of Economic Counselors rose hesitantly. One started to speak, but Harrington shut him off. "This is a meeting of government officials. By rising you have just ceased to be one, and your opinion is no longer of value to me."

Ushers moved around the table herding them out.

"Now, if I may continue, ladies and gentlemen.

"Seven. Employment. The government is from this date the employer of last resort. All unemployed persons will be registered and those capable of working will be assigned to public works projects to be designated by the Secretary of Labor. Those refusing to accept work will be denied all social benefits.

"Eight. Crime. The crime rate in this country has reached crisis proportions during the depression. In order to restore law and order, I propose to institute a uniform federal crime code. All police forces will come under the direct supervision of a Department of Domestic Security which is herewith established under FBI director Harlan Worth. Criminal courts are herewith federalized and will henceforth be under the control of the Attorney General. Registration of all citizens will be effected, and each of us will from the date of registration be required to have in his possession a National Identity Card."

Harrington glanced around the room, absorbing the looks of distaste on most of the faces. "We are being overwhelmed by crime. There is no other solution. In addition, something has to be done about the massive immigration from the Latin American countries. We now have more than thirty million resident illegal aliens. Something has to be done before we are inundated. Identity cards are part of the solution."

Harrington stood up. "That concludes the cabinet meeting, gentlemen. I will go on television with this program at twelve o'clock noon. The referendum is scheduled for December 30. We will begin implementing the provisions of these proposals immediately, however, and the necessary decree laws will be issued as soon as my personal staff can get them drafted. This is an emergency beyond anything the republic has ever suffered in its history. We cannot hesitate." He turned and stalked out of the room, his big body moving with elastic force and vitality.

Doyle felt Maria's arm slip through his and followed her down the corridor to her office. Her green eyes were bright with excitement. "Well, what do you think? He's buying everything we put up to him. We'll get our program through in spite of this ignorant countryman. He doesn't even understand half of it."

"It sounds a little drastic, Maria," Doyle said, stifling a yawn.

"Don't be a fool, darling. Of course it's drastic. This big, powerful, bumbling country has been drifting along for decades without direction. Now we can harness its forces and make it genuinely efficient for the first time. Don't you see? It's a chance we'll never get again."

"Maybe. But you're going to have every businessman and labor leader in the country after you. Not to mention all the civil rights people, the rich and the poor, and God knows who else. It's a program designed to antagonize everybody."

"Not everybody," Maria said smiling. "Just the power elites. The little guy is going to see what he wants to see. A job, the rich being soaked, the immigration of cheap labor stopped, a crackdown on criminals. Of course, these are only sops." She waved an impatient hand. "Taking all the money away from the rich is a joke. They haven't really got very much and it's meaningless anyway. Just pieces of paper saying they own parts of factories. Confiscating the wealth just means changing the name on the pieces of paper, but it's a grabber. It'll draw votes."

Doyle watched her stride about the office, her body moving sinuously under the clinging jersey of her dress. "Goddamn it, Steve," she said, eyes blazing, "We're

294

going to impose a new era on this country, can't you see it? He's making you head of the joint chiefs, and I'm going to draw up the economic plan. We'll be running the country, you and I."

"I've a feeling he may not see it quite that way," Doyle said as she came into his arms.

CHAPTER SEVENTEEN

Harrington submitted to the ordeal of being made up in the White House television studio as Matt Skille went over a list. "Carey for the Treasury, Simpson for Interior, Beckwith for Commerce, Jordan Cummings at State and that fills out the Cabinet. Two more Supreme Court judges have resigned, which now brings it to four."

Harrington grinned. "Maybe if they all resign we can just forget about it, huh, Matt?"

Skille smiled nervously. "Sure, Josh. Now what about Doyle? Are you going to put him in permanently?"

"How's he reacting?"

"Reacting? Oh, hell, Josh, he's a fucking Indian. You can't tell what he thinks."

"Can he control those Neanderthals over at the Pentagon?"

Skille shrugged. "If anybody can. He's punched his ticket. Without him you wouldn't be here."

"What did he say about the program?"

"I doubt if he understands it or cares. He takes orders, Josh. I think you ought to keep him."

"All right. For now. But I owe him too much. Sooner or later he's got to go. Now what about those freaks in Management and Budget? Can we keep them under control until we can get some of our own people in place?"

"Sure, Josh. They think we're dummies. That Vicente broad has delusions of grandeur. She figures she's going to be your Richelieu. But she's bright as hell and we can use her. Especially right now. The economy is on the verge of collapsing, and the banking system is about to come apart. She and those young geniuses may just be able to keep it going until we've got total control."

"All right. But are you sure the people are going to buy all that kooky economic crap?"

"Josh," Skille said patiently. "We've got the polls the previous administration did. These are just the things people want. Soak the rich, stop crime, punish the bankers, and do something about the stock market. We're on the verge of revolution. But it's all words. Once we get control, we can do whatever we damned please. Jesus, Josh, don't you understand?"

"Understand what, Matt?"

"You've got total control. You can do whatever you damned please."

"So you took the king's shilling, Jordan," Doyle said, watching the former Pentagon intelligence chief carefully barber a cigar and light it.

"It's my patriotic duty, Steve," Cummings said, drawing in the smoke and exhaling with a light cough. "Goddamn emphysema is getting worse. Besides, he's having trouble getting people. If some of us don't help him, he's going to wind up totally in the hands of the freaks from the far left and the far right."

"Yes," Doyle said. "They're beginning to gather. I'm not sure which are worse."

Cummings shook his head. "You miss the point. There is never much difference between fanatics, but in our time there is almost none. State capitalism, which is what Cooley wants, or socialism, which is Esterhazy's dream, come out to the same thing. All the control of the means of production is in the hands of a few bureaucrats, with no contrasting forces to balance that massive economic clout." He shook his head. "No, Steve, if there is any single lesson that history teaches over and over again, it is that to maintain any kind of freedom you have to disperse the centers of powers as widely as possible. We did it with a natural genius for more than two hundred years. Then the consensus died. The world just got too complicated for us, and our system caught intellectual arteriosclerosis. It hasn't been working since the Vietnam war and the continued economic crisis which succeeded it. Something like this was historically inevitable. It's the price of maturity."

"What's going to happen?"

Cummings shrugged. "It's already happened. Josh is a shrewd Kentucky politician, almost totally unideological, but a practical man who has watched the system fail for thirty years. Now he's got power. He'll try to make it work. He's basically a decent man. Maybe he'll eventually decide to turn the power back to the people."

"But you don't think so?"

"No, Steve. I don't think so. It isn't in the nature of the animal. The intoxication of being number one is too great. You've seen it happen at all levels of the bureaucracy. Petty tyranny is satisfying, but think of the heady wine at the very top." He shook his head. "Almost none of them have ever gone gracefully into retirement, and Josh will be no exception. With the difference, of course, that nobody can force him out."

"You think there is an alternative, Jordan?"

"You could kill him or somebody could. But the way things stand, it would only bring in another dictator, one maybe worse than Josh. No. Right now I see no way out. Anyway, our major problem at the moment is to preserve our place as a world power. That fanatic who was killed was about to commit national suicide, and the damage he's done is going to be tough to repair. The Germans and Chinese think we're maniacs and the Russians are more and more convinced of our weakness. It makes for a highly unstable world, one which could go up in atomic smoke if we're not careful. Never forget, Steve, we've been the balance wheel for forty years, ever since World War II. Our alliances with the Germans and the Chinese have kept the Soviets in check. We can't afford to have that break up. A realignment would tempt the other side too much."

"You think the Germans or the Chinese might join the Soviets against us?"

"No. Not really," Cummings said, ignoring a long ash as it fell onto his tweed jacket. "It isn't in their self interest. But if we weaken enough, the temptation might be there. The trouble with this country is that it always thinks in terms of solutions. There are none. There are tactical, temporary accommodations, nothing more. Every so-called solution simply generates the next problem. Once we finally understand this, our policies can become rational. Until we do, we're international adolescents."

Maria rolled her body across on top of him and hit the channel seven button on the remote selector box.

Doyle came awake, his mind and body fighting consciousness.

"Wake up, darling. The new president is about to address the nation. Again." She lay across him nibbling at his ear, her tongue drawing small circles along his jaw.

"You want to watch him or make love to me?"

"The two things are not mutually exclusive, lover," Maria said, giggling. "But it would be wrong, in the words of one of our great presidents." She raised herself up astride his hips, and wiggled once, flipping herself away as he reached for her.

"Look at the screen, General. Your commander in chief is about to address you." She lit a cigarette and sat cross-legged on the bed watching the big wall screen as the picture cleared and Joshua Harrington appeared seated behind a small desk, which was completely bare except for an elegant brown leather desk set.

"He looks like that anchorman from the seventies," Maria said. "Like everybody's father."

"Cronkite," Doyle said, surprised. It was true. Harrington's craggy, kindly face projected the same sense of trust and sincerity as the old television personality, without any real facial resemblance.

"My fellow Americans, I come before you this evening as the head of a nation torn and divided more grievously than at any time since the Civil War. The assassination of a president and the rebellion of elements of the armed forces are only symptons of the crisis we face. An economic depression of frightening dimensions has settled upon our country. We have become confused and lost the confidence and dynamism which made us the leaders of the world. Our enemies sense our weakness and our allies fear it. The magnificent governmental system which has been the wonder of the world for more than two centuries is on the brink of collapse."

As he spoke he stared directly into the camera, eyes moving only imperceptibly to follow the teleprompter with letters almost six inches high to compensate for his nearsightedness.

"There would be no point in my hiding from you the gravity of this crisis. The rebellion is ended and tomorrow we will bury our dead president. But even as I mourn for him with you, I must, in your name, take up his burden. I will need your help as no man in this lonely and awesome office ever has. We must together close the wounds which divide us, recover the confidence and dynamism which have made us great, and return to the discipline and civilized behavior which are the mark of mature societies. As you know, I have asked for special powers to govern by decree in this great emergency. Congress, in its wisdom, has granted me those powers. I wish solemnly to assure you today that I accept this burden with humility and an intense awareness of the responsibility which has fallen to me."

"Jesus, he's good," Maria said, dragging deeply on the cigarette. "Look at the hypocritical old bastard. He's playing on his voice like an organ."

Doyle propped himself against the headboard of the bed, watching Harrington as he, seemingly unrehearsed, followed the signals of his off-camera television advisor. Every move of his hands, every gesture of his head had been programmed and practiced. He went through the program he had outlined at the early morning cabinet meeting, softening the language, blurring the lines, but retaining all its essential elements.

"No one is more aware of the drastic, even draconian, nature of this program. No one is more aware of the dangers it presents." He paused. "No one is more aware that it is in fundamental violation of the constitutional guarantees on which this nation is based." As he spoke, Maria hugged her shoulders and slipped herself between Doyle's legs, propping her back against his chest.

"I'm cold, Steve."

He pulled the blanket up around her shoulders, crossing his arms in front of her, feeling the soft firmness of her breasts through the thin material.

"But, my fellow Americans," Harrington continued, his face tense and turning slightly to present a firm jawline to the camera. "I can see no alternative to these measures except chaos. The chief justice and three members of the Supreme Court have resigned. Four of my cabinet have found the measures too draconian. I have accepted their resignations with great regret and sadness. But the responsibility is mine, and I must come before you today to say that I cannot bear it alone.

"I must have your support in this hour of our nation's greatest danger. I have therefore decided to hold a national referendum, the first in our long history, to seek your approval of this program and to ask for your support and trust of me in this crucial time. It will be held on December 30. I ask you to look within yourselves, to examine what I propose and to give me the backing which I will need both here at home and before the world to bring this country out of chaos and despair into prosperity and strength. Thank you."

"He'll win," Maria said, turning her face to Doyle. "He'll win and win big."

"I know," Doyle said.

"Do you trust him, Steve?"

"Trust him?" he shrugged. "Listen, Maria, this country was the luckiest piece of geography on earth for two hundred years. Anybody with brains and energy and a little luck could make it. There was an instinctive realization of this. We all agreed on the rules, or about eighty percent of us did. Hell, I'm a West Virginian hillbilly and you're an Italian immigrant's daughter. The president is a steel worker's son."

"What's that got to do with anything" Maria said impatiently. "I've heard all those clichés until I want to vomit."

"The reason a cliché is a cliché is because it's true," Doyle said. "Only it isn't any more. It hasn't been for a couple of decades, maybe a hell of a lot longer. People began to realize that we were an old country sometime during the last thirty years. All of a sudden the guy working in the steel mill knew he wasn't going to be a doctor or a lawyer. It sank in slowly. People got bitter and resentful without really knowing why. Kennedy's death and the Vietnam war were a sort of watershed. The people who fought that war were the sons of the lower class. There were goddamn few sons of the elite out in those jungles. Their families kept them in college, or they left the country or got into jobs that protected them."

"So what? Why should they fight a war they didn't believe in?"

"No reason. No reason at all. But the ones who did fight it, who had no choice, came back pretty goddamn bitter. The divisions in our society congealed in those years. We became like Europe. Pragmatism gave way to ideology. People became aware of class and privilege. Nobody gives a damn anymore whether anything works. It has to conform to a preconceived set of values. The universities became infested with half-assed Marxist economists, historians who rewrote history, invariably to make the United States look bad, and disillusioned powerless intellectuals of all kinds who, because they were excluded from power, were determined to bring down the system. Well, it looks as if they have, but, as usual in revolutions, they'll be the first ones with their backs to the wall if I know Josh Harrington."

"Are you going to help him?"

"Yes," Doyle said, running a hand through her hair, lifting her lips to his. "I'm going to help him. And you are too. Because there is no other way. The world's too dangerous and life is too complicated for the kind of chaos we've been going through. The country's been tearing itself apart too long, the wounds are too deep. He's our last chance to survive."

"My God, Steve. Do you really know what you're saying?"

"Yes. He's the last Caesar."

The Destroyer

Warren Murphy

In the sacred lexicon of heroes, one finds a great similarity among the inhabitants. A hero is brave, a hero is made of righteous mettle, has the strength of an ox, the wisdom of Solomon, and (mostly with American heros) an overdose of libido. Oh, yes, he (always a he) is ruggedly handsome, too. The Destroyer is not in this category of hero. The Destroyer is something else again. The Destroyer, well, The Destroyer just is. . . . In the following pages we will attempt to let The Destroyer and its faithful chroniclers describe just what this, this, er, force/power/hero thing is all about. To begin, we'll let Ric Meyers, novelist in his own right, and Number One Destroyer fan, give you one of the best commercials we've seen:

When was the last time you saw a hero? Not one of those mindless, looney-bin rejects who line the bookracks: The *Exterminator, The Extincter, The Ripper, The Slasher, The Wiper-Outer, The Mutilator, The Ix-Nayer,* all those same series, with their same covers, their same plots, and their same moronic machine-gunning leads who figure the best way to solve a problem is to shoot it.

No. A real life-saving, mind-craving hero for the world today.

Not Tarzan, he won't help. He's in Africa. Not Doc Savage,

he was in the thirties and forties. Not James Bond. He was left behind at the turn of the decade.

For the seventies and eighties, the world is in. It's *The Destroyer*.

Why *The Destroyer?* Why the phenomenon that has writers, editors, literary agents, ad men—people who deal in words, and who you think would know better—following these tales of Remo Williams and his Korean teacher, Chiun, with the same kind of passion and faith that only a few like Holmes and Watson have instilled?

Why has this . . . this . . . *paperback* series drawn such high reviews from such lofty heights as *The New York Times, Penthouse, The Village Voice,* and the *Armchair Detective,* a journal for mystery fanatics?

Honesty.

Look beyond the facts that *The Destroyer* books are written very well and are very funny and very fast and very good.

The Destroyer is honest to today, to the world, and most importantly to itself.

And who is *The Destroyer?* Who is this new breed of Superman?

Just sad, funny, used-to-be-human-but-now-isn't-quite Remo. Wise-assing Remo, whose favorite line is: "That's the biz, sweetheart."

What's this? A hero who doesn't like killing? Not some crazy who massacres anything that moves with lip-smacking pleasure?

No, Remo doesn't have the callous simplicity of a machine gun to solve the world's problems. He uses his hands, his body, himself. What he's saying with "that's the biz, sweetheart" is that you knew the job of fighting evil was dangerous when you took it.

But somebody has to punish these soul corrupters, and reality has bypassed the government and the police and the media and the schools and has chosen Remo.

And who's he to argue with reality?

The other fist backing up *The Destroyer* is philosophy.

Yes, that's right. Philosophy.

It isn't just the incredibly drawn supporting characters who are written so real that you see them on the street everyday. Not just the "future relevancy" of the books' strong stories, even though *The Destroyer* has beaten the media to such subjects as radical chic, world starvation, detente, and soap operas. Not only that, but *The Destroyer* gets it better with a more accurate view. Chiun was delivering the truth on soap operas long before *Time* magazine's cover story. When the iterati was pounding its collective breast over the struggle of "the noble red man," Remo was up to his neck in the movement, and delivering some telling truths about "the Indians from Harlem, Harvard, and Hollywood."

No. What's different here is the philosophy of Sinanju, that forbidding village in North Korea—it's real—which spawned Chiun and the centuries of master assassins preceding him. The philosophy culled from its early history, a history of starvation and deprivation so severe that its people became killers for pay so the babies wouldn't have to be drowned in the bay.

Kind of chokes you up, doesn't it?

Chiun too. He'll tell you about it. And tell you about it. And tell you about it. And he'll tell you other things.

Chiun on Western morality:

"When a Korean comes to the end of his rope, he closes the window and kills himself. When an American comes to the end of his rope, he opens the window and kills someone else. Hopefully, it's just another American."

Chiun on old girlfriends:

"Every five years, a white person changes. If you see her again, you will kill her in your eyes. That last remembrance of what you once loved. Wrinkles will bury it. Tiredness will smother it. In her place will be a woman. The girl dies when the woman emerges."

Chiun on Sinanju:

"Live, Remo, live. That is all I teach you. You cannot grow weak, you cannot die, you cannot grow old unless your mind lets you do it. Your mind is greater than all your strength, more powerful than all your muscles. Listen to your mind, Remo. It is saying to you: 'Live.' "

Philosophy. It makes the incredible things they do just this side of possible.

And it says that Remo and Chiun are not vacuous, coldhearted killers. Nor are they fantasy, cardboard visitors from another planet with powers and abilities, etc., etc.

They're just two a-little-more-than-human beings.

Chiun must have been reincarnated from everybody's Jewish mamma. Remo is the living embodiment of everyman, 1980s style.

Will Chiun ever stop *kvetching* about Remo being a pale piece of pig's ear and admit the love he feels for him?

Will Remo ever get the only thing he really wants, a home and family?

Keep reading and see. *The Destroyer* today, headlines tomorrow.

Remo Williams, The Destroyer, didn't create the world he's

living in. He's just trying to change it. The best way he knows how.

And for the world's greatest assassin, that's the biz, sweetheart.

* * *

Remo Williams, the ex-Newark cop who was "executed," only to be transformed into The Destroyer, doesn't have a helluva lot to say. He's mostly a doer, fixer, a remover. When he does say something it's mostly to Chiun. Or a smartass remark to the head of his secret agency, CURE.

Chiun, however, has much to say. Here are some passages from his personal journal:

These books are mistakenly labelled *The Destroyer* series. I say mistakenly labelled because you and I know who is the star of the series and it is certainly not the ex-Newark policeman with the attention span of a five year old and the self-discipline of rice pudding.

But all is not lost. Despite the inept, inaccurate writing of Murphy, you have been able to glimpse the awesome magnificence of the glorious House of Sinanju.

It is suggested in the books that the House of Sinanju is a house of assassins and I am the chief assassin. Oh, how clever is Murphy to be able to twist a simple truth into such a cunning distortion, merely to sell more copies of his awful books.

The House of Sinanju is a way of life. For ages past, the Masters have demonstrated the potential that exists in every man to use his body and mind to its fullest limits.

And what of karate, where people sometimes break boards with their hands and more often break their hands with boards? And kung fu? And judo? And tai chi chuan? These are all nice games and might even be able to assist a grown man in protecting himself from a berserk child, if applied properly. They, too, were stolen from the Master of Sinanju, but they are each like a ray while Sinanju is the sun.

If you wish to emulate the Master of Sinanju, you must study his words. You can find them in the Murphy fictions. Forget the stories that he tells you in those books because he always gets them wrong anyway. However, anytime I am speaking between those little marks like this (" "), pay attention. Those talking are called direct quotations and they are correct because I write them all down so even the scribbler cannot get them wrong.

You must study them carefully and then destroy them so

that they do not fall into the wrong hands. Otherwise, I promise you absolutely nothing, except wisdom, strength, courage, and self-respect.

* * *

OK, so who is Warren Murphy? Murphy is an ex-newsman and press agent for politicians. He studies politics and sociology (in New Jersey) . . . when not testing a new wife or besting the tables at Vegas. Very regular guy. . . . We'd be great friends if we didn't fight over Remo and money so much. But he is the fastest, bestest writer of pop/cult adventure today. Not only that, sooner or later he will bust loose with a really important American novel. Meanwhile, *The Destroyer* will go on for another ten years, at least, and outlive most other series. Unless some shrewd producer makes a film out of the series . . . then anything could happen. *The Destroyer* could become the hottest property of the century. Excuse me, Number 41 just arrived (manuscript) and I can't wait to see if that crazy guy is gonna keep that sexy Ruby Gonzalez in the story!